BONE
LAKE

BOOKS BY STACY GREEN

NIKKI HUNT SERIES

The Girls in the Snow

One Perfect Grave

Lost Angels

The Girl in the Ground

The Trapped Ones

Her Frozen Heart

Her Last Tear

LUCY KENDALL SERIES

The Girl in the Pink Shoes

Little Lost Souls

The Girl in the Cabin

The Lonely Girls

BONE LAKE

STACY GREEN

bookouture

Published by Bookouture in 2023

An imprint of Storyfire Ltd.
Carmelite House
50 Victoria Embankment
London EC4Y 0DZ

www.bookouture.com

ISBN: 978-1-83790-710-6
eBook ISBN: 978-1-83790-709-0

PROLOGUE

AUGUST 2001

Amy jumped at the sound of thunder rattling the stained-glass windows in the attic above her bedroom, almost spilling the wine cooler she'd snuck from the kitchen all over her nightstand and plush, rose-colored carpet. Most of the windows on the first and second floors were modern, but the stained-glass panes that lined the stairwell to the attic were original to the home and needed repairing.

Amy rolled her eyes at the sound of her mother's irritated voice from downstairs. The woman was predictable as hell. Amy didn't need to make out the words to know Sandy Kline was complaining about the windows needing fixing, just as she did every time it stormed. Amy's dad would inevitably say something about taking care of scheduling the repairs for her mom given her busy schedule, knowing her mother would take the comment as a personal dig, as she insisted on overseeing any work needed on the historic Victorian. Amy's father would eventually get tired of the arguing. He'd grind out his nightly cigar in the crystal ashtray next to his favorite chair, grumbling about Sandy Kline knowing everything except her ass from a hole in the ground. He wasn't wrong, either.

Amy slipped her headphones on and hit play on her Discman; the Beastie Boys' distinctive voices filled her ears. Most of her friends didn't get the group's appeal, but Amy loved the raw voices and fun vibe. Boyband crooning didn't interest her, because life wasn't all sunshine and rainbows.

Especially her family's.

She skipped ahead to "Sabotage," her favorite song and the perfect soundtrack for the miserable day she'd had. Diary in hand, Amy settled against her pillows with her four-colored pen. She always chose the color that matched her mood. Blue meant she was sad, green was happy, black for the boring, mundane things. Red represented anger or a bad day, and Amy's diary had been filling up with red lately. Until the last few weeks, her entries had been about summer fun and working at the pool. Summer had started out great until her now ex-boyfriend had become jealous. But the red wasn't about him. Not tonight, and not for the last several nights.

Usually writing in her diary helped Amy feel better, but seeing the words on the page only made her feel worse now. Her dad once told her that money didn't buy happiness, but Amy hadn't really believed him until the last few months. Money hadn't stopped her family from completely falling apart.

Bobbing her head with the music, Amy glanced up to see her bedroom door slowly opening. She slammed the diary shut as her little brother, Matty, slunk into the room, closing the door behind him.

Amy paused the music. "Why are you still up?" Matty was small for a ten-year-old boy, and he still had enough baby fat that he looked even younger. His eyes were round as saucers. "You have a bad dream?"

Before he could answer, she heard a thud downstairs, followed by hushed voices. Matty hurried to her bedside.

"Someone else is in the house."

He looked so terrified that Amy couldn't tease him for being such a scaredy-cat. "No, they aren't. You've lived here since you were born. You know it's an old house. It makes weird noises. Dad calls it settling."

Except that had sounded like a hell of a lot more than just a creaking house. Their father's deep voice floated up through the old floor grates. "Get out of my house."

Amy tried to keep a calm face even though her own heart had started to race. "Mom and Dad are probably having an argument." It wouldn't be the first time that a screaming match sent one of her parents to sleep at a hotel.

"But why is he up? He went to bed early, remember?"

She did remember. Her father had a really big presentation tomorrow.

Amy listened as the voices rose and fell downstairs. Her father was angry, and it sounded like her mother was crying—both common in their house lately.

And then Amy heard another sound.

"Why should I? I want what's mine."

Amy's blood ran cold at the stranger's voice. It was definitely a man, and he sounded angry. Why in the world would anyone come to their home at 1 a.m.? Praying that she'd just let her imagination get the best of her, Amy reached for the phone on her nightstand. She looked at her brother, knowing she had to do something to reassure him. But there was no dial tone. She pushed the buttons on the phone, but nothing happened. If the phone lines were cut, Amy knew the intruder in the house was dangerous. She'd learned that much from TV.

Matty watched her, terror building in his eyes. Amy's mind raced through their options. Her bedroom door didn't have a lock on it because her parents wouldn't allow it, and Matty's room was at the opposite end of the long hallway, closest to the curved staircase leading to the main floor, but it didn't have a lock either. Her father kept a pistol in his nightstand, but even if she and Matty reached her parents' room unseen, Amy had no idea how to use it.

She didn't see any other option. Someone had to go for help.

Amy got out of bed and held her hand out to Matty. "Tip-toe," she whispered.

He shook his head. "We should hide."

"You're going to get help," Amy said.

Her little brother's eyes widened as he realized what she meant. "No way."

"Matty, the phone isn't working. Mom and Dad are arguing with someone, and you're the only one small enough to get help. You can get into the dumbwaiter, down to the basement, and escape. Get to next door. Find someone. Call the police." She tried to ignore the swirling butterflies in her stomach, but her hands still trembled.

"Maybe they don't need help," he whispered.

Amy shook her head and put her finger to her lips. She opened the door as slowly as possible to keep quiet and peeked into the hallway. She pulled Matty out of her room and crept toward the attic door. Amy turned the handle and it squeaked. Holding her breath, she waited to see if anyone downstairs reacted, but the argument just intensified. She eased the door open and pulled her brother up the narrow, dusty stairs, the wind rattling the stained-glass windows her mother had never fixed.

When their great-grandfather had built his Victorian dream home on the lake, the servants' quarters had been located in the attic, and her grandfather had a dumbwaiter installed so the servants could be more efficient. Two years ago, Matty had discovered it and locked himself inside for hours. He wouldn't go into the dumbwaiter without arguing.

"Turn on the light," he whimpered.

Amy could barely see the steps, let alone a white cord to switch on the light. "I think they're in the kitchen," she hissed, trying to hide her nerves. "The back window up here faces the backyard. He might see it from the kitchen."

"Amy, please." Matty's voice shook as they reached the top of the stairs. "I'm scared."

"Shush." She hadn't been up here since January when she'd helped her father store the Christmas decorations. Family heirlooms crowded the attic floor, making the walk across in the dark treacherous. "Stay behind me and try to follow my steps."

She navigated through the maze of stuff, focusing on the moonlight streaming in the dormer window at the back of the attic. Central air conditioning hadn't been installed up here, and the stale, hot air made it difficult to breathe.

"I can't do it," Matty said. "I'll get stuck."

"You didn't have anyone to move the rope that time." Amy stepped into the stream of moonlight and grabbed the frayed rope. She pulled on the metal handle, but it didn't budge. Sweat beaded on her forehead, her heart hammering in her ears. Amy tried again with both hands and pulled as hard as she could. The door moved a tiny bit, and the voices downstairs grew even louder. She had to get Matty out of the house if they were going to get help. Amy figured she could block the attic door with enough old crap to hold off the intruder, if he came all the way upstairs, while Matty ran to the neighbors.

Panic nearly choking her, she yanked again and again, tears rolling out of her eyes. Her back ached, her shoulders weak and numb. She tried again, and the door finally gave in. Amy slid the dumbwaiter's door open. It wasn't very big, but Matty wasn't, either.

"Amy—" he started.

"Listen to me." She crouched in front of him and grabbed his shoulders. "The dumbwaiter goes all the way to the basement, remember?" The Victorian's basement was more like a dugout cellar, and she and Matty both hated it, but it was the safest route out of the house.

"I can't, Amy." The moonlight illuminated the fear in his blue eyes. She had to be brave for Matty.

"Yes, you can. Remember what I told you about directions?"

"The pool is on the east side of the house," Matty whispered.

"That's right," Amy said. "The cellar is at the corner of the house. To the left of the pool, but on the north side of the house." Matty struggled with directions, so Amy always made sure he understood.

"They're locked from the outside."

"No, remember a couple of weeks ago, the padlock broke and Mom hasn't replaced it." Her parents had argued about it yesterday. Amy looked into Matty's eyes. "When you open the heavy doors going outside, make sure you look around and see if someone is out there first. If the coast is clear, run to the Kettners' house. That means straight north, through the woods behind the house, until you reach the road. That's Miller Avenue. The Kettners live in that big house on the curve."

"What if the bears are out?"

"The black bears are north of here, in the real woods. Only animals out there will be more scared of you than you are of them, I promise."

A muffled scream came from downstairs. They were out of time.

Amy shoved her brother into the dumbwaiter. "I'll operate the rope until you reach the bottom. Remember to make sure no one is around before you make a run for it."

Their closest neighbors were nearly a mile down the road, and even taking the shortcut through the woods, Matty's little legs would take at least twenty minutes to reach the Kettners', if not longer.

"Don't walk right along the road," she told him. "Don't be seen."

Amy thought she could hear her mother sobbing downstairs.

"Amy," the little boy said, choking back sobs. "What about you?"

"Get to the Kettners and tell them to call the police. I'll meet you there." She held up her right little finger. "Pinky-swear."

Matty gulped and locked his finger with hers.

Amy kissed his forehead. "You're a tough kid, you know that? And brave as hell. Don't ever let anyone tell you different." She could feel her control slipping, and if she freaked out, Matty would never leave the attic. "I love you, buddy." She slid the cover down and grabbed the rope.

Amy had no idea how long it took for the dumbwaiter to reach the basement, but it finally did, the rope going slack. Amy prayed her little brother would remember what she'd told him. She searched the attic for something to use as a weapon, but it was too dark to find anything.

Choking back her terror, Amy crept down the attic stairs and listened through the closed door. Her mother wasn't crying anymore. Her father had gone quiet. She gently opened the door, checked the hall, and then stole into her parents' room next to the attic. Heart in her throat, she ran across the room and opened her father's nightstand drawer. A mix of relief and absolute horror filled her. His pistol was there, meaning her father couldn't defend himself. Is that why he was so quiet?

A hard lump formed in her throat. She had to help her parents.

She didn't know if the pistol was loaded or how to take the safety off, but she hoped it would be enough to scare the intruder.

The gun felt heavy in her hands. Amy took one step at a time, holding it out like she'd seen on cop shows. She stepped carefully, trying to avoid the creaks in the hardwood flooring that even the heavy stair runner couldn't silence. Her heart pounded so hard, she was certain the intruder had to hear it. She rounded the final curve of the stairs, relieved to see the nightlight in the foyer.

Ten feet in front of her, the front door still had the deadbolt on. The front room—the formal front room for guests, her mother called it—was as dark as the rest of the house. Amy leaned over the thick banister, looking down the hall to the lit-up kitchen. She stifled a scream at the sight of her father lying face down in the hallway, blood surrounding him.

Tears streaming down her face, Amy raced to her father.

"Daddy," she whispered. She checked for a pulse. Nothing.

Amy couldn't breathe, couldn't think straight. Her father was gone. Where was her mother?

Sliding glass doors leading out to the pool stood wide open. Had her mother escaped?

Amy stood frozen, staring at her father.

What would happen to her family now?

A tall figure dressed all in black suddenly appeared in the open back door. He didn't seem surprised to see Amy, but the mask covered everything but his eyes.

They looked familiar.

Amy pointed the gun and fired, her heart sinking at the empty click. Her dad refused to keep it loaded. The bullets were probably right there in the nightstand. The man snickered and turned to walk away. As he did, Amy caught a glimpse of the watch on his right wrist, and an anger like she'd never known consumed her. She dropped the pistol, grabbed the biggest kitchen knife out of the block on the counter, and ran out the back doors.

A few feet from the pool, the man in black bent over her mother's bleeding body.

Her mother's chest moved. She was still alive, but for how long?

The intruder bent down and kissed her mother's lips.

Amy saw a flash of silver slide over her mother's throat, slicing it wide open like her father's had been. Amy screamed like a wounded animal. Knife raised, she stalked toward the man. He grinned, revealing his perfect white teeth. Amy attacked first, sinking the knife into the man's side. He grunted, his big hand closing over her wrist like a vice.

"This is a pleasant surprise." He wrenched the knife from her hand. "You should have stayed in your room, Amy."

ONE

FOUR MONTHS AGO

Nikki watched as investigative reporter Caitlin Newport spoke directly into the camera, her voice poised but emotional. "In late August 2001, when she should have been preparing for her junior year of high school, Amy Kline, along with her parents, was viciously murdered in their home by an unknown assailant. Their youngest child, Matt, managed to escape to a neighbor's home. The Kline murders were on every news channel across the state, with multiple law-enforcement agencies fighting for jurisdiction, but twenty-two years later, we still have no idea who slaughtered poor Matt Kline's entire family." The director called 'cut' so the makeup artist could attempt their finishing touches.

Nikki tried to relax as he refreshed the concealer hiding the dark circles beneath her eyes. She normally didn't wear a lot of makeup, but being on film apparently required a pound of various creams and powders.

Sitting across from her, Caitlin's nervous energy was contagious, but not in a good way. Why had Nikki agreed to do this?

The producer called for action once more.

Caitlin smiled encouragingly at Nikki. "Agent Hunt, you're

a criminal profiler, having trained at Quantico with some of the agents who first developed profiling techniques."

She rattled off a list of cases that Nikki had assisted on out east, along with her mentor's famous name and résumé, and then quickly established Nikki's Minnesota background, including the murder of her own parents and eventual return to the area.

Caitlin looked into the camera, her expression grave. "Agent Hunt has an intimate knowledge of the Washington County area, and I believe her unique skills are vital in moving the Kline family murders out of cold storage—" She stopped and scowled at the producer hovering behind Nikki. "Cold storage? We can't use that term if we want to be taken seriously."

"We'll reshoot some of your questions," the producer said. "Keep going."

Switching back into presenter mode, Caitlin explained the goal of the documentary: drumming up new interest and leads in one of the most heinous unsolved murders in the state. "Agent Hunt, can you explain your process?"

Nikki remembered the advice Caitlin had given her that morning and focused on her friend's face. "Profiling is no more than studying behavior and comparing it to reams of information collected by my predecessors. It's not a magic wand but a system that ultimately tells us what sort of perpetrator committed the crime. If we know the type of person who committed the murders, then we have a good idea of how he or she might act in the days following the crime, which is absolutely crucial."

"In partnership with the Washington County sheriff's department, we've been given exclusive access to case files," Caitlin said. "Agent Hunt has been gracious enough to sit down with the information and create a profile of the killer. Agent Hunt, I'll ask you a couple of questions about your background and then we'll dive into the case."

Nikki hoped her flop sweat wasn't obvious on camera. She reiterated that profiling was a tool, and just one of many at law enforcement's disposal. "Let's start with the crime scene first. No sign of breaking and entering, which meant the Klines either knew their killer or he posed as someone with authority to gain entry to the house." She glanced at her notes. "Looking at the photos of the Kline home, it's likely there's at least some degree of premeditation here."

"So an organized killer, then?" Caitlin asked. "The scene left was so bloody. Isn't that the sign of a disorganized offender?"

"Well, we aren't discussing serial offenders, and that's really where organized versus disorganized is most useful," Nikki explained. "We don't know the motive behind the Kline murders, and there's no evidence to suggest additional crimes. In general, organized defenders are planners, and everything they're doing is part of a ritual they must perform to find release. It's part of a fantasy they've been working on for years. Disorganized killers don't plan, and they're often driven by some sort of emotional trigger."

Caitlin nodded, her eyes wide. "Can you expand on that, Agent Hunt?" She'd already told Nikki that her producers wanted to focus on organized versus disorganized because pop culture had turned them into buzz words any true crime fan understood.

"By their nature, organized killers are older, at least mid-twenties. They have the patience and ability to operate under the radar, and the lack of forensic evidence left in such a bloody attack suggests experience—or at the least—planning. They clean up after themselves because they've been thinking about this for a while. Disorganized killers are the impulse killers. They may drive somewhere with the intent of killing someone, but they haven't planned it out. That's often why the goriest crime scenes are committed by disorganized, impulsive killers.

They rarely clean up because they didn't have a plan to begin with and don't have the stuff to do so. Most of the time, they're under thirty with a menial job—"

"How do you know that?" Caitlin asked. She'd given Nikki a list of the questions, so she had a ready answer.

"Those under thirty years old are more likely to be unstable, still trying to find their place in life. The disorganized killer leaves a lot of clues at a scene, including, sometimes, their DNA."

"But the Kline scene was very bloody," Caitlin said. "Yet they don't have the killer's DNA."

Nikki had seen the photos: Mr. Kline cut down near the stairs, left to bleed out. His wife outside near the pool, her throat slit so deeply, her spinal cord was visible. And Amy Kline, her naked body floating face down in Bone Lake. "Exactly, which tells me that if we have to label him, we're looking for a mixed offender, meaning he shows traits of both. Based on the violence left at the scene, these appear to be emotionally charged murders, which is consistent with disorganized offenders. But this killer didn't leave any usable forensic evidence. That means he came prepared to protect himself, so there's at least some degree of premeditation. Thanks to Matt Kline, we know Amy likely interrupted the killer. Perhaps he wasn't expecting her, or she put up a fight and took longer to kill than he anticipated, which left no time to clean up."

Nikki looked down at the photo of Amy's body, out of sight of the camera. "The working theory at the time was that Amy's ex-boyfriend, Ben, was the culprit. Unlike Amy's parents, she had been raped before she'd died, according to the medical examiner. They believed Ben had shown up to see Amy and got into an argument with her parents, who he then slaughtered. Amy must have been in her room. When she realized what was going on, she helped Matt escape and then confronted Ben. Ben was a few years older than Amy and the parents didn't approve of him." Nikki held up the photo of the tire tracks taken just outside the Klines' driveway the next morning. "Both Amy and her parents drove four-door sedans, but a larger vehicle, either a truck or SUV, had made those fresh marks. And that's exactly what Ben drove."

"But he had an alibi?" Caitlin asked.

"Yes. I've gone over the witness statements, statements from friends, the autopsy, all the police files. As a profiler, there's one thing that sticks out to me, and I think it's something crucial the original investigators might have missed."

Caitlin was on the edge of the leather chair.

"Sandy Kline's throat wasn't just cut, it was severed down to her spine, with no sign of hesitation marks. An act like that is almost always driven by rage."

"Are you saying the police have been wrong all these years, and the murders had nothing to do with Amy Kline?" Caitlin's eyes were wide.

"I'm saying that Amy may have been sexually assaulted in an effort to make it look like she was the one he was after. If Sandy Kline were the real target, a diversion like this would ensure he was never found."

The producer called cut and announced a five-minute break.

Caitlin grabbed Nikki's arm, motioning her to wait until the studio cleared.

"Was it that bad?" Nikki asked.

"Not at all," Caitlin said. "You really believe the police were looking the wrong way from the start?"

"It's certainly possible going by the information I've looked at, but remember, I haven't conducted interviews or gone into too much depth."

"Liam said the same thing months ago when I told him about the documentary idea." Caitlin had been seeing Nikki's partner for more than a year. They'd met when Nikki returned to Stillwater, along with her team, to help solve the murders of two teenaged girls. "The violence to Mrs. Kline really bugged him. And I've uncovered some information that suggests the Klines weren't the all-American perfect family."

Nikki smiled at her friend. "If anyone can get to the bottom of the case, it's you. I'll help in any way I can, as long as the office approves it." She didn't think it would be a problem. Profiling was such a hot topic that her boss had jumped at the idea of Nikki being involved in the documentary. The more the public understood it wasn't a magic tool, the better. Television shows had made profiling into something nearly godlike, able to ride into town and rescue the damsel in distress.

In reality, profilers were often brought in after all other leads were exhausted—and not a damned thing about the job was glamorous. It didn't mean flying in a private jet or even first class. The local police provided them with the case materials, which the profiler spent hours and sometimes days going through, looking for patterns. The greats had learned to spot the patterns and connect the dots, not because they were mind readers but because they'd dedicated their careers—and, in truth, their entire lives—to understanding and predicting behavior. Since they were usually invited in weeks, if not months, after the crime had occurred, profiling could be tedious. Constantly defending your methods despite years of proven success was an exercise in patience.

"About the profile," Caitlin said. "We'll discuss it on camera, but how do you think the Klines' killer would have acted after the murders?"

"He might have seemed agitated in the weeks after, but the more time that passed, the more confident he would have become. If I'm right in my theory about Sandy, he would have been able to figure out that the police were looking the wrong way if he watched the news footage of them arresting Amy's boyfriend. A feeling of superiority would have grown. He would have become more and more comfortable in his choices, possibly even snooping around the investigation. Not in an obvious way, but just a prolonged interest in it, more than the average person."

"How would he have been acting in the days leading up to it?" Caitlin asked.

"That's a lot tougher to answer without knowing the motivation," Nikki said. "We'd need to know a lot more about why he did it for that behavior to even stand out in people's memory, and those are always shaky, especially in a case this old." She thought about the crime scene photos. "He was older though. He might not have cleaned up the scene, but he also didn't make a mess. He kept his wits, and we've seen over and over again in first-time offenders that age makes a big impact on behavioral reaction."

"So, not a twenty-year-old college dropout who still lives at home with his parents?"

"No, I don't think so. He must have had his own place because the Klines lost so much blood, including the spatter in the hallway from Mr. Kline, that he would have had blood all over him. I suppose if his parents gave him plenty of privacy, but given the late hour, and the vehicle—neither one of Ben's parents owned a truck, and Ben drove an old, blue Chevy S-10 pickup. None of their vehicles' tires matched those tracks. In my opinion, whoever killed the Klines was physically fit, with the means to own a large vehicle, and his living situation didn't draw any attention to him."

"How certain are you that Sandy knew him?"

"Almost certain." Nikki caught the glint in Caitlin's eye. "Why do you look like a cat gearing up to pounce?"

"My producer received a tip this morning about information that could change the course of the case, and it allegedly has to do with Sandy."

TWO

PRESENT DAY

Nikki scowled and flicked the iridescent beetle off her tomato plants. "Beat it." She and Lacey had spent the summer working on the garden—the first one Nikki had planted since she'd been a teenager. It had done well for its first year, yielding zucchini, yellow squash, and green beans. Those had already been harvested for the year, but late August meant tomatoes. She'd waited all summer for those tomatoes, and she'd be damned if the invasive Japanese beetle destroyed her plants. Nikki didn't want to use harsh chemicals on the food and couldn't bring herself to drown the beetles in dish soap and water. Rory had finally used potassium bicarbonate, which killed the eggs, and the pests had slowly thinned down, or so Nikki had thought. As she surveyed her plants, she counted twelve shiny green beetles gnawing away.

A gentle breeze from the east brought the rich aroma of the wild bergamot flowers at the end of the garden. Nikki had read the leaves could be used for tea, but she'd never tried it. Her parents had practically lived on iced tea, and even though two decades had passed since their murders, tea still made Nikki queasy.

She picked up the hose she had dragged out with her and sprayed the plants down. Most of the beetles took off, but they'd be back. The battle never ended. Nikki snagged four of the best-looking, fattest tomatoes off their drooping vines, carefully putting them in the container she'd brought outside. The solitary diamond on her ring finger sparkled in the midday sun. Rory had wanted something bigger than a carat, but Nikki had put her foot down. They'd had a small wedding in June, followed by a reception at Rory's parents'. Lacey had been the flower girl, throwing daisies at everyone she passed.

Nikki was still processing it all. After her divorce, she hadn't expected to find love again, and she definitely hadn't planned on getting married, but Rory had changed all of that. He loved her and six-year-old Lacey deeply and wanted them to be an official part of the family. He didn't want to replace Lacey's late father, but they had filed paperwork for Rory to legally adopt Lacey not long after they were married. It should have been a simple process, but Tyler's parents had to butt in. They were terrified that the adoption meant they would lose access to Lacey, despite knowing Nikki would never do that to her daughter. She wanted Lacey to remember her father. Their divorce had been amicable, and he'd been a good, brave man. They'd just fallen out of love. She would never hurt his parents like that. In an effort to show how important they were in Lacey's life, she'd allowed Lacey to spend the last two weeks of the summer with them at their cabin near the Boundary Waters, close to the Canadian border. She and Rory hoped the gesture would alleviate some of her grandparents' concerns, allowing the adoption to move forward.

Nikki picked up the bowl of tomatoes and headed back to the house, enjoying the pleasant summer breeze. Hopefully Minnesota's hot months were behind them, and they would have more than a few weeks before the cold and snow arrived.

Kevin the cat greeted her with a loud yowl. Lacey had

convinced them to adopt the yellow tabby at Christmastime after they'd explained their busy schedules just couldn't accommodate a dog right now. Lacey had bonded with the cat right away, naming him Kevin after her favorite character in the movie *Up*.

"Oh no, I can see a tiny part of the bottom of your bowl." Nikki rolled her eyes. She shook the bowl, evening out the food, and sat it back down. Kevin looked up at her with disgust. Knowing this was another battle she'd never win, Nikki found the food and dumped a little more into the bowl. Kevin ate like he was starving for thirty seconds and then hopped up in the open kitchen window and started licking his rear end. "Typical male."

She checked the time. Rory didn't normally work on Sundays, but he'd left earlier to deal with a supply issue. Rory owned a successful construction company, and they were due to start a big project in the next week. Nikki needed to finish the paperwork for her team's last case—a rapist they'd tracked across the Midwest and taken down in Wisconsin—but she hated how quiet the house was without Lacey.

She scanned the kitchen for her phone and found it on the table. Sheriff Miller had called three times in the short time she'd been outside. Since Nikki's return to Washington County, she'd worked several high-profile cases with Miller, but things had been quiet for the last year. She hadn't talked to Miller in over a month, and instinct told her this wasn't a social call.

Nikki unlocked the phone, feeling more on edge when she saw that Miller hadn't left her a message. He never left sensitive information in a message, especially at the beginning of a case when a victim hadn't been identified or their family hadn't yet been found.

Definitely not a social call.

She hit 'call back.'

"Miller." He picked up quickly. Any hope Nikki had of the

call not being about something awful disappeared. She had worked with Miller enough to recognize the tone of voice. Someone was either dead or missing.

"It's Nikki. What's going on?"

"Double homicide, two teenaged girls. They rented an Airbnb for the weekend. Cleaners arrived this morning and discovered them. A third is missing. Is there any way you could come to the scene? I know the new boss starts tomorrow, but I have a feeling I'm going to need your team."

Special Agent Hernandez, Nikki's supervisor, had been offered a plum position at FBI headquarters in D.C. The decision had been a difficult one, but turning down a promotion in the Bureau often set agents back several years. Hernandez's replacement was due to start bright and early tomorrow morning. Getting involved in a case without his authorization would piss him off out of the gate, and that seemed ill-advised, but Nikki couldn't ignore Miller's plea.

"I'm getting the sense that I've walked into a shitstorm that's just gaining speed," Miller continued.

"Why? What am I missing?"

Miller told her the address.

Nikki's stomach bottomed out. "I'll be there in forty-five minutes."

THREE

Nikki jumped in the shower, her thoughts racing. Normally, after a request from any law enforcement officer, she called Liam, her second-in-command of the unit and her protégé. Over the past couple of years, she and Liam had both allowed personal involvement to leak into cases, resulting in a lot of pushback from the FBI brass, so she felt less inclined to involve him until she knew more about the case. Plus, she didn't want Hernandez's replacement to be angry at him as well as her from day one.

Thanks to several high-profile cases, Nikki's notoriety had only grown when she'd returned to Stillwater and worked her first case with the Washington County sheriff's department. The bigwigs at Quantico and D.C. had been initially thrilled about her team's success, but it was more about politics than people. During her first month at Quantico as a recruit, Nikki had been shocked at how many well-educated and experienced agents knew little about the middle of the country. Most of them seemed to think the Midwest was basically Chicago and farmland, which was only part of the truth. Much of the Midwest was rural, the agricultural lifeline of the country, so

Nikki never understood why recruits from places like New York and Boston acted like the Midwest didn't matter. In some of her colleagues' eyes, the only time someone from the middle of the country mattered was if they wound up dead and on national news. Every agent in the Bureau wanted to jump on those cases because the Midwest was safe and stuff like that "never happened there."

Nikki knew firsthand that wasn't true. Unlike her time at the University of Minnesota, Nikki couldn't be anonymous at Quantico. Every single person knew who she was and what had happened to her parents, and it seemed some of them expected her to crack at any moment. Her roommate at the time had likened it to the way Clarice Starling had been treated at the beginning of *The Silence of the Lambs*. It had only made Nikki more determined to succeed.

When she'd accepted the offer to start the unit in Minnesota, she'd been instructed on how important it was that the Bureau's reputation in the Midwest improved, because they were getting pushbacks from Washington. Nikki had ignored it all and did her job, and the agency had loved it, especially the effect it had on their overall crime numbers. That had allowed Nikki more freedom within her unit than a lot of others, but it also meant a higher profile. She'd made her own investigative mistakes when a serial killer she'd been chasing for years took Lacey but had managed to smooth it over with the department because of the extreme circumstances. They'd all been pulled through an emotional wringer and come out stronger.

Liam, on the other hand, hadn't been so lucky. Last summer, when two little girls had been taken during a fireworks celebration, he had made the mistake of omitting that his girl-friend's son might have had information about the kidnappings. Liam had been suspended without pay for two weeks, despite Nikki and Miller's protests. He'd spent the past year doing everything by the book, and the entire experience had brought the team closer.

Nikki towel-dried her wavy hair and threw on comfortable clothes and tennis shoes before making sure her notebook and pen were in her bag, along with her FBI badge. She left a message on Rory's cell, letting him know she had a case and may not be back tonight.

Before she pulled out of the driveway, Nikki double-checked that her gun remained locked in the case beneath the seat. She didn't always have the weapon on her person, especially at a crime scene.

She drove down the county road, taking Highway 15 north toward Scandia, a small village in northern Washington County. Scandia had been settled by the Swedes, with many families remaining in the area for generations. Highway 15 ran along the western side of Big Marine Lake. Boats of all kinds floated in the big, popular lake, the recreation area and beach overflowing with young people trying to enjoy the last week of summer—a stark contrast to the last time Nikki was at the lake nearly two years ago. A missing young woman had been discovered in the lake days before Christmas, and Nikki had almost become a victim of the serial killer responsible. She shook the memories out of her mind as she passed the final bit of the lake and turned her focus to Miller's call.

She still couldn't believe the timing, and the seasoned, cynical cop in her didn't believe this would turn out to be a coincidence. Not after the documentary that had just premiered on Netflix. 23816 Lofton Avenue North, nick-named Lilydale after the original builder's wife, was infamous to anyone who'd lived in the area in 2001, when three members of a well-known family had been slaughtered. Nikki had been in college, with no desire to return to her hometown. She'd heard about the murders in college, but the pain of losing her parents had been too fresh. Nikki had managed to avoid learning any real details about the case until Caitlin asked her to do an initial profile, using police reports, witness interviews and statements, crime-scene photos and the coroner's report. Like many of the cases she'd cut her teeth on at Quantico, the case had long been cold, with few leads. She hadn't had as much access to the case files as a consultant, but she'd done her best with what Caitlin had been able to share with her.

Liam's girlfriend, a renowned journalist, had spent the better part of the last year working on a documentary about the killings for Netflix. Local newspapers referred to the unknown killer as the Butcher of Bone Lake. The lake hadn't been named after the murders, but by the Swedes, who initially called it "Bonny Lake." That had been shortened to Bone at some point.

The show had premiered last night, on the anniversary of the murders, and the location Miller had told Nikki on the phone was the exact same house. The documentary had been advertised for weeks by not only Netflix but also local news. Caitlin's ultimate goal was the case getting attention and a new investigation, which Nikki had warned her was a long shot unless tangible evidence had been uncovered. The case would definitely be back in the spotlight, and not with the kind of attention Caitlin had intended. Had the killer reacted to the documentary by attacking the residents of the house again, or were they dealing with some kind of copycat?

Several newer homes had been built since 2001, but the north side of the lake had developed at a much slower rate, with only two new homes going up since the murders. As she drove down Lofton Avenue, Nikki noticed Fox 9 and KARE 11 news vans hugging the shoulder, while a couple of reporters and cameramen tried to line up their shots. The woman from Fox 9's eyes recognized Nikki as she drove by. The reporter shouted at her cameraman. Nikki ignored both of them and followed the road until she reached the gated driveway near the intersection of Lofton and 238th Street, which wrapped around the north side of the lake.

A young Washington County deputy whose name Nikki couldn't remember stood in front of the gate with a clipboard. He jogged to her window.

"Agent Hunt, right?"

Nikki held up her badge, and the deputy opened the gate for Nikki to pass through. Giant willow trees lined the driveway, blocking most of the house. Pea gravel crunched beneath the jeep tires as the three-story Victorian came into view. Despite the severity of the situation, Nikki had to tamp down her excitement about seeing the house inside. She'd been here a lifetime ago with her mother during a parade of the area's historical homes but didn't remember much other than the sheer size of the place. Her late mother had loved old houses and passed that down to Nikki. The first summer after Nikki and Rory had met, she'd been working a kidnapping case at the F. Scott Fitzgerald house in St. Paul. As grand as that place had been, the Queen Anne Tower-style house eclipsed it.

Nikki shut the engine off and grabbed protective gear out of her bag, along with her notebook and pen. As she got out, she took in the property layout. Maple and birch trees surrounded the house, which sat less than a hundred yards from the lake. A pontoon boat was anchored next to a large floating dock. Out on the lake, people watched the action from their boats, as though it were some kind of production instead of a triple murder scene.

She headed up the stone walk, taking in the house. Bright purple pansies decorated the wraparound front porch, which also featured two Adirondack chairs and a small wicker end table.

Another deputy guarded the double-doored entryway. Nikki showed her badge to the deputy and then put on her booties. Like a lot of old houses, the front door led into a vestibule, the passage between the outer and interior doors with a closet and an area for shoes. Nikki didn't see any sign of forced entry or blood, but as soon as she stepped into the hallway, the heady scent of copper assaulted her.

How much blood had been spilled in this house?

The front room was set up like a parlor, although with modern furnishing, including a small cabinet piano. At the back of the room, two wooden doors stood open, revealing the modern living room, a large flat-screen television the focal point. A victim lay perpendicular to the television, only bare legs and feet visible behind the overturned chair. Remnants of a porcelain vase were scattered around the room.

Despite years of seeing horrific crime scenes, Nikki gasped at the sight of the woman's face. Someone had beaten her so badly they would need dental records or fingerprints to identify her.

"For once, I beat you here." Courtney, head of the FBI crime lab, stood in the corner of the room taking pictures. She winced. "Not the right choice of verb."

Courtney had been one of the first people Nikki had requested for her new unit in St. Paul when she'd arrived from Quantico several years ago. Courtney had been a rising star in Virginia during Nikki's tenure, and when Nikki learned that Courtney had been looking for an opportunity to come back to the Midwest to be closer to her family, Nikki had given the information to Hernandez, and he'd pulled the strings to get Courtney promoted as the Minnesota Bureau's Head Criminal Analyst. Nikki's team had solved more than one tough case thanks to Courtney's brilliance. She and Courtney had bonded quickly, and she'd become Nikki's closest friend.

Nikki tried to ignore the reek of soaked blood and bodily fluids as she crouched down next to the girl. Blood stained the girl's blue tank top. She swallowed back nausea. "If I didn't know better, I'd think an AR-15 did this."

"I wish," Courtney said. "It would have been more merciful than this. I just hoped they died quickly."

"Any idea who she is?"

"Not yet." Miller appeared in the open doorway to the dining room. "The other one is in here."

The dining and kitchen area had been modernized since the original murders. Nikki had seen a less open floor plan in the photos from 2001. A young, dark-skinned woman slumped in the corner of the dining room, her face as beaten as the other victim's. Her skull had been cleaved down the middle, blood smeared and sprayed on the wall behind her. Defensive wounds on the girl's hands showed she'd put up some kind of fight. Hopefully she had managed to get some of her attacker's DNA.

"An axe?" Nikki asked, examining what remained of the young woman's head.

"Maybe, or a hammer or crowbar," Miller said. He pointed to the blood spatter on the walls. "But this is obviously where she fell."

Nikki examined the wide swath of blood the girl's head had left when she'd slid down the wall. She peered at the skull, careful not to touch anything. "Back of her head was probably bashed in, but not here since the wall doesn't have any damage besides blood." She looked at the hardwood floor. Blood droplets led into the kitchen. Someone had yanked the drawers open, likely in search of a weapon. Nikki scanned the area but didn't see any sign of a knife block. "Who found them?"

"Cleaning service," Miller said. "This place is an Airbnb, and checkout time was 10 a.m. The crew arrived about twenty minutes later and called it in."

Nikki hadn't used Airbnb very much, but the house couldn't have been cheap. "Who signed the rental agreement?"

Miller checked his notes. "Alexia Perry. She said that a couple of friends might join her while she was staying at the property, but assured the property management company it would be no more than five people. I cross-referenced the email address she gave the property manager and found Alexia on social media. I think she's the one missing."

Nikki eyed the two tied trash bags next to the back door. Red Solo cups and paper plates were visible through the thin plastic. Two different kinds of vodka sat on the counter, along with a half-empty simple syrup and several empty beer cans. "Looks like Alexia had a party."

"That's what I'm thinking," Miller said. "Which means our suspect list could be extensive."

He led Nikki up the impressive, L-shaped staircase. She stopped on the landing to look out the bay window, which overlooked the front of the property. Bone Lake glimmered in the sun, peaceful and idyllic, unlike the scene inside the beautiful, old home.

They continued climbing to the second floor, to another, larger landing with a bay window, this one accompanied by a built-in window seat.

Miller pointed to the locked door on their left. "Smallest bedroom, they use as office and storage. Property manager is the only one with a key. One of the girls appears to have stayed in the big room next door."

The large room sat at the front of the property, providing an incredible view of the lake. The four-poster double bed appeared to have been hastily made. A carry-on-sized suitcase lay open on the floor, clothes scattered around it. "Looks more like a messy girl than someone searching for stuff. Have you found her purse? Cell phone?"

"I waited for you," he said. "Plus, the cleaning service called the property management company. Death investigator took one look and decided to call the medical examiner to the scene. She's on her way. That's why we haven't touched the bodies. I'm hoping we'll find phones or ID in their pockets."

Nikki snapped on latex gloves and checked the armoire

across from the bed. "Extra bedding and pillows." She shut the door and crouched next to the open suitcase. The owner had packed a couple days' worth of clothing, but Nikki didn't see any sign of a wallet. She unzipped the pink toiletry bag and examined the contents. She held up a pack of pink pills. "She brought her birth control but didn't take it yesterday. Of course, the actual box, with the prescription and her name, isn't here." Her gaze landed on the bottle of Fenty foundation. She held up the bottle for Miller to see. "Shade 390. Unless there's another Black girl we don't know about, this room belongs to the victim in the dining room."

They exited the room and followed the curved hallway, and Nikki immediately recognized it as the stretch of hallway with the bedrooms that belonged to the victims in 2001. Caitlin's documentary team had spent a few days getting interior shots of the house, so Nikki knew the room to her right had once belonged to Amy Kline, who'd been found floating face down in the lake, stabbed several times. The original investigators believed that an injured Amy had gone to the lake and tried to escape in the family's fishing boat but had fallen overboard due to blood loss. Unlike today, the day after the Kline massacre had been humid and foggy, resulting in Amy's body not being spotted until nearly noon.

The documentary used photos from the original case, sans the victims' bodies. The re-creation of the blond-haired girl floating in the lake, with fog still hanging overhead, had chilled Nikki when she had watched it.

"Looks like the person who stayed here brought more stuff with her." Nikki's eyes landed on the designer purse sitting on the nightstand. She quickly found a matching wallet and searched for the identification. "Alexia Perry, eighteen." A chill went through Nikki as she read the license's details. "This says she's 5'8" and 130 pounds. The white female downstairs is too small." She looked at Miller, who nodded.

"We haven't found anyone matching Alexia's description," he said.

They both hurried across the hall to what had been the Klines' master bedroom. It had been occupied by someone as well. While Nikki checked their belongings, Miller headed to the last bedroom next to the locked attic door.

"A female stayed in here," he called out. "Judging by the length of the joggers on the bed, it's the girl from the dining room." His voice grew closer. "You find anything?"

Nikki held up the wallet she'd found in the duffle sitting at the end of the bed. According to his driver's license, five and a half foot, one-hundred-forty-pound Chandler Glover had also been staying at the house. "Yeah, a Chandler Glover's driver's license." She looked back at Miller. "So where is he?"

The medical examiner had arrived by the time Nikki and Miller made it downstairs. Miller headed out to update his deputies about the possibility of two more victims—or suspects—in the area.

Nikki joined Dr. Blanchard in the parlor. She stood over the dark-skinned victim with her clipboard, notating what she saw.

"Dr. Blanchard, have you found anything—"

She held up a bagged iPhone. "It was in her back pocket, still has battery. Locked screen showed a notification. She's got one of those pockets on the back of her phone case. Her name is Vivienne Beckett. Someone named Olivia B texted her last night."

Got home safe. Talk tomorrow? The iPhone's settings blurred the home screen, making it impossible for Nikki to make out anything of substance.

"I'll let Miller know," Nikki said. "We found a driver's license for a Chandler Glover, but there's no sign of him."

"Agent Hunt?" One of Courtney's criminalists appeared in

the doorway, holding a shattered iPhone. "This was in the downstairs bathroom."

The slick latex gloves almost made Nikki drop the other phone. The frozen screen showed another message. *I'm home. Still creeped by what u did.* Nikki tapped the screen, hoping the phone would respond, but nothing happened. She slipped it into an evidence bag. "We need to find out who it belongs to."

The downstairs bathroom was on the other side of the house. Nikki would expect to find the phone closer to the other victim if it belonged to her—kids were never far from their phones these days. She turned the iPhone over in her hand. Finding Olivia had to be a top priority. She might be able to identify the victims as well as shed light on what had happened.

Miller returned. "A driver's license was with the phone. Vivienne Beckett, eighteen years old." She showed Miller the cell phone from the bathroom. "Someone called Olivia sent Vivienne and whoever owns this phone a text saying she got home safely. She didn't stay the night." Nikki dreaded telling the teenaged girl about her friends and how close she'd come to being a victim. "Once we get an address, I'll head there to interview her. She could be crucial."

"I'll have a deputy track down Vivienne's parents." Miller held up the driver's license they'd found in Chandler's room. "I found Chandler's parents through public record, but I haven't notified them. I had our social media liaison go through his online accounts and came up with a phone number." Miller punched in the numbers on his phone and waited. "It's ringing. Nope, voicemail."

"Nik!" Courtney called from the kitchen. "There's a phone vibrating in here somewhere."

She and Miller hurried to join her.

"It just stopped, but it's somewhere in this area." Courtney gestured to the kitchen.

Miller hit redial.

"It's over here somewhere." Nikki went to the corner of the kitchen, where the pantry and infamous dumbwaiter were located. Could one of them have tried to do the same thing little Matt Kline had done in 2001?

The dumbwaiter door opened easily. A flashing iPhone was jammed between the moving seat and the door. The bottom of the dumbwaiter was missing, the earthy scent of a root cellar filling the air.

Nikki shone her phone's flashlight down the passage. In 2001, the cellar had consisted of dirt floors and walls, more suited to a storm shelter. Since then, a cement floor had been poured over at least part of the cellar, and she could see a shelving unit and gardening tools in the corner.

She also saw a man's bare foot.

FOUR

Miller used a crowbar to break the padlock on the basement door, which was located in the narrow hallway between the kitchen and the door that led to the covered porch. Damp earth and stale air greeted them as they descended the narrow, rickety steps. Miller shone his big flashlight over their heads, searching for a light, but they didn't see anything.

They quickly made their way to the center of the space, near the back wall, where Chandler had fallen from the dumbwaiter. His right leg was bent at an odd angle, likely broken. His dark hair had been slicked back from his pale, clammy face, and his arms outstretched like a snow angel.

"He's breathing." Nikki dropped to her knees and checked his pulse. "Pulse is slow but steady. We need EMS." She knew Miller had sent the ambulances away when they had discovered the two bodies, and it would take at least ten minutes or longer for a crew to get to the house. "Radio it in, but send Blanchard down."

The wooden stairs shook as Miller ran upstairs.

Nikki touched her hands to the young man's clammy face. "Chandler, can you hear me?"

To her surprise, he emitted a faint groan.

"Just relax." Nikki kept her tone gentle. "We're going to get you out of here."

Chandler tried to speak, but no sound came out.

Blanchard hurried down the steps with her medical kit.

"He's lost blood, but I haven't tried to move him." Nikki angled her flashlight so that Blanchard could move without falling. "I don't know the source. He did respond to his name."

Blanchard knelt next to Nikki, stethoscope already in her ears. "Pulse is okay. Judging by his cracked lips, he's dehydrated." She leaned over and squeezed his bare toes on the leg that hadn't been broken. Chandler moaned again, moving his foot around. Blanchard repeated the exercise with both of his arms and he tried to pull away. "All good signs he's not paralyzed." Blanchard slipped her hands beneath him, cradling his neck. "We need to find the source of the bleeding. If it's a head wound, time is of the essence."

"Chandler, we're going to roll you just a little bit so we can see your back." Nikki cradled the flashlight against her ear. Chandler's eyes fluttered open.

"Pupils reacted to light," Blanchard said. "Chandler, can you hear us?"

His nodded his head.

"Okay, just hang on."

Nikki and Blanchard carefully eased Chandler up, trying not to disturb his broken leg. Nikki slipped her hand next to Blanchard. "I've got him. You assess."

"No head wound," Blanchard said. "At least not one that's bleeding. He likely has a concussion." She moved to examine Chandler's back. "Two stab wounds, neither in life-threatening places, but he's lost plenty of blood and infection has likely set in."

Nikki gently eased him back to the floor. "Chandler, can you open your eyes again and try to talk to me? I'm the FBI, and

I'm here with the sheriff. Something happened last night. Do you remember anything?"

Chandler squeezed his eyes shut. "Libs, the girls... are they okay?"

Nikki didn't want to send his body into further shock, and, technically, Chandler had to be considered a suspect. He could have attacked the girls and tried to escape through the cellar. "Do you remember what happened last night?"

Tears leaked out of Chandler's eyes. "Everything was okay... and then he was in the house."

"Did you see his face?" Nikki's mind raced with questions.

"No. Dressed in black."

Nikki didn't want to push too much right now, but she needed answers. "Who else was here when the attack happened?"

"Viv, me." He winced in pain. "Alexia and Libby. They're okay, right?"

She didn't want to tell him about his friends before EMS arrived. "What's Libby's last name? We need to call her parents."

"Brown."

"Do you think Alexia could be involved? We haven't been able to find her."

Chandler shifted, suddenly becoming aware of his leg. Pain was etched across his pale face.

"The ambulance is on the way." Miller reappeared on the stairs. "How is he?"

"Preliminary exam is good," Blanchard said. "No immediate signs of paralysis or major head injury. He's come around a bit."

Nikki asked Chandler about Alexia again, but he could only focus on the agony in his legs. Blanchard offered to wait with him until EMS came.

"Chandler, I'll see you at the hospital," Nikki told him. "It's going to be okay." She couldn't imagine the PTSD the kid would have to endure in the upcoming months and maybe even years.

Nikki motioned for Miller to follow her upstairs. She told him what Chandler had said. "The other victim is Libby Brown. He's in too much pain to say much else. Still no sign of Alexia?"

"No," Miller replied. "I searched the whole house again after you found Chandler. She's not here. I'll put out an APB saying we need to locate her whereabouts, that she could be in danger. If she's involved somehow, we don't want to set her off that we know. In the meantime, I'm setting up a search grid, ten-mile radius." He pointed toward the east side of the house. "More populated over here, so I've got two deputies canvassing all the neighbors. I've got three more searching west/northwest of the house, which is mostly timber and fields. That's the most likely escape route if you're not going out the front door. Chisago County sheriff's going to search on his side of the line, and we'll meet up in the middle."

"What about Vivienne and Libby's parents?"

"Once I track down Libby's address, I'll contact both families. According to Facebook, Alexia's mother's name is Shanna Perry. Working on getting her contact information. If the dad's involved in her life, he's not on social media."

"We need to talk to the property manager," Nikki said. "Especially since Alexia is the one who rented the Airbnb. I can track her down and have Liam go to the hospital. I assume you want to stay here?"

He nodded. "We're locking down the property. Media is already trying to barge in. It's not happening. I don't know if that damned documentary had anything to do with this, but I'm not going to let these kids' murders be fodder for entertainment."

"Hey, guys." Courtney joined them, her face paler than usual. "I picked up the remote to dust for prints, and the television came out of sleep mode." She turned and headed toward the living room, motioning for them to follow her.

Dread swept through Nikki as she and Miller entered the living room. She immediately recognized the question on the screen: *Are you still watching Netflix?*

Nikki's stomach lurched as she realized what the group had been watching. "*Bone Lake: An American Horror Story.*"

FIVE

"We need to keep their interest in the 2001 murders out of the press," Nikki said. "This thing will turn into a circus really quickly."

Miller glanced at his phone and swore. "That's not going to happen. We found this on Alexia's Instagram account." He held his phone for Nikki to see.

"Watching *Bone Lake: An American Horror Story* at the murder house! Binging starts at 8 p.m.!"

Alexia had tagged more than a dozen people, including someone called Olivia Barton. *Bingo.*

"Looks like we've found our Olivia," Nikki commented. "But our suspect list just opened up quite significantly." Alexia had over two thousand friends on Instagram, and the message had been reposted multiple times.

Nikki scrolled through Alexia's feed. She'd posted on Instagram about the documentary at least ten times between 8 p.m. and midnight. Much of it was harmless commentary on specific scenes, but Nikki's worry intensified as she continued.

"Her last post was at 12:17 this morning. 'Cat's out of the bag! Did you spot me in the doc?'" She looked at Miller. Nikki had only watched the documentary once, but she would have remembered seeing Alexia. "What's she talking about?"

"No clue, but maybe Olivia can answer that. I'll track down her address. We need the names of everyone who stepped foot inside this house over the weekend. Have you called Liam?"

"Not yet," Nikki said. "I'll call him on my way to talk with Olivia." She glanced out the front window and saw Chandler being secured in the ambulance. "I'm going to see if he remembers anything else."

Nikki jogged down the steps to the ambulance and approached the rig. Blanchard had already gone back to the victims inside, more comfortable with the dead than the living.

"Is he any more alert?"

The paramedic attending to Chandler's IV nodded. "In and out, but he knows where he is."

Nikki climbed into the rig, keeping her voice low. "I'm sure he'll be taken to surgery, so I'm hoping to ask him a few more questions before you guys head to the hospital." She squeezed in next to him and patted his hand. "Chandler, it's Nikki from the FBI."

Chandler's eyes flooded open. "My mom..."

"She'll meet you at the hospital," Nikki assured him. "Chandler, I know you're in pain, but can you tell me how many people were here over the weekend?"

"Bunch during day," he mumbled.

Nikki had suspected as much after seeing the overflowing kitchen trash and liquor bottles. "How many actually stayed over?"

"Four," he managed. "Others left later. After documentary."

"Is that the reason you guys rented the Airbnb?" Nikki struggled to keep the judgment out of her voice. She knew that at their age, in another lifetime where her own life hadn't been touched by violent crime, Nikki and her friend group probably would have done the same.

Chandler nodded. "Alexia... her thing."

She wanted to ask what Alexia had meant about seeing herself in the documentary, but the painkiller flowing through his IV was starting to take effect. He struggled to keep his eyes open, so Nikki prioritized. "How many others were here?"

"Seven."

"Seven more people?"

"Total."

"Can you give me names?" Nikki pressed. "Could Olivia tell us?"

"Who?"

"Olivia Barton. Was she here last night?"

"Oh yeah, Livvy. Livvy and Libby. Get it?"

"I do." Nikki squeezed his hand. "Olivia was here but left, right? She texted someone that she got home safely."

"Yeah. Olivia."

"You remember where she lives?"

"Townhouse."

"Thank you." Chandler was fading into painless sleep. "Hang in there."

He mumbled something, then his eyes closed.

Nikki jumped out of the ambulance and went back inside to find Miller. She told him what Chandler had said. "A few others stayed to watch the documentary and left. Hopefully she can fill in those blanks. What about the phone in the bathroom? We need to get it unlocked, especially if it's Alexia's. She's in presumed danger, so no need for a warrant. You guys have the Cellebrite software, right?" Cellebrite allowed police to unlock a victim's phone, without a warrant, quickly.

"We just trained someone in it," Miller answered. "I sent the phone back to the government center with a deputy. Hopefully we'll have something within the next twenty-four hours. In the meantime, I've got the office using her social media photos for the APB. I hate to do this when we can't get ahold of her parents, but Alexia is eighteen and in danger. Surrounding counties are on alert, too."

Nikki was worried about Alexia. While interest in true crime was understandable, and popular, Alexia's obsession with the Bone Lake murders could have had something to do with her friends' deaths, and put Alexia in danger too.

Miller looked at his watch. "The property manager is waiting at the Water Street hotel. She's got the rental information. Can you meet with her while I run things here?"

"It might be a better idea to speak to Olivia first. She's going to hear about her friends' deaths on the news if she hasn't already."

"I'll let the property manager know you'll be delayed," he said.

Nikki logged onto her work laptop and ran a search for Olivia Barton. There were only four in the metro area, but three were adults. Just as Chandler had said, she lived in a townhouse in one of the new developments in northwest Stillwater. She didn't think calling the girl about the tragedy was the way to handle it, even if Olivia had already heard. It was better to ask these questions in person—especially if Olivia didn't know what had happened.

Nikki drove past the line of emergency vehicles, glancing in her rearview mirror. The imposing house seemed to swallow the entire reflection. She waved at the deputy manning the roadblock Miller had set up a hundred yards away from the long driveway. Two reporters from the local news tried to get Nikki's attention, but she ignored them and told Siri to call Liam.

Liam listened while she filled him in on the morning's awful turn. He was silent for several seconds. "You're kidding, right?"

"No, and don't tell Caitlin. She'll hear about it soon enough."

As much as she liked Caitlin, Nikki knew she'd be front and center the second she found out, and the longer Nikki could put off her barrage of questions, the better.

"They took the boy, Chandler, to Lakeview in Stillwater. His parents are meeting him there. Miller's got to stay at the scene and lead the search for Alexia, but he needs to notify the other families first. Can you go and assist while I talk to Olivia and the property manager? And get Kendall and Jim on standby. We're going to have several people to track down—there's a list of people who may have been present at the house from an Instagram post. I'm hoping Olivia will be able to help us narrow down the list." The two junior agents were primarily Liam's responsibility, but Nikki had spent time in the field with both over the last year, and they were solid investigators.

"What about the two victims? Were they killed the same way as the Klines?"

"No. Those poor girls were so badly beaten in the face we couldn't identify either of them at first." Nikki still couldn't believe the beating Vivienne and Libby had both endured, so much of it centered on their faces. Had that been intentional or had the killer's rage gotten out of control? "Vivienne Beckett had her ID in her back pocket, and Chandler confirmed the other girl is Libby Brown."

"I can't believe this happened again at that house," Liam said. "I'm not superstitious unless it's about football, but that's some tragic coincidence."

"I'm not sure it's a coincidence," Nikki clarified. "We know they watched the documentary because Netflix was paused. We may have a copycat." Nikki would rather chase down a serial killer than a copycat, because she'd learned from experience that copycats' behaviors were much harder to anticipate. "Miller's got the job of notifying Vivienne's parents and Deputy

Reynolds will go to Libby's. They're trying to coordinate so neither one finds out from the other or the media. Blanchard is taking them to the medical examiner's office in Minneapolis. Miller's expecting you."

"I'm on it, boss."

SIX

Olivia Barton lived with her mother in a lovely townhouse overlooking Lake McKusick. The in-demand area featured amazing hiking trails and views, and the Barton condo sat on the cul-de-sac—a prime piece of real estate in any neighborhood. The development was among Stillwater's newest, and the home prices reflected the area's popularity. A black Kia Telluride and an older-model Toyota Camry were parked in front of the townhouse.

Nikki parked behind the Camry, breathing a small sigh of relief at the sight of the Kia. Before she'd left the scene, Nikki ran a records search for Olivia's address. Cross-referencing with the DMV showed a 2020 Kia Telluride registered to Nina Barton. She'd been afraid Olivia would be home alone. All of the victims had been entering their senior year of high school, and Nikki didn't want to deliver news like this to a minor without at least one parent present.

She made sure her pen and paper were in her bag and locked her gun in its case before sliding out of the jeep. The lake shimmered beneath the afternoon sun, with several people jogging or walking around the trail that circled the lake. Dread made Nikki's feet feel like lead as she walked up the pristine sidewalk. She took a deep breath and knocked.

A brunette with crow's feet and a bright smile opened the door. "Can I help you?"

Nikki held out her ID. "I'm looking for Olivia Barton. Are you her mother, Nina?"

The woman's eyes widened. "Yes, I'm Nina Barton. Olivia's upstairs."

"Do you know where she was last night?"

"Of course," Nina answered. "She spent the weekend with friends at an Airbnb they rented. She had an early shift this morning, so she didn't stay last night. What's this about?"

They hadn't heard about the massacre.

Nikki lowered her voice. "Ms. Barton, there's no easy way to say this. Sometime after your daughter left the lake house, two of Olivia's friends, Libby and Vivienne, were murdered, another badly injured, and one more missing."

Nina stared at Nikki as though she'd sprouted a second head.

"We haven't been able to locate Alexia," Nikki continued. "I need to speak with her right away."

Nina's dark eyes filled with tears. "You're serious. This happened last night... at that house?"

"I'm sorry to come unannounced," Nikki said. "But it's not the sort of thing you discuss over the phone. Would you mind getting Olivia?"

"Yes, of course," Nina stammered. "Can I tell her privately? Before she comes down?"

Nikki didn't believe Olivia was a suspect, but she would have preferred to see the girl's reaction. Given the situation, Nikki decided not to push. Her mother giving the news might help Olivia stay calm enough to talk with Nikki. "That's fine."

Nina started for the stairs. She stopped and looked at Nikki. "My daughter isn't a suspect?"

"Technically, anyone who came to the house over the weekend is a suspect, but Olivia's text brought me here. I'm just hoping she can tell us about the party, who was in the house over the weekend, that sort of thing."

"All right. Come in." Nina closed the door. "Make yourself at home."

She headed upstairs. Nikki listened to the sound of her footsteps, followed by a knock and a door opening. She could just hear Nina's voice but wasn't able to make out the words. Olivia's raw scream a few moments later chilled Nikki to her core. It was a sound she'd heard loved ones make a thousand times, the pain and shock nearly unbearable.

Minutes later, Nina descended the stairs, tears streaking her face, holding her daughter's hand. Olivia's rich, brown hair was tousled, her eyes still bleary with sleep and fresh tears. She clutched her phone. When she saw Nikki, she pushed her mother aside, jumping the last two steps. "Is it true?"

"I'm afraid so."

Olivia's legs folded, and she collapsed on the bottom step, sobbing. Her mother sat next to her and wrapped her arms around the shaking girl. Nikki gave them a few moments. Nina smoothed her daughter's hair and kissed her temple. "It's okay, honey. But the agent needs to see the video."

Nikki leaned forward. "Video?"

Fighting sobs, Olivia unlocked her phone and handed it to Nikki. "Last night... Alexia sent me a Snap video after I texted her that I'd got home safe." So the other phone belonged to Alexia, Nikki realized. "I was already asleep." She burst into fresh tears.

"Snapchat?" Nikki recognized the app. She'd learned from Caitlin's teenaged son that even texting was too much for some of Gen Z. They recorded video messages instead. She recognized the marble sink from the downstairs bathroom.

"I'm so done right now," Alexia said into the camera. Her

eyes shone with anger, her cheeks pink. "I'm not in the mood for a lecture from perfect Libby." Alexia rolled her eyes. "I stand by my choice and—" A bloodcurdling scream came from somewhere inside the house. Alexia dropped the phone, which explained why it had been found busted on the floor. Nikki choked up as she realized that if Alexia hadn't broken her phone, she might have been able to call for help.

"I would have called the police if I'd seen it before Mom woke me up." Olivia rocked back and forth. "They would still be alive."

"I don't think so," Nikki said. "It appears everything happened quickly. By the time Alexia heard that scream, it was probably too late for the other girls." Mascara from the night before stained her cheeks. "It's our understanding that you didn't spend the night because you had to work early this morning."

Olivia burst into a fresh round of tears. "I lied. I just didn't want to stay there."

"I'm so sorry," Nikki said. "Can we sit down somewhere?"

Nina ushered her daughter into the kitchen and Nikki followed. Nina flushed as she moved a pile of invoices and folders off the table. "Sorry, trying to catch up on some stuff. Please, sit."

Nikki waited until Olivia and her mother sat down. "Olivia, I know this is really difficult, but what can you tell me about the weekend? Why didn't you want to stay Saturday as well?"

"That place gives me the creeps," Olivia answered. "Especially upstairs. I couldn't sleep Friday night, so I made up a story about my boss making me come in earlier." She took a few moments to compose herself. "You wanted to know about the weekend. Where should I start?"

"The beginning," Nikki said.

"Well, Alexia rented the place because she wanted to watch the documentary premiere there, which we all thought was a little weird, but Alexia is persuasive. Five of us…" Her mouth trembled. "Came Friday. I stayed over that night. Yesterday we had a party—a last summer party."

"Do you know how many people came through the house over the weekend?"

"A lot," she said. "People were coming and going all day Saturday. Alexia said we weren't supposed to have a ton of people and had to be careful about the neighbors, so we kept everything in the back, by the pool."

"Who stayed to watch the documentary?"

"Alexia made everyone else leave after pizza so we could watch the documentary as a smaller group. There were seven of us, including me. I said I had to leave because I had to work early this morning."

"Who else besides you five?" Nikki asked.

"Brett Dalton and Luke Webb. Luke's kind of Alexia's boyfriend." Olivia's eyes widened as though just remembering something. "Some guy showed up at the house not long after we started watching the third episode. Alexia saw him drive up and went outside. When she came back in, she told us it was the property manager checking on things. Then Luke said something about the property manager being a woman, and Alexia got huffy with him. He got mad and left. He was Brett's ride, so Brett left with him."

Nikki scribbled the names into her notebook. "What time was this?"

"Around eleven, I think."

"Is Luke the jealous sort?"

Olivia shrugged. "I don't know if I'd call it jealousy. More like abandonment issues. His mom left when he was little." Her eyes widened. "Wait, you think Luke could have done this?"

"I don't know," Nikki answered. "That's why I've got to talk to everyone. Do you think he's capable?"

"No way. He didn't make it past dissecting the frog in anatomy. Legit threw up."

Nikki jotted the information down, resisting the urge to tell Olivia that she'd known more than one murderer who couldn't stand the sight of an injured animal but had no issue gutting the human being he felt had wronged him. Libby and Vivienne had been beaten in a rage. Could Luke have snapped?

"What about the guy who stopped by last night, the one Luke was upset about? Did you get a good look at him?"

Olivia shook her head. "It was dark. He had a gray Chevy truck."

"Was he tall, short, white, black?"

"He was white, and probably six feet."

"Did Alexia seem rattled when she came back inside after he left?"

"I wouldn't say rattled. More like amped up."

Nikki quickly texted Miller the information about the gray Chevy pickup. "And you guys went back to the documentary?"

Olivia nodded. "After Luke and Brett took off, yeah. I left right after the last episode finished."

Nikki confirmed the timestamp of Olivia's text. "When you left, it was just Alexia, Chandler, Libby and Vivienne at the house?"

She nodded.

"Did you notice anything odd?"

"No."

"Did you see any sign of Luke or Brett?"

"No, but I wasn't looking. My mom said someone is missing?"

"Alexia Perry," Nikki answered. "How well do you know Alexia?"

Olivia's lips trembled. "We've been friends since elementary school. I probably know her better than anyone. She could still be alive, right?"

Nikki nodded. "Why was it important to her that you all watch the documentary?"

"I guess she's a bit of a true crime buff," Olivia said. "She did a paper about the murders last year for her psychology class. Since then, she's been kind of consumed with it. I couldn't understand it, because it's just awful, but Alexia wants a career in criminal justice."

"Tell me about her as a person," Nikki continued. "Sounds like she's a resourceful kid."

"That's an understatement." Olivia wiped her eyes with the back of her hand. "Alexia's a hard worker. She knows what she wants and how to get it. I envy that about her. She's not afraid of taking risks."

Nikki thought she sounded like a type A personality: someone who would overachieve. "What was she wearing last night?"

"Black bike shorts and a pink Nike crop top," Olivia said.

Going by her social media photos, Nikki could see that Alexia was taller and stronger than most of her friends. She had an athletic build and ran both cross-country and track at Stillwater High School. She was strong enough to put up a good fight, and yet there hadn't been any sign she'd done so at the house after hearing the scream. If she'd tried to escape and gotten injured or lost, Miller's searchers should be able to find her by nightfall. The woods behind Lilydale were thick, but they weren't like the big northern woods that could swallow a person whole.

Nikki's cell phone rang, Miller's private number on the caller ID. "I have to take this. Excuse me." She walked to the small entryway for privacy and updated Miller. "Hey, Kent. I'm with Olivia right now. We've got another couple of witnesses to track down. They did have a party, and three other people, including Olivia, stayed to watch the documentary." She explained Alexia's fight with Luke. "His name is Luke Webb. I'll see if Olivia has his number."

"I should be able to find him without it," Miller replied. "I called because Dr. Blanchard found a bright red acrylic fingernail tangled in Vivienne's hair. Alexia's last social media photos show her with the same color on her nails."

Nikki told him about the video Alexia had sent Olivia. "It's a fraction of a second, but there's genuine horror in her eyes, Kent. She's definitely another potential victim. Perhaps she just had an altercation with Vivienne, or lost the nail helping her friend during the attack."

"Blanchard said the nail looks like it popped off from some force. She and Courtney both looked at the picture Alexia posted with her red nails on Friday afternoon, and they both said they were long and had some outgrowth, so it wouldn't have taken much force to pop the acrylic off. Given the nail's location in Vivienne's hair, our theory is she stopped to try to help her friend and that's when the nail came off."

Nikki thought about the overturned chair and busted porcelain vase scattered over the hardwood floor and the disarray in the vestibule. The downstairs bathroom was at the end of the main corridor, which meant Alexia would have had a straight route to the door. She must have seen Vivienne. She must have stopped to check on her and lost the nail. She must have exited out the side porch, which was the only entrance that didn't have a security camera mounted on the outside. "That has to be how the killer came inside then, as well. The only other entrance is the main door. Surely that narrows down our suspect pool to someone who knew the floor plan."

"Somewhat, but this is an Airbnb," Miller reminded her. "The property manager is putting together a list of renters from the last year."

"It's a start, along with all the kids who came through here over the weekend."

"What's the motive here?" Miller asked. "A sick copycat?"

"That's my first instinct, given all the media attention the documentary has received the last several months."

"Did Olivia say anything more about this gray Chevy truck?"

"Just that the guy was about six feet and white. Alexia said it was the property manager, but we know that's a female." She checked her watch. "I'm going to finish up here and head back downtown to meet her."

"Can you ask about Alexia's parents? I still can't get ahold of either of them."

Nikki ended the call and rejoined the two anxious women. Olivia's mother clutched her daughter's hand, likely thinking of how close she'd come to losing her. "Olivia, we're trying to track down Alexia's parents—do you know how to get ahold of either one?"

Olivia made a face. "Her dad's in California with his other family, and her mom's in New York for work. She's a bigwig at J.P. Morgan Chase."

Nikki nodded. "What's Alexia's relationship with them like?"

"Her dad left with his new girlfriend before the divorce was final, when Alexia was eleven. She sees him a couple of times a year, hates his guts. But he's a legacy at UCLA and pulled some strings to get her early admission."

Nikki didn't have the statistics in front of her, but UCLA had one of the tougher acceptance rates. "What sort of strings?" Nikki immediately thought of the USC scandal with the woman from *Full House*.

"Alexia is a track star. She's one of the best in the state and had offers from a couple of schools here when she was a junior. She's also a national merit scholar. Her dad just pushed the early admission notification. That's how I understood it, anyway. She's really excited about getting out of

Minnesota, even if it means tolerating her dad every once in a while."

Nikki jotted the information in her notebook and hoped she could read the messy script later. "What about her mom?"

"Shanna's nice, but I think Alexia resents her for the divorce. She works a lot and travels to New York a fair amount."

"She's the head of investments at the Minnesota branch," Nina said. "I think the title is Executive Director, Head of Investments. She handles my retirement fund. I have her cell phone number."

"It's in my phone." Olivia started to get up, but her mother shook her head.

"I've got her business card right here in my wallet." Nina reached for the stuffed handbag at the end of the table and dug inside, swearing under her breath. "I'm so disorganized. Here it is. Her cell's on there too."

"Any idea when she left for New York? When she'll be back?"

"She left Friday afternoon," Olivia said. "Our check-in time was at 2 p.m., but Alexia had to wait for her mom to leave for the airport."

"Are you telling me her mother doesn't know about the Airbnb?"

Olivia flushed. "Alexia said that her mother would just rag on her for being interested in true crime stuff. She wants Alexia to go into finance or something lucrative."

Nikki asked one of the questions that bothered her the most. "How did you all get to the Airbnb?"

"I drove." Olivia looked confused.

"What about the other girls?"

"Alexia picked up Libby and Viv. Isn't her car there?"

Nikki shook head. "Do you know the make and model? The year?"

"It's a Volvo," Olivia said. "Blue, four doors. I don't know the model, but it's not even a year old. Her mom bought it for her eighteenth birthday. Brand new."

"And you're certain the car was at the lake house when you left after the documentary?"

"Yes." Olivia reached for another tissue. "I don't understand. If you can't find Alexia or her car, what does that mean?"

"It's too early to tell," Nikki said. She checked Volvo's website and pulled up their sedans. "Look at these and tell me if any of them are the right model."

Olivia didn't hesitate. "It's this one, the S90. It's a hybrid." She returned the phone, and Nikki fired off a text to Miller so he could put out the APB.

"I just have a few more questions," Nikki said. "Is there anyone else who came to the house over the weekend that stood out for the wrong reasons? Someone Alexia didn't want there?"

Olivia contemplated the question. "I can't think of anyone. I mean, there were maybe fifteen or twenty people throughout the day. The only one I remember Alexia complaining about was Eric." She looked at her mother. "Remember, I told her that if he couldn't hang out, then I wasn't either?"

"Eric is your boyfriend?" Nikki asked.

"No, just a good friend. Alexia doesn't like him because he doesn't worship her." Olivia put her hand over her mouth. "Oh my God, how can I talk about her like that?"

"She didn't want Eric there?"

"She never said anything until he showed up, and then she was pissy. But she got over it."

"Did Eric stay late last night too?" Nikki asked.

"Not to watch the documentary," Olivia answered. "I took him home around five, I think. He works on a farm and had to be up super early this morning. He's usually asleep by 8 p.m."

Nikki asked for Eric's number and address, along with the names of the other people who were in the house Saturday. She tore a clean page out of her notebook and slid it across the table to Olivia. "If you have their phone number or address, I need that too. Their place of work, that sort of thing. Whatever helps us track them down the fastest." She'd also have one of the junior agents sift through the hundreds of kids in Stillwater High School's senior class to cross-reference any previous run-ins with the law. They also needed to talk with Alexia's track teammates and coaches, along with anyone else at the school she could have confided in. Nikki struggled to see why someone would brutally kill Vivienne and Libby if they were intent on getting revenge on Alexia, unless they were talking about a true violent sociopath. Thankfully, fewer existed in society than television depicted.

After she retrieved her phone from upstairs, Olivia took the pen Nikki offered and started writing. Her hand trembled, the pressure so strong, Nikki could hear it scraping the table through the thin sheet of paper.

"Is there any place you can think of that Alexia might go if she were in trouble?"

"Libby's," Olivia said. "They've been best friends since kindergarten. Do you think Alexia is okay?"

"Honestly, Olivia, I don't know what to think right now. But I'm going to do everything possible to find the answers."

SEVEN

Nikki took a photo of Olivia's list of names and sent it to Liam and Miller, along with the details about Alexia's missing car and her mother's whereabouts. She let Liam know they had more than twenty high school kids to track down. The already under-staffed sheriff's department had their hands full with the search for Alexia, but every single person who'd been in the house since the group arrived Friday needed to be interviewed. Nikki asked Kendall, Liam and Jim to split the list into three groups and cover as much ground as possible. Miller was still trying to contact Alexia's parents while his chief deputy shadowed Chandler at the hospital. Nikki planned on joining Miller at the station to interview Alexia's boyfriend, but she had to meet with the property manager first.

Nikki's eyes took a moment to adjust to the ambience at the Water Street Inn. The historic hotel in downtown Stillwater had a cozy feel, along with its modern furnishings. Nikki stopped at the front desk and asked for directions to the small conference room, where Sera Everett took care of her local business.

The concierge directed Nikki across the expansive lobby to

a conference room overlooking the peaceful riverfront. Nikki could see the sun shimmering on the water and pedestrians on the historic left bridge that had been turned into a walking trail.

She spotted a petite woman with shoulder-length, ash-blond hair sitting at the table, her nose in her laptop. Nikki recognized her from the billboards she'd seen all over the metro area.

She knocked, and Sera Everett looked up from her laptop, motioning Nikki inside. "I hope this is okay. We should have plenty of privacy."

Sera didn't look as glamorous as she did on the advertisements, wearing little makeup and dressed casually in a soft, navy T-shirt and khaki shorts. Her eyes were red, her skin pale.

"I can't believe this has happened. When the cleaning service called, I thought it was a joke. But then they texted me a picture."

"Of one of the victims?" Nikki asked, shocked.

Sera nodded. "I deleted it and told her to do so as well, and warned her that if it was leaked online, she and her whole crew were fired and wouldn't work around here again. She won't share it."

Sera sounded sincere, but a photo could be shared with dozens of people in an instant, and countless apps promised to store secret photos. Nikki's mind drifted to the Kobe Bryant tragedy a few years ago and the first responders who'd taken photos. His widow had the means to move heaven and earth to make sure the photos had been destroyed, but the average person didn't.

"Please make sure she keeps to that," Nikki said. "The sheriff is still notifying the families. And I can assure you if those photos go public, we'll find a way to charge your employee. The photos being public could have a negative effect at trial too."

Nikki expected pushback, but Sera only nodded. "I'm just

happy to hear you say trial. Do you think you can find the sick person who did this?"

"We're going to do everything we possibly can," Nikki said, opening her notebook.

"Today only solidified that I don't want children." Sera shuddered. "This world sucks."

"It does sometimes," Nikki agreed. "You're a real estate agent, right?"

Sera nodded. "Yes. Everett Property Management is a side hustle."

"How so?"

"I only do it for a few select clients who've purchased high-end and usually historic homes." Sera adjusted her tortoiseshell glasses. "As I'm sure you know, Airbnb is taking over the hotel industry. Most people who use a property manager to rent their home are using it as a vacation house, and in general, those are a dime a dozen."

"I've never used Airbnb," Nikki said. "How does it work?"

"Well, most of the time, the property owners either hire professionals to list the house and take care of all the administrative and practical stuff, like cleaning and repair, or they handle the rental themselves. Their vetting process for renters isn't nearly as stringent as my clients'."

"Who are?" Nikki prodded.

"People I've sold homes to," she said. "The Castle House in the historic district is one of them. These are historical homes, many with owners who are retired and have zero interest in Minnesota winters."

"I remember seeing the Castle House sold for nearly a million dollars a few years ago." The Castle House had been named after its first owner, James Castle, an attorney, Minnesota senator, and United States representative. The four-story, second-empire Victorian was nearly 4,000 square feet, with a four-story centered tower above the dormer roof. It had a distinctly Gothic feel, which Nikki loved.

Sera nodded. "To a wealthy banker who wants to spend the summers here in Stillwater near the river. They don't want the place to sit empty in the winter, but they also don't want just anyone staying in the house. That's where I come in. Everett Property Management started as a result of those clients. I've only got six homes right now, including the Victorian on Bone Lake." She slid the file sitting next to her laptop over to Nikki. "Alexia Perry turned eighteen a few weeks ago, and she wanted to have a small get-together with friends. I was leery, but I agreed to meet with the friends. We sat right here at this table and discussed the house and the owner's expectations."

"Who owns the house now?"

"Matt Kline still owns it." Sera's voice softened.

Nikki was shocked. She would have assumed he'd sold it. Why would he want to keep the house where his whole family perished?

"The house was built by his great-great-grandfather, and it's an important part of the area's history. After the murders, the house went to him. He was still a kid, in the custody of his aunt Peggy. The house sat empty for a few years before they started renting it out. After his aunt passed away last year, Matt contacted me. He explained he didn't want anything to do with the house but couldn't bring himself to sell it. It's on the National Historic Registry, you know. He wanted to make sure no more ghosthunters or mediums had access to it. I agreed to take the property on."

Nikki could only imagine how many ghosthunters and so-called psychics had gone through the house trying to exploit the Kline tragedy. Nikki never discounted the possibility of the supernatural, but proving the existence of spirits was a million-dollar industry for people with little moral compass.

"Matt told me Peggy had allowed all sorts of groups—as

long as they didn't cause damage—to come through the house. He didn't fight her on it because he wanted her to have the extra income from the renters."

The Klines had been worth millions at the time of the murder, and Caitlin's research had uncovered Matt had inherited everything, with his aunt as custodian. Nikki knew she'd put the money into a trust for Matt. By all accounts, she'd done right by her nephew instead of siphoning money out of his trust, which happened far more than people realized. He'd gone to Yale School of Medicine and started out as a promising cancer researcher, as his father had been, but he'd become addicted to painkillers and lost his job. Caitlin had discovered Matt still lived in the area, but he'd refused her interview.

"But the house was listed through Airbnb," Nikki clarified. "How exactly does that work?"

"Alexia requested the rental, and we set up the meeting after speaking on the phone. Payments all go through Airbnb, once I've vetted the clients." She looked ready to cry again. "I had a gut feeling Alexia was planning a party. I almost drove out and checked Saturday, but I had to attend a funeral a couple of hours away."

"Where was this?" Nikki asked, knowing she'd need to check the details. Sera reached for a leaflet in her bag, and passed over the order of service.

"Don't blame yourself," Nikki said, folding the paper and putting it into her pocket. "As far as the Airbnb arrangement, when you book a stay, you get a percentage, similar to a real estate agent?"

"If I were greedy, that's probably how I'd do it," Sera said. "But I'm not, and like I said, this is a side gig. I charge an hourly rate, because, honestly, there isn't a ton of work that goes into this most of the time. I coordinate the cleaning crews and screen renters, but I spend maybe twenty percent of my work day on the property management." She shrugged.

"I assume you have rental records?" Nikki asked. "I understand your clients are private, but we have to speak with anyone who spent time in the house in the last few months. We'll be able to get a warrant."

"I have no problem giving you the information, but can I reach out to the clients and ask if I can give you their names?"

Nikki considered her options. She didn't like giving any possible suspects a heads-up. "Let us get the warrant so we do things by the book. Not all of the families have been informed, either."

Sera nodded. "Well, once you have it, the names are yours."

Nikki thanked her. "You said Matt Kline reached out to you?"

She nodded. "Peggy had health issues and couldn't deal with the bookkeeping, so they hadn't been renting the house for a few years. Matt wanted nothing to do with it, but he couldn't let the house go, either."

Nikki understood the sentiment, but she couldn't imagine how hard the decision must have been for Matt. "How often do you see him?"

"We've only met once, around a year ago," she said. "Everything else is done by email or text. I keep a log of my hours, send them at the end of the month, and he pays me."

"What was your impression of him?"

"Sad and brilliant," she said. "He's soft-spoken, but when I mentioned my mother had died of cancer, he asked what kind. He spent several minutes explaining cancer research to me, even though he's not in the field anymore, why it's so hard to isolate the right genomes, that sort of thing. I understood about forty percent," she added ruefully. "He's a fireman now. He's passed every random drug test and says he's been clean for five years."

"Have you had any issues with him? Late payment, that sort of thing?"

"No," she said. "Today's the first time I've even called him in months." She picked at her manicured nails.

"Matt's aware of the murders, then?" Nikki hadn't been able to find his current address or phone number, which didn't surprise her. His name was well-known, and Caitlin's documentary would have made him even more desperate to keep himself hidden.

"He's not answering his phone, and I didn't leave it on the voicemail. He's reclusive and freaked about the documentary, I guess."

"I'll need his phone number and his address,' Nikki said. "I'd like to speak with him in person. We don't want to tell him this over the phone, and there are a few things I need to clarify."

Sera reached into her briefcase and then handed Nikki her business card. "He's on Birchwood Drive in Stillwater, corner lot. I can't remember the house number, but it's got light green vinyl siding. You won't miss it."

EIGHT

Nikki wasn't much of a golfer, but as she drove towards Stillwater Country Club, she couldn't imagine more perfect weather for the sport. Despite the events of the day, the blood spilled at Bone Lake, the sun was shining brightly over the lush green grass, the lakes sparkling. She could almost pretend she hadn't seen the carnage earlier, but like so many other victims, Libby and Vivienne's broken bodies were imprinted in her memory.

Miller had given her Brett and Luke's location, and she was hoping to catch them by surprise, even though the Luke that Olivia had described didn't sound like the type to commit such a violent crime, even with assistance.

All Nikki could think about on most of the drive was Matt Kline. His story of escaping the murder of his whole family echoed so much of her own dark past. And she felt awful that what had happened to these poor girls was going to force him to relive everything again. Nikki's instincts told her these cases weren't linked, but perhaps all of this could help Caitlin get the original one reopened and finally get justice for Matt and his family.

The Stillwater Country Club was a beautiful course, designed by noted golf architects. Its position overlooking the St. Croix Valley provided incredible views of the lush, green landscape. A single membership cost over two thousand dollars a year, which meant nearly all of the clientele were upper middle class.

Miller had texted Luke Webb's license plate number and the make and model of his vehicle shortly after they had ended the call, with the additional note that his driving record was clean. Nikki circled the parking lot in search of the black Mustang convertible. Since he'd turned eighteen three months ago, Nikki didn't have to worry about questioning a minor without parents.

She spied the Mustang and parked in the space nearest the car, next to a Range Rover that likely cost a year of her salary. Nikki wished she'd worn something other than shorts and a basic T-shirt, but she'd rushed to the scene and hadn't had time to stop at home for a change of clothes. The country club had a dress code, but Nikki had a badge and two dead girls, with another missing.

Nikki debated holstering her gun, but decided against it.

As she neared the clubhouse, the group of seniors sitting outside under the green-and-white-striped umbrellas eyed her.

"Excuse me." A dyed redheaded woman wearing designer golf clothes called out to Nikki as she ascended the stone steps. "There is a dress code here, young lady."

The snobbery in her voice would have made Nikki laugh in any other circumstance, but she flashed her badge without looking at the group. "FBI."

The dyed redhead looked more curious than shocked. Nikki wouldn't have been surprised if they'd followed her inside.

The bright, airy clubhouse was bigger than it looked from outside, boasting a full bar and multiple meeting rooms. Nikki bypassed the bar and headed for the front desk, where a bored-looking high school girl sat glued to her phone.

"Hello." Nikki wasted no time, showing the girl her badge. "I'm looking for Luke Webb."

The bleached blond eyed Nikki up and down. "How do you know he's here? I can't just leave the desk and look for him."

"Because his car is in the parking lot. If you don't want to find him, I'll start asking around myself. I'm sure most of these members will be interested to know I'm here on an urgent FBI matter."

The girl rolled her eyes. "What, like a bomb threat?"

Nikki couldn't believe the audacity of the girl. "No, like a double homicide. Now, are you going to help me, or do I just start asking random members?"

The teenager finally seemed to grasp the severity of the situation. "Jesus, all right. Let me see when he checked in." She unlocked the iPad sitting next to her, her long nails tapping against the screen. "He arrived about forty-five minutes ago. I don't know if he started on the course right away, but he'd be on the first few holes. Unless you want me to page him?"

"No, thanks." Nikki grabbed the paper map of the course and headed back outside.

The group she'd all but ignored on the way inside must have worked quickly, because several heads turned in her direction.

She smiled at a shy caddie. "Hi, I'm looking for Luke Webb. Do you know what hole he's at?"

The caddie checked his clipboard. "Should be on the fourth, but you're not really supposed to just walk out."

Nikki held up her badge. "Thanks."

She strode out onto the green, well aware of the whispering golfers.

"That's the famous FBI agent. Why is she here? Did someone threaten the club?"

Nikki resisted the urge to roll her eyes. Didn't these people realize they weren't the center of the universe? Deep down, she knew that she was being just as judgmental. Nikki hadn't forgotten the way the rich, country-club kids at Stillwater High treated everyone else. She wanted to believe times had changed, but so far, she'd seen nothing to support that.

Nikki recognized the tall, sandy-haired, muscular guy preparing to tee off at the fourth hole from the social media photos she'd examined before driving over. His trendy pink golf shirt was also hard to miss. As he shifted into his stance, ready to swing, Nikki made her move.

"Luke Webb?"

He stumbled, nearly dropping the nine-iron. "What the hell, lady? Don't you know basic etiquette?"

Nikki held up her badge and introduced herself. "I need to talk to you about what happened at the lake house last night."

Luke looked at his friend, who shrugged.

"Is this Brett?" Nikki pointed at the shorter man with dark hair and brooding eyes.

"Yeah, but what's this about?"

She studied the two young men, uncertain if their shifting body language meant they had something to hide or if they were just confused and too busy to be bothered. "Murder."

The two of them stared at her and then at each other.

"What are you talking about?" Luke finally asked.

"I'm sorry to deliver the news this way, but..." Nikki kept her voice low. She could see other golfers milling around and inching closer, trying to overhear what business the woman in cutoff shorts had with two of their members. "Vivienne Beckett and Libby Brown have been murdered. At the house on Bone Lake. Chandler Glover is injured, and Alexia Perry is missing."

To the outsider, Nikki's delivery would likely seem cold and uncaring, but she wanted to assess Luke and Brett's reactions without her own emotions getting in the way. If one or both of them was involved, catching him off guard in front of their parents' wealthy peers was the fastest way for Nikki to get the information she needed. Nikki watched as shocked expressions took over their faces.

"You're serious?" Luke asked. He leaned against his nine iron, the end of the club digging into the green from his weight. Brett stared in shock.

"I'm afraid so," Nikki answered. "Is there somewhere we can talk privately?" Another golfing party had arrived to play the fourth hole. "We're holding them up."

She waited for one of the boys to argue about losing their spot, but they both stowed their clubs and asked the caddie to take care of them. Nikki motioned for the boys to lead the way so she could keep an eye on their body language. Luke's shoulders sagged, his head down and his hands in his pockets as he walked. Brett trailed behind, seemingly in a daze.

"I need to go home," Luke said. "God, has anyone talked to Viv's and Libby's parents? What about Alexia's mom? She's in New York."

"Yes, the sheriff is notifying the families," Nikki said. "We're trying to reach Shanna Perry."

The patio crowd had thinned, so Nikki asked the boys to sit at one of the umbrella-covered tables.

"Why aren't you out looking for Alexia?" Luke demanded. "She's missing, right? That means she's alive."

"We have a lot of people out looking for her," Nikki said, opening her notebook. "What time did you two leave last night? Or this morning?" She didn't mention that Olivia had already given them a timeline of the evening's events.

"Before the documentary ended," Luke said. "Alexia was in a mood, and I didn't want to deal with it."

"What do you mean, in a mood?"

"She's a control freak, everything has to be perfect, even when it's just a group of her friends. Personally I thought her idea of watching the documentary at the murder house was creepy and shitty. Damn it, Lex." Luke's voice cracked on the last word. "How did this happen?"

"That's what we're trying to figure out," Nikki said. "When did you leave?"

"During the third episode," Brett answered.

Luke nodded. "We got to my house before midnight. My dad was still up."

Nikki thought she detected a hint of defensiveness in his tone. "You haven't spoken to Alexia since then?"

"I called this morning, but it went to voicemail. I texted her that I was sorry for pissing her off." Luke caught Brett's eye, an unspoken conversation between them. Nikki let the moment pass, wanting to see if they decided to share without being prompted.

Brett ignored him. "A couple of weeks ago, the three of us were hanging out at my house, drinking. Alexia went on about the party and how she wanted to study serial killers: people like whoever murdered the Klines. She said wouldn't it be cool if she could find him. Solve the case. Luke laughed at her and told her to stay in her lane. That didn't go over too well."

Nikki kept her eyes on Luke as his friend spoke. The words seemed to resonate, although he said nothing.

"When she told us she'd booked the Klines' old house, Luke and I both told her that was in bad taste, but she never listened." He looked at his friend for a beat. "Dude, come on. I'll tell her if you don't."

Luke shook his head and looked at the ground.

"Vivvy and Libby are dead," Brett spat, his face red. "I don't give a damn about anyone's secrets."

"Tell me what?" Nikki pressed.

"After he showed up last night, Luke accused Alexia of cheating with Matt Kline. She was in contact with him, trying to get inside information about the house and the case."

Matt Kline, the sole survivor of the 2001 massacre and the

owner of the house, the same one who refused to have anything to do with the house? "Why did you think this?" Nikki asked.

"Because she told Libby she'd been reading about repressed memories and thought she could somehow get close to Matt and then start grilling him, I guess."

In recent years, true crime fans and internet sleuths had helped solve some cases, but Matt Kline had been interviewed by dozens of law enforcement over the years. Caitlin heard that he'd also tried hypnotism to remember anything that might help bring his family's killer to justice, but hadn't been able to confirm since Kline refused her interview. How had an eighteen-year-old high school girl managed to get so close to him?

"That's part of the reason me and Brett went last night." Luke finally spoke. "I don't know how much investigation she actually did, but it kind of freaked me out that she wanted to stay there." His jaw tensed. "I shouldn't have left."

"You could have easily been a victim," Nikki said. "As for Matt Kline, what made you think she went through with contacting him?"

"Because he showed up Saturday night, drunk. Said he didn't know Alexia was the one who'd rented the Airbnb, went on about how the property manager should do a better job screening. Alexia took him outside and they talked for a while." Luke's face reddened. "We tried to listen since the windows were open, but they walked down to the dock."

"How did things end?" Nikki asked.

"He left, and she didn't seem too upset over it," Brett answered.

"What was her explanation for his visit?" Nikki asked.

"She said she'd flirted with him at a bar a couple of weeks ago, and that's it." Luke shrugged. "I don't know if that's the truth, though. I have my doubts."

Nikki explained she would have to speak to Luke's father to confirm their alibi, and neither seemed to have any issues. She gave them both a card and told them to call her personally if Alexia tried to contact them.

Nikki jogged to the jeep and called Miller, but his phone went to voicemail. She didn't leave a message, instead calling Liam. She didn't want to show up at Matt Kline's place alone, in case he really had been involved.

"Was just about to call you." Liam sounded out of breath. "Caitlin heard it on the news before I could tell her. She's devastated."

"It's not her fault, even if the documentary did have something to do with it—"

"Let me finish," Liam cut in. "Caitlin knows Alexia, and she knew the girls were staying at the house last night. She actually thought about stopping by, but then decided it would be weird."

Nikki sat stunned, trying to process the information. "How does she know Alexia?"

"Because she interviewed her for the documentary a couple of weeks ago."

NINE

Nikki drove down Birchwood Avenue, still trying to process what Liam had told her. The five-minute drive took Nikki past downtown Stillwater, towards the old Jaycee ball fields, a more working-class area of Stillwater. Most of the homes on the quiet residential street had been built in the mid-eighties, giving the residences more character than many of the newer subdivisions built in the last decade. Large maple and oak trees surrounded Matt Kline's modest ranch, the foliage likely blocking any security cameras the houses beside his might have.

A couple of weeks ago, Caitlin had told Nikki, Liam, and Miller about the new allegations that had turned up regarding the Kline murders, but she couldn't reveal her source because she'd signed an ironclad confidentiality agreement. Since the case was still open, Miller had promised to look into it when he had the time, but they'd all agreed that without more information from the source, the investigation likely wouldn't get very far. Caitlin's producers wanted to use the source's information to add a fifth episode in a few months, with an update into the hopefully reopened investigation.

If Nikki didn't know Caitlin, she probably would have assumed the "source" had been thrown in for ratings. That might have been the producers' intention, but Caitlin had made the documentary because she wanted to help find the Klines' killer, just as she'd helped free Rory's brother, who'd been wrongfully imprisoned for Nikki's parents' murders. Caitlin wasn't a saint—she also wanted to build on her brand as a documentary filmmaker—but she wouldn't have shared anything with law enforcement if she didn't believe it had at least some merit.

Nikki parked behind Liam's silver Prius. She stifled a snicker as his tall frame unfolded from the small car. "Any updates on Alexia?"

"Miller's getting drones in the air. His guys have cleared the woods surrounding the house. No sign of her." Liam leaned against her jeep. "And guess what? Alexia contacted Caitlin last summer when news about the documentary came out. She pitched it as wanting to let the community know that the younger generations haven't forgotten and want justice. Then Alexia claimed her mother had an affair with Matt's father not long before the murders, and she had proof."

"You're kidding." Nikki remembered the original investigation had turned up allegations of cheating by both Mr. and Mrs. Kline, but they'd never been substantiated because the investigation was centered around Amy.

"Alexia was adamant her mother didn't have anything to do with the Kline murders. She wanted to prove that she was a brilliant investigator, that she could dig up things the police at the time couldn't." Liam shook his head. "Alexia claimed her mother's affair was over months before the attacks. Shanna parlayed their dirty deeds into a large severance and helped get her hired at Bank One, which later merged with J.P. Morgan Chase. She was already out of state when the murders took place."

Nikki struggled to make sense of the new information. "You said Alexia had proof? What sort of proof? She wasn't even alive then, and Shanna's not going to volunteer anything if her name's never been brought up."

"Shanna kept a diary," Liam continued. "Still does, and Alexia said her mother never threw any of them away because she liked to read them sometimes and remind herself how far up the corporate ladder she'd climbed. Alexia found it one day when she was looking for a pair of Louboutins to borrow. She took pictures of every entry about Kline and then contacted Caitlin. At the time, she was seventeen, and Caitlin couldn't interview her without her mother's consent. Alexia was insistent her mother wouldn't cooperate, so one of the producers asked when she turned eighteen. Once they found out her birthday was in July, they started planning the follow-up episode. Caitlin hasn't been happy about it because her producers are trying to subvert Shanna Perry in the whole process."

"What do you mean?"

"Shanna doesn't know Alexia spoke to anyone about the documentary. She doesn't even know Alexia found the diary and took photos. But the producers have decided to run with Alexia's story, anyway." Liam shook his head. "If Shanna Perry threw a fit over the images being shared—which she should—I guarantee you it would have been Caitlin's ass, not the producers'."

"Any idea how Shanna met Ted Kline?"

"Shanna told Alexia she worked at the cancer institute when Kline was there. She had an accounting internship."

"I wonder how much of Alexia's opinion about the murders was influenced by things her mother said about the family over the years, even if she never mentioned the affair. She had to have some thoughts on it."

"Me too," Liam said. "Don't you remember Caitlin's source

also said she believed that Matt Kline saw more than he'd been able to tell the police that night?"

"I do, but that was barely touched on. Caitlin couldn't confirm that with Matt Kline, could she?"

"He refused her interview requests. That's why she didn't want to put that information in the documentary. But Alexia told producers she had an intimate relationship with Matt and believed she could get him to come around for the final episode. So that information's at the very end of the fourth episode, with a sneak peek of one that's not even completely filmed."

"They took her word?"

"She had texts, according to Caitlin's producer. She claimed Matt told her he saw the killer that night. The producers insisted on using it."

"Weren't they worried about Matt's safety? Or his reaction?" Nikki couldn't imagine if someone had used her to get information about her parents' murders. She would have been mad enough to do something about it, and since Matt had shown up at the Airbnb last night, he must have been too.

"Caitlin showed me the emails between herself and her producers. She told him that because the case is still technically open, they have to be careful about making statements they can't prove," Liam said. "Like she told her asshole executive producer, as far as we know, the killer is still out there. Netflix has promoted the hell out this documentary, and it's been on the news. If he's alive, he'll likely watch it, and that could put Matt in danger. Caitlin worried Alexia was putting herself in harm's way, but she couldn't change anyone's mind."

Nikki still couldn't believe Alexia had done such a thing to Matt Kline. What else was the young woman capable of doing? "She seduced him, I assume?"

Liam nodded. "That's Caitlin's understanding."

"Didn't Alexia worry about his reaction once he found out how she'd used him?"

"She told Caitlin he didn't know her real name or have her real number. She wasn't worried in the least."

Nikki gazed at the small home where Matt Kline lived. "Maybe she should have been."

TEN

The dumbwaiter creaked as it slowly dropped from the second floor, past the kitchen, and into the dark, dank cellar. Matt's sweaty hands clung to the rope. *Don't cry*, he told himself. *Amy sent you for help. Mom and Dad are hurt.*

He reached the dirt floor and used the screwdriver to open the door. Musty dirt and stale air triggered his allergies, but he held back the sneeze. He couldn't be heard.

Matt crept out of the cramped wooden box. His toes touched the cool earth, and he tried to get his bearings in the darkness. Which way was the cellar door?

The pool's at the back, he remembered.

Earlier in the summer, he and Amy had gone into the woods behind the house to look for pink and yellow wildflowers. Even though the patch of massive, leafy trees wasn't all that big, Matt still felt like he'd been swallowed up whole.

"Don't be a scaredy-cat," Amy had said. "There's nothing in the woods to be afraid of, except maybe snakes, and there aren't poisonous ones around here."

Big deal, Matt thought. A snake was a snake and so was a spider and all the other critters roaming the woods.

"What if we get lost?" he'd asked his big sister in a small voice.

"Easy. Use the lake as a starting point, okay?"

Matt had nodded.

"The house is on the north side of the lake. That means we're walking north, and Miller Avenue isn't as far as it seems."

"But what if I get messed up and don't know where north is?"

Amy had stopped walking and looked down at him with a bemused grin. "Long as you're walking this direction, it's north. Here's a trick I learned a long time ago to help me remember directions." She pointed north. "Never eat shredded wheat." She pointed in each direction as she spoke. "East is always to the right of north. And the sun sets in the west. Remember that and you'll never be lost."

Matt didn't realize he was crying until he tasted the salty tears on his lips. He couldn't see anything, not even moonlight through the cellar doors. He put his hands in front of him and walked slowly forward until his fingers touched the wall. Heart pounding, he inched around the room until he felt the rickety wood steps that led outside.

He climbed up on hands and knees and then pushed on the cellar door. It didn't move. Had the lock been fixed without Amy knowing again?

"Maybe it's stuck," he whispered to the darkness.

Matt tried again, with all his strength, and the heavy door inched open. Trying not to think of who might be waiting for him outside, Matt heaved the door open and climbed into the fresh night air, barely managing to keep the wood from smacking the side of the house.

He couldn't make any noise.

He stared into the side yard, his mother's lilies blowing in the breeze. The pool was north. So were the woods.

Certain whoever had come into the house could hear his

pounding heart, Matt crept to the corner. He peered around the rosebushes and saw his mom lying near the patio doors, her arms at a weird angle. He could see blood on the concrete.

Why wasn't Mommy moving?

Matt reminded himself that eight-year-olds don't say mommy anymore and inched toward his mother. Amy had said to run straight through the woods to the road, but he couldn't leave his mom like that. Matt dropped to his hands and knees and crawled to her.

A deep slash ran across her throat. He remembered how they'd taught him to check for a pulse in science class. His shaky fingers touched his mother's wrist. Her skin felt cooler than normal, and he didn't feel any blood pumping.

"Mom?" he whispered.

A scream broke the stillness.

Amy!

Matt ran toward the front of the house, certain the scream came from that direction. The front door was open, but he didn't see anyone.

"Stop!" Amy screamed.

Matt started for the lake and saw his sister on the ground, on the path leading to the dock. He ducked behind the big hedges.

A man loomed over Amy, pinning her arms. Amy kept fighting, her knee going into the man's stomach. She managed to free her hand. Matt saw her red fingernails scrape the man's face, leaving red streaks.

"Bitch." The man raised his hand, the knife blade unlike any Matt had seen before. It didn't look like a fishing knife or a hunting knife.

The blade came down, sinking into her chest.

Amy stopped struggling.

Matt turned and ran for the woods.

ELEVEN

Nikki pointed to the neighbors across the street from Matt Kline's house. "That looks like a Ring camera on the doorbell. If it's on, it should have recorded Matt Kline arriving home last night."

"That's the first thing I did when I got here," Liam answered. "It's definitely a Ring, but no one answered. I left my card inside the screen door."

"What about the houses next to him?"

"Gray split-level on the right has cameras facing his door and garage, so we may be able to see Matt driving down the street. He's emailing me last night's videos, but I'm not sure they'll be much help. House on the left side only has a front door camera, and it's off." Liam unlocked his phone. "I'm going to pull up this house on Zillow. They should have the most recent floor plan. I'd like to know what we're walking into if possible."

"That's a good idea." Nikki's thoughts jumped to the murder scene. "Lilydale is pretty much the same as it was in 2001, right? The house is on the National Register of Historic

Places, which means any structural changes have to be approved by them."

"So?"

"Miller said the killer had to have knowledge of the house," Nikki said. "Between people renting it as an Airbnb and sites like Zillow, it wouldn't be that hard to get a copy of the floor plan. Did you speak with Matt Kline's boss?"

"On the way here," Liam answered. "He was suspended last week for an internal incident. Fire chief wouldn't tell me more, but unless he's working somewhere else, he's here."

"He's got a trust, right?"

"Set up by his aunt after the murders. Between the Klines' estate and life insurance, the trust's opening balance was five million, and Matt couldn't use it until after he graduated college. Caitlin couldn't find definitive information on the balance. I did a little research on trust interest. It's tough to come up with a median interest rate since 2001, but if the trust earned three percent a year, even with taxes and other fluctuations, the trust should be over eight million by now. So he doesn't have to work."

Matt Kline had refused Caitlin's interview, and all the Stillwater fire department would say was that he'd been an exemplary employee and they weren't going to talk about his personal tragedy. "So much for the exemplary employee. Although I have to wonder about the timing of his internal incident." Was it possible that Matt Kline had something to do with the attacks? If Alexia had told Caitlin the truth, he had to feel betrayed and angry.

Nikki holstered her gun and slipped the heavy Kevlar vest on, just in case they were walking into a volatile situation. Liam did the same.

Nikki scanned the exterior of the house for a security camera but didn't see one. She wasn't surprised. Witnesses of violent crime were often at one end of the fear-spectrum: terrified, with locks and intensive therapy, or stubbornly brave, sometimes to the point of recklessness, like Nikki.

"I'll check the backyard and make sure no one can climb out of a window before we can get into the house." Liam disappeared around the corner.

Nikki crossed the wooden deck and knocked on the front door before taking a defensive position next to the frame. "FBI. We have an emergency and need to speak with you."

Nikki strained to hear the other side of the door. It sounded like someone was stumbling around, either trying to make an escape or come to the door. She knocked again.

Heavy footsteps came from the other side of the door. Several locks clicked, and the door flew open. Nikki looked up into the bleary, red eyes of Matt Kline. He was about Rory's height, his dark hair barely long enough to need combing. He was also naked.

"What the hell? Half the neighborhood heard you banging on my door."

"Could you put some clothes on, Mr. Kline?" Nikki texted Liam to come back to the front.

"Answer my question." His tone was hostile, his eyes blazing with anger, not fear.

"It's about what happened last night."

Matt rolled his eyes. "She called the FBI?" He started to slam the door shut, but Liam arrived in time to jam his size twelve foot in the doorway.

"That's not why we're here." Nikki had hoped to deliver the news in a gentler way, giving Matt the benefit of the doubt, unless he gave them more reason to suspect them. "Two girls were murdered at your Airbnb last night."

She watched for any signs on his face, any subtle movements, eyes dilating, or even a defensive posture in his shoulders. Matt Kline had none of those. He stumbled backward, pressing his fist against his mouth as though fighting for control. "What are you talking about?"

"I'm sorry to be blunt, but you need to get dressed, and we need to talk."

Five minutes later, Nikki and Liam sat across from Matt Kline at his kitchen table, one of the few pieces of furniture he owned other than the recliner in the living room. No pictures hung on the dingy walls. An empty bottle of Jim Beam sat on the cheap end table next to the recliner. His big, flat-screen television, flanked with two different gaming consoles along with dozens of games, provided the only real evidence Matt hadn't just moved into the place.

He'd thrown on sweats and a dingy T-shirt.

"I don't handle the Airbnb stuff," he said. "I have a person who does that. You should talk to her."

"I have," Nikki said. "But we still don't know what happened..."

Matt's eyes darkened. "Shocker."

Nikki ignored the jab. She certainly couldn't blame Matt for resenting the police. "The documentary producer explained that Alexia approached them with information." Nikki chose her words carefully. "Some of that information included things you'd told her, I'm afraid."

Matt's cheeks flushed with anger. "I trust two, maybe three people. I knew better than to bare my soul to some girl I met at a bar."

"Tell me how the two of you met."

"I was playing pool at the bar I always go to, and she came up and challenged me for the table. She kicked my ass, and we started talking."

"How long ago was this?" Liam asked.

"July fifth," he said. "I'd worked a twenty-four-hour shift on the fourth, then slept like the dead the next day. I didn't want to go out, but a buddy convinced me."

"Which bar is this?" Nikki asked.

Matt sipped the beer he'd taken from the fridge. "The Harbor Bar, not far from here."

"I know it." Rory loved a good dive bar, and he'd managed to turn Nikki into a fan of them as well. The Harbor wasn't far from their house in southwest Stillwater, near Lake McKusick. "John is a by-the-book guy," she said, thinking of the owner. "He always checks IDs, and you've got to be twenty-one to enter."

"She must have had a great fake, then," Matt said. "Couple of guys from the department and I like to have a few drinks after our shift. I'd seen Alexia sitting alone at the bar a couple of times before, and she flirted with me any time she crossed my path."

It likely didn't take much for Alexia to turn heads. Tall and lean, with blue eyes and blond hair, she looked every bit the California girl.

"I came in by myself the night I met her."

"She approached you?" Liam clarified.

Matt nodded. "Yeah, challenged me for the table and then bought me a beer after she kicked my ass. We had some drinks and talked. I got pretty drunk, but she seemed fine. She insisted on driving me home. One thing led to another. Like I said, the owner always checks IDs, so I didn't ask. But seventeen is the age of consent in Minnesota."

"We're not here about that," Nikki said. "What happened the next day?"

"Nothing," Matt said. "She left while I was asleep. Left me her number. I wasn't going to call her again, but she frequented the bar, so we started hanging out a lot." He rolled his eyes. "She told me that she'd moved from California for a job at the university and to be closer to her family. I bought it."

"How often did you talk about what happened to your family?" Liam pressed.

"At first, not a lot. She told me she'd heard what happened, but she wasn't going to ask me about my family. I could share if I wanted to." Matt's eyes clouded with anger. "She didn't bring it up after that, so I started to think she actually didn't care about my past."

Nikki felt for Matt Kline. She remembered what it had been like after her parents were murdered. Everyone wanted to know how she was doing, but most people just really wanted to be able to say they knew her well enough to check in on her. Some people didn't care how they received attention, as long as they were at the center of it.

"What made you open up to her?" Liam asked.

"Couple of weeks after we met, she shows up here, crying. She told me that her friend in California had been killed in a home invasion, and she was devastated. She gave me this whole spiel about the friend's secret life and how it caught up with her, how their other friend found them dead. She knew what to say to get me to talk. That's when we got drunk and ended up talking about the murders."

"What did you tell her?" Nikki asked.

"Well, her friend in California was conveniently part of a love triangle," Matt said. "Alexia never asked me straight out about the rumors of my parents' affairs, but she talked about her friends and how she'd pleaded with them not to cheat because of what her own parents did."

"Which was what?" Liam asked.

"They both cheated on each other." Matt took another long swig of beer. "When she was nine years old, she caught her father. He bought her silence with a horse. I told her mine bought me a remote-controlled car, top of the line."

Had Alexia planned her story to get Matt Kline to trust her?

"Did you tell her that you saw the person who killed your family?"

The muscle in Matt's jaw flexed. "I told her that I saw the guy with Amy, but I didn't get a good look at him. She promised she wouldn't say anything. I never told the police because I didn't actually see his face."

Nikki understood that Matt was a child at the time—a scared little boy who'd lost his whole family. But he'd denied the original investigators a lead. "You must have gone ballistic when you heard about the interview in the documentary," Nikki said.

"I didn't even know about that until last night."

"Is that why you went to the house to confront Alexia?" Nikki leaned forward. "We have a witness who says you and Alexia argued."

Matt glared out of the window to his empty balcony. "I don't want to watch the documentary, but I almost caved, so I was driving around last night. The family attorney called me and asked why I hadn't told him about the new developments. I didn't know what the hell he was talking about until he told me about the sneak peek for the new episode." His sharp jaw set hard. "I remembered my property manager had said a girl and her friends rented the house for the weekend." His voice trembled with anger. "Then I called the phone number she'd given me, but it was out of service. I didn't think I'd be able to find her because I didn't even have a photo. Then I remembered seeing an A. Perry on the Airbnb rental service. She'd told me her name was Lisa Riley. I drove to the house..." Matt closed his eyes, the lingering trauma etched into his face. "I hadn't been out there in years. Never wanted to see that godforsaken place again. But I couldn't just let her get away with using me, so I drove out there. I thought she was going to pass out when she saw me."

"Did you argue with her?" She already knew the answer,

but Nikki wanted to compare Matt's version of events to Luke and Brett's.

"She told me a few things—none of which I believed," Matt answered. "I called her a coward and asked how much the producers were paying her. She insisted it was all about justice... but I know she just wanted to be famous. I told her she deserved whatever was coming to her. Then I left."

Nikki glanced at Liam and knew he was thinking the same thing. "What did you think she had coming to her?"

"Misery."

Nikki sensed that Matt wasn't telling them everything. "And then you came back here? Do you know what time that was?"

"I was too amped up to go home, and I knew if I went to the bar I'd end up in a bad way, so I drove around, thinking. Came home around 4 a.m. And no, I don't have an alibi other than that."

"You remember the route you took?" Liam asked.

"Some of it, but I was so freaking angry, I don't remember half the drive."

"I don't blame you," Nikki said. "After my parents' murders, I used to drive my dad's old Chevy around at all hours just to feel close to him."

Matt didn't respond, but she could tell the words resonated with him.

"Why did you get suspended?" Liam asked. "Drinking?"

"None of your business," Matt snapped.

"We can make it our business." Liam's voice matched Matt's harsh tone.

"Do what you have to do," Matt said. "But what happened at work didn't have anything to do with any of this mess."

Nikki wasn't sure she bought that, but Matt wasn't going to tell them what had happened. "How'd you end up being a fire-fighter instead of a doctor? You went to med school, right?"

Matt looked at the table. "I'm sure you know that, too, because everyone else does. Yeah, I got into grad school and then started using drugs to keep up." He glared at her. "But I've been clean for nearly five years."

She didn't think his drinking habit met the requirement for sober but didn't argue. "And the firefighting?"

"Needed something to do. I volunteered at first but then got the training. They know about my drug issues in the past, which is why I agreed to monthly testing. I was eventually hired on part-time." He shrugged. "Suppose it's an adrenaline thing too."

"You're still part-time?"

"I've been full-time for four years," he answered.

Matt allowed a cursory search of his small home. There hadn't been any sign of Alexia or that Matt had been involved in something violent, but she hadn't been able to look through his clothes or trash. Still, his shock at the news struck Nikki as genuine.

She and Liam both gave Matt their business cards.

"And I'm sure we'll have more questions for you," Liam added. "You don't have plans to leave town for any reason, do you? No vacations or anything?"

His underlying meaning wasn't lost on Matt. "I'll be here the next time you want to question me, Agents."

TWELVE

Nikki hadn't been inside the Washington County sheriff's department in several months, but it looked the same. Located in the massive county government center that also housed the county attorney's office and the jail meant the parking lot was always at least half-full, even in the middle of the night.

Liam had stopped to charge his Prius after they left Matt's, and she didn't see any sign of him in the parking lot. Hopefully he hadn't gotten stuck in the never-ending construction traffic.

The lobby always reminded her of a corporate building, with its gleaming tile floors and giant ficus near the front door.

Nikki smiled at the young deputy sitting at the admin desk. "Hi, Sydney. How are you feeling?"

Sydney grinned and rubbed her protruding belly. "Fine, but I'm getting too big to be chasing bad guys, so I get to hang out in here until I go on maternity leave in a few months."

"Best advice I can give you is to get as much rest as you can now because the next eighteen years are going to be exhausting."

Sydney laughed and hit the buzzer to allow Nikki into the

sheriff's area. "Sheriff Miller's in the bigger interview room." Her smile faded. "He said he'd come from the hospital."

"What about Vivienne's and Libby's parents?"

"They came to the hospital," Sydney said. "Blanchard had them identify the girls there instead of bringing them all the way to the metro area. Sheriff didn't say much when he got back. That's always a bad sign."

Nikki thanked her, refusing her offer to walk her down to the conference room. She didn't envy Miller making the notifications. A cop carried those memories forever.

The sheriff's department was a bit of a maze, but Nikki had been here enough that she could have found the room with her eyes closed. Photos of Stillwater and Washington County over the years lined the corridor walls. Nikki had never stopped to look at them, but the sepia photo of Lilydale caught her eye now. It had been long after the building was completed. Although the front yard still had a wild look about it, Nikki also recognized the big, towering willow trees.

She read the inscription beneath the photo: *August Erickson, his wife, Lily, with good friends F. Scott Fitzgerald and his fiancée, Ms. Zelda Sayre. Scandia, Washington County, Minnesota, 1919. Photograph donated in 1998 by generous supporters of the retired officers' fund Ted and Sandra Kline.*

Nikki knew Sandy Kline's ancestors had built the George Barber mail-order Victorian, but she didn't know much about the family history before the Klines' murders. The connection with the Fitzgeralds sent a weird chill down Nikki's spine. She'd worked two brutal crimes in homes that had some connection to the celebrated writer, and he and Zelda had left the area for New York City after they married.

If only Nikki's mom could see her now. She'd want a detailed description of every nook and cranny of each house. Her mother used to joke about joining one of the cleaning services just to get a chance to see inside homes like the Victorian on Bone Lake.

As Nikki studied the expressions of both Ericksons, she wondered if the home had ever been a happy place. People rarely smiled for photos, but even still, the entire family looked miserable. Then again, the nineteenth century wasn't exactly fun for most of the settlers, no matter their wealth. As much as she adored old houses, it might be time to tear the place down.

Miller sat alone in the conference room, staring at the wall as Nikki entered.

"Kent, you okay?"

"Not really," he answered. "I just had to explain to two devastated families their girls were beaten to death during a sleepover."

Nikki wanted to tell him that she understood, that the emotion was part of what made him a good cop, but Miller already knew those things. "I'm sorry."

He nodded, clearing his throat. "I know."

"Were Vivienne's and Libby's parents able to tell you anything new?"

"Not really," he answered. "They've been friends since grade school, along with Alexia. Alexia is definitely the leader, and headstrong, according to both girls' parents. She's used to getting what she wants, but all four parents said she had a good heart, that their daughters never had a problem putting their friend in place." Miller rubbed his temples.

"How well do the parents know her mom and dad?" Nikki asked.

Miller retrieved the small flip notebook he kept in his breast pocket. "Rumor mill is the dad cheated with a younger woman, and that caused the divorce, but they don't really know either of Alexia's parents that well. Both Vivienne's and Libby's mothers said the girls liked Alexia's mother."

Liam strode through the doorway. "Freaking construction." He dropped his bag in the chair next to Nikki.

"That's why I told you not to go completely electric."

"Yeah, yeah." He glanced at Miller. "How was the hospital?"

"As bad as you can imagine," the sheriff answered. "And still no signs of Alexia or her car. We're pulling all of the CCTV in the area, but it's still rural enough out here that not every intersection has them, plus there are a couple of gravel roads they could have driven through. Drones are looking for the car too."

"We know someone let the killer inside, since there was no forced entry, and it wasn't Chandler, but I don't know that intimate knowledge of the house is going to help us narrow things down." Nikki explained she'd checked all of the major real estate sites, and even though the house had been off market forever, any structural changes had to be approved by the historical society. "The floor plan is online. It's accurate."

"Do you think it's the same killer from 2001?" Miller asked Nikki.

"I don't know," she admitted. "Sandy Kline's throat was cut, and all three victims suffered multiple stab wounds. Vivienne and Libby were beaten," Nikki said. "My theory about the original killer is that he's older; he'd have to be in his forties at least, which means he's in his sixties now. Would he still have been capable of such brutality? And does the motive seem the same? If it was love, lust, passion... jealousy over Mrs. Kline or Amy, how could the same be true for these girls? We know Alexia was interested in the old case. Did she find the killer? Was this all about keeping his identity hidden?"

"We have to keep Matt Kline on the suspect list," Liam said. "He doesn't have an alibi, he has keys to the house, so he wouldn't need to break in. He showed up a few hours before mad as hell, then drove around and doesn't remember much of it. He has a history of substance abuse and a motive."

"He also doesn't have any defensive wounds and consented to a search of his house before we left," Nikki reminded him. Liam was right about everything he'd said, but she had her reservations about focusing too much on him. "No sign of Alexia or any female, for that matter."

"He's wealthy," Liam said. "I'll see if he owns any other property."

"Courtney discovered something after I left for the hospital," Miller said. "I printed out the photos she sent."

He handed them to Nikki. She recognized the side porch at Lilydale, the screened-in oasis that led to the north side of the house and the woods.

"If you're walking through the living area to the porch," Miller explained, "this would be the back right corner, behind the loveseat. The porch is off-limits to guests, with a heavy fine if they're caught breaking the rules. Chandler insisted they followed those rules, and no one had been in that room, and yet the door was unlocked. She swabbed for prints and DNA on both the outside of the porch door and inside."

"You're saying someone who came to the party earlier in the day unlocked the door and snuck back in that night?" Liam asked.

"Makes the most sense to me. Either that or one of the girls unlocked it for some reason." Miller looked at Nikki. "Either one of those takes some planning and patience. Just like the Kline killer."

"You're right, but the level of rage here is different," Nikki countered. "The beating to both Libby and Vivienne—which didn't happen to the Klines—seems different. Statistically, you're more likely to see that from someone under twenty-five. And with so many teenagers having access to the house, I think we've got to look there first."

Liam nodded in agreement. "And if a teenager did this, he's probably going to be in panic mode at this point."

"Right." Nikki looked at Miller. "And he likely is known for having a short fuse. In the last few weeks, there's probably been a stressor that made him start acting more extremely just in day-to-day life. He probably feels like he got the short end of the stick in life and likely isn't part of the popular group. He's been rejected before, possibly by one of these girls."

"He could have been fantasizing about attacking a girl and then finally snapped," Liam continued. "He tried to put that fantasy into motion, but he didn't stop and think about the logistics because of his rage. He just attacked."

"We need to focus on post-murder behavior when we're talking to the kids who came to Bone Lake at any point over the weekend. Make sure your people know we're likely looking for someone who's all of a sudden acting oddly because he's probably not emotionally equipped to handle the stress. Most of these kinds of murderers can't, so their behavior starts to change as soon as the adrenaline wears off. Lack of sleep, obsession with the case, overall agitation and singular focus—behaviors that make friends and family think something's wrong."

Liam drummed his fingertips against the table. "To play devil's advocate, we need to think about how Matt Kline would act post-murder too."

"The same," Nikki said firmly. "If he hasn't been able to go into the house for years, then I don't see him suddenly conquering it on the anniversary of the murders."

"Except he really liked Alexia and found out she'd played him," Liam argued. "She's going to lay his whole life bare in the extra episode."

"Have Caitlin or the producers spoken to Matt about this?" Miller was fuming. "It's an open case, and I don't appreciate not even getting a courtesy call about these new allegations."

Liam flushed. "Caitlin has an email drafted to you that's

been ready to send for more than a week. The producers claim this is information the original investigators could have easily learned if they'd done their jobs. Her executive producer knows they're walking a tightrope, but he also wants ratings. He asked her to wait until after the first episodes aired before going to the police with the new information." His eyes flashed with anger. "Convinced her that they should do the investigative work to substantiate everything Alexia said before bothering the police. Caitlin didn't even know about the sneak peek until the documentary premiered yesterday."

Nikki shared his disgust. She knew Caitlin understood the legal system as well as anyone, and she wouldn't have wanted to send Miller on a wild goose chase. Her producers had used that against her. "That also means Matt didn't have any advance warning, right?"

"Caitlin tried to contact him repeatedly, but he refused to talk. She didn't want to leave the information in a message." Liam looked at Nikki. "To answer your question, no one from production told Matt about Alexia's interview. Tell me he couldn't have done this."

"Of course he could have." She couldn't hide her irritation. "But he doesn't have a record, right? Yes, drugs, but nothing violent," Nikki said. "You're telling me he did all of that during the early-morning hours, came home, was so detached he didn't leave any bloody clothing lying around. But before that, he did something with Alexia. Do you really think that's the person we spoke to today? That Matt Kline is capable of that kind of psychopathy?"

"People snap, especially when trauma's involved." Liam glanced at his notes. "According to Matt, he drove around aimlessly on the backroads until about 4 a.m. Can't remember the exact route, but most of it was on gravel roads that didn't have security cameras. He did stop to fill up with gas but didn't get a receipt. He thought it was closer to the time he came home, which doesn't help as far as an alibi goes."

"And he gave us permission to check his financial records." She shifted in her chair. "Matt's Chevy Sierra looks fairly new. Any idea what year it is?"

"Let me pull up the registration." Miller opened his laptop. "This thing is so slow. We need new ones." He squinted at the screen as he typed. "Okay, here it is—2020 Chevy Sierra pickup."

"GPS." Nikki looked at Liam. "Those Chevy trucks have OnStar navigation. Get a warrant and we should be able to find out his exact route."

"Shouldn't be too hard," Liam said confidently. "Finding a judge willing to look at the warrant on a Sunday will be the hard part. I'll text Kendall and get her on it."

"Have you reached Alexia's parents?"

"I spoke to her mom about half an hour ago," Miller said. "She's flying back from New York today. She's hard to read over the phone. Very upset, but controlled too. Let's go back to the weekend guests." They'd sent the list of names Olivia had given them to their junior agents so that Miller's deputies could focus on the search for Alexia.

"Going by her list, an additional fifteen people came through the house." Liam checked his texts for the information Kendall had sent. "Kendall and Jim are tracking those people down and interviewing them. They intend to speak with everyone today. Sheriff, what did the families say? Were you able to get anything more from Chandler?"

Miller had gone to the hospital to interview Chandler and his mother. "He's in shock, but stable. He was able to tell me that they'd started watching the documentary as soon as Netflix dropped it."

Netflix usually premiered all of their new content at 12 a.m. Pacific, but Caitlin's producer had convinced them to make it available by midnight Central Time, as the 2001 murders had taken place between midnight and 1 a.m. Another carrot to dangle at the killer, if they were still alive.

"Episode one was an hour and fifteen minutes," Miller reminded them. "Chandler said they were about fifteen minutes into the second episode when Matt Kline showed up."

"Matt's visit was short, and he and Alexia spoke outside," Liam continued. "Luke didn't hear much of that conversation, did he?"

"Unfortunately not," Nikki said.

Miller checked his notes. "Well, Chandler said that he and Libby eavesdropped at the window while the others theorized on Matt Kline's bizarre appearance. They had no idea that Alexia was in contact with Matt, much less that she had been talking to Caitlin."

"She told them after the last episode?" Nikki asked. Luke and Brett hadn't mentioned anything about Alexia's involvement in the documentary, but they'd left before the group finished watching. "How did Luke act when Matt showed up?"

Miller flipped through his dogeared notebook. "Stunned. He asked her how she knew Matt. Couldn't remember if Alexia told them it was Matt or if they'd figured it out. When she came back in, Luke met her at the door and demanded to know how she could do that to him. Luke accused Alexia of sleeping with him to get information so she could get famous. She thought that was funny. Sounds like that's when Luke had enough and left with Brett."

"Meaning she embarrassed him," Miller said. "He could have gone back to punish her."

"Maybe, but he appeared genuinely shocked, and that doesn't give him reason to attack the other girls."

"And they finished the documentary after the boys left?" Liam clarified.

Miller nodded. "Chandler said Alexia promised to tell them

everything after they finished watching. When they saw the sneak peek, they couldn't believe it. Vivienne and Libby both thought she'd overstepped. Chandler said he went to the kitchen to avoid it all."

"He say what time?"

"After two for sure."

"Backing up, did Chandler say anything about how Alexia acted after Matt left? Was she rattled at all?"

"Alexia never gets rattled, according to him. If she does, she hides it well. She took it all in stride and came back inside like nothing happened."

"Luke and Brett's story lines up for the most part," Nikki said. "Alexia sent the video to Olivia at 2:39 a.m. Matt Kline said he stopped at a Shell station four blocks from his place to fill up. He doesn't have a receipt, but he can have the bank confirm the activity. He then claims he stopped at the liquor store next door to his house. He paid cash there, because the machine was broken. We're still trying to confirm that.

"Thanks to the video Alexia sent Olivia, we know the attack started around 2:40 a.m.," Nikki continued. "Hopefully Matt or his GPS can show us he was nowhere near there, and we can cross him off the list." She had a feeling it wasn't going to be that easy, however. "Does Chandler remember anything else about the attack?"

"He was in the kitchen trying to clean up some of the mess when he heard a scream. Libby ran in, terrified. She told him to go for help and pointed to the dumbwaiter. He was the only one small enough to fit inside. He'd just shut the door when he heard another scream, and then the dumbwaiter busted. He blacked out, and the house was silent when he woke up. He kept listening, hoping for any sign of his friends, but nothing. He'd passed out from the pain when you discovered him."

Liam tore a sheet of paper out of his notebook and drew a crude layout of the Airbnb. "That confirms the killer didn't enter through the back patio doors. They had to have come in through the screened-in porch, just like we thought. Someone left it unlocked."

"That's the easiest access to the living room," Miller agreed. "Vivienne was attacked first, then Libby. Alexia's being in the bathroom might have given her a chance—"

"I don't think so," Nikki interrupted. "It's a straight shot from that bathroom to the front door. If the killer is attacking the girls in the living room area, Alexia should have gone out the back. We know she didn't because of her nail in Vivienne's hair."

"Chandler said Alexia wouldn't go down without a fight," Miller told them. "She liked being the center of attention, but she was loyal to her friends. He said she would have tried to help and fight, not run." He looked at his notes again. "Oh right. Luke Webb's dad called not long after you stopped at the country club. He said the family's devastated and wants to do whatever they can to help. Took it in stride when I asked for security tapes. He emailed the last twenty-four hours from the front and back entrances of the house. He said he watched them, and the boys never left after returning home, but we need to check them ourselves."

"How did it go with Vivienne's and Libby's families?" Liam asked.

"About as awful as you'd expect. Vivienne's mother passed out." Miller's voice was tight. "Reynolds is going to follow up with the family and friends who didn't come to the house. Just to make sure we're all on the same page, we agree that the suspect's likely someone who knew the girls and knew they could get into the porch door. We don't know if Alexia was the intended target and the others collateral damage, but her digging into the Klines' case and using Matt is the best motive we've come up with?"

"I wouldn't say it's the best because nothing I saw from

Matt today suggests he did anything," Nikki said. "I can't get past that porch door being unlocked. Matt wasn't inside the house. Hopefully Kendall and Jim can track down everyone they need to today. We also need to know exactly what information Alexia told Caitlin and the documentary producers."

"Caitlin's getting all the information together and bringing it over," Liam said. "She has copies of the original investigators' notes, the files, information from the assistant district attorney—everything we'd ask for if we were pulling from the archives. What about the K9s?"

"En route," Miller answered. "As luck would have it, they were at a training conference in Green Bay. I'm meeting them on the scene as soon as they're back in town. I don't know how much light we'll have left, but my first priority is tracking Alexia out of the house. Shouldn't be hard for the dog since we've got plenty of her belongings to use as scent. We're getting drones up in the air in the next hour or so. They'll keep an eye out for her, but they can search for the car much faster than we can on foot. Hopefully one of them will spot it."

"Have you talked with Courtney since this morning?" Miller asked. "She sent me the information about the screened-in porch, but I haven't heard anything else."

Nikki read the text Courtney had sent during the drive over. "She collected a lot of forensic evidence from the bodies and the scene, but given the foot traffic over the weekend, it's going to be difficult to narrow things down, not to mention the whole Airbnb angle. Her team collected dozens of fingerprints, and they'll all have to be cross-referenced with the victims as well as Matt Kline." Airbnbs, like hotels, created a unique problem for investigators. Even the best cleaning crew missed things, and without corroborating evidence, anything taken from the house—fingerprints, fibers, hair—would be under higher scrutiny. "And Matt Kline's a firefighter, which means his prints are in the system. Courtney can compare them to the ones she took from the scene. Matt insisted he only went as far as the entryway last night and hasn't been in the house in years. Let's find out if that's true." Fingerprints could last for a while, but if Matt truly hadn't been in the home in years, his prints would have been long scrubbed away.

"Did Matt confirm what Alexia's implied, that he saw the killer?"

"He saw the man with Amy." Liam's knee bounced with nervous energy. "But not enough to identify him."

Miller's dark eyes found Nikki's. "You think he's telling the truth about that?"

"Yes," she admitted. "He was pretty defensive and upset that Alexia broke his trust. But right now, it doesn't matter if he saw him or not. The public will think he did, and that means so will his family's murderer, assuming he's still alive."

"We need to put a car on his place," Miller said. "Keep an eye on his movements and whomever might be following him."

"That's going to be tough, since the media descended on him as we were leaving," Nikki said. "I called Lieutenant Chen. He's going to handle that end for us." They'd worked with Chen on the last big case in Washington County that Nikki's team had been involved with, and he'd earned a promotion at the Stillwater Police Department and trust from Nikki and her team. "He's also going to do a little digging on Matt Kline, find out if he's got more skeletons in his closet. Anger issues, that sort of thing."

"The media wants a statement," Miller said. "The public thinks it's the 2001 killer or a copycat. Matt Kline hasn't made it onto their suspect list, but I'm sure he will."

"Why would the 2001 killer come back and risk getting caught, especially the night the documentary actually premiered?" Liam said.

"Ego," Nikki replied. "Someone who is used to being the star and getting what they want regardless of others. Your basic sociopath." She shrugged. "It's probably a long shot, but it would be a good idea to look at all of Caitlin's files to see if we can find any other common denominators." She looked at Miller. "Ben Hinson was Amy's ex-boyfriend and the only serious suspect. They looked at a few other people, like a gardener and some contractors who'd done work earlier in the summer, but they all had alibis. Any idea what Ben's up to now?"

"He's one of the first people I thought of," Miller answered. "He's not hard to find. He owns a chain of rent-to-own stores across the city. I had my assistant check his record, and he hasn't had as much as a speeding ticket since 2001."

"We need to speak to him. And let's not forget that Alexia's claim that her mother had an affair with Mr. Kline makes her a new suspect in the original case. Matt has also said both his parents were having affairs. Whoever Mrs. Kline was sleeping with is a suspect in their deaths too. Our responsibility is to solve this current case, to find Alexia and get justice for Libby and Vivienne, but there's a chance we're looking at the same killer, and we need to run down that lead. What time is Shanna Perry's plane landing?"

"Seven. She's supposed to come straight here. I'd like you both to be here for that if you can."

Nikki had already let Rory know she'd likely be spending the night at the sheriff's office. This would be the first night they hadn't slept in the same bed in months. So much for low-profile cases.

THIRTEEN

AUGUST 2001

Mary Katherine sat up in bed, startled awake by the loud bangs on the front door. She heard her father, Vic, cursing as he hurried down the hall of their modest ranch-style home. The front door creaked open—her father still hadn't replaced the hinges like he'd promised her mother.

"Matty Kline." Her father's baritone echoed through the house. "What in the world are you doing on my doorstep at one o'clock in the morning?"

Mary Katherine didn't hear the response, but her father shouted for her mother to call the police out to the Klines' beautiful house on the lake. Mary Katherine sprang out of bed and ran down the hallway, her bare feet smacking the cracked vinyl.

Her mother was already in the kitchen on the phone. Vic ushered Matty inside the house, and Mary Katherine's stomach rolled the same way it had on the rollercoaster at Valleyfair the other day. Amy and her friend had taken Mary and Matt to the popular amusement park in a suburb of Minneapolis, letting them ride all the big kid rides that Mary Katherine's parents normally didn't allow. It had been their little secret.

When she'd gone swimming with Matt in the Klines' pool

earlier in the day, Mary Katherine had secretly envied that the sunburn he'd received at Valleyfair had already turned tan. Her fair skin meant endless applications of sunscreen with zero chance of getting anything darker than new freckles. Matt teased her about being a ghost, but he was the one who looked pale now. His face had gone white, like she'd seen in the movies, and his eyes were like dark orbs. His hands trembled, his bare legs full of fresh scratches.

"You're bleeding." Mary Katherine hoped her father didn't send her back to her room. She pointed to the dark spot of blood where Matt had stood seconds ago. "Your foot's bleeding."

Matt didn't seem to hear her, but Vic knelt down and gently lifted his right foot. "Hoo, boy. Looks like you stepped on a nail. You'll need a tetanus shot." Vic squeezed Matt's shoulder, something Mary Katherine had never seen him do, as her dad had never been big on displays of affection.

"Matty doesn't like needles." Mary Katherine walked closer to her best friend, her heart racing just like it did on the big rides. Between camp and being neighbors, she and Matty had gotten into all sorts of scrapes over the years, most of them Mary Katherine's fault. Matty always thought everything through, worrying about getting hurt or in trouble, while Mary Katherine acted on impulse. Matty was usually the one who kept them from doing something stupid like "poking an eye out"—one of her mother's favorite warnings.

Her gaze slid down to his feet again, and this time she noticed burrs stuck to his shorts. He was getting over his fear of the dark, but he hated the woods, and that was the only place he would have gotten the prickly nuisances.

Mary Katherine's mother, Tonya, brushed past her with a first-aid kit. She ushered Vic out of the way and crouched in front of Matt, who kept staring at Mary Katherine, like a living statue.

"What happened, honey?" Tonya lifted his foot just as Vic

had done and winced. "We'll clean this as best we can, but you will need a shot. I called your mom, but no one answered. Do you know what's going on, sweetheart?"

"Tonya, obviously he does or he wouldn't be here." Vic glanced at Mary Katherine and then back to her mother. He mouthed "bad."

Mary Katherine could only stare at her father and wonder what he meant.

Matt blinked. He finally looked at Tonya. "He killed them. He killed all of them."

At nine years old, Mary Katherine knew plenty about death, most of which she'd learned from the nuns at church. They tried to make it sound like a wonderful thing, telling the children that all the good people will go to heaven. Mary Katherine prayed it was true, but she'd seen what happened when people died. She remembered seeing her grandma in the coffin, still and stiff and cold. Mary Katherine would never forget the sound of the coffin slowly lowering into the ground. What happened to her body now? Did it just rot away? If Grandma's body was in the ground, then how could she go to heaven?

Dying happened to everyone. But killing was a sin. Sister Amelia had talked about killing when she went over the seven deadly sins. Wrath, envy, pride, gluttony, love, lust, and greed all led to the same bad ends, the nun had told them. "Every single killing, every life taken by another, falls into one of these seven deadly sins. They are the ugly thoughts that drive the sinner's wicked actions. And it's often part of the reason people become victims. The sins drive them to make poor decisions, putting them in the path of a terrible evil."

The lesson had been sobering because Mary Katherine had all of those bad thoughts. She could never kill anyone, but what if she made a mistake or a poor decision and someone killed her for it? She and Matty had discussed the idea at length after school. Matty went to public school, and he'd only been told that God is good and wise and wants everyone to love each other. He knew the Ten Commandments were important, but their church sounded a lot less stressful than Our Lady of the Holy Savior.

Matty didn't even know what being baptized meant until Mary Katherine had explained it to him. Amy had overheard and explained that in the church the Klines attended, the person chose when to be baptized, because it was their decision to join God's flock.

Mary Katherine hadn't known choice was an option. Believe and obey God or you'll burn in hell had been the mantra she'd heard as long as she could remember. She'd been aghast when Amy had told her she'd never been baptized.

"Amy, if you die without being baptized, you won't get into heaven." Mary Katherine had been so frightened that Amy promised she'd get baptized soon. She'd even said it at Valley-fair, when her friend joked about the rides being dangerous.

If Amy had been killed... that meant she was gone forever. And if she hadn't been baptized, Mary Katherine would never see her again, not even on the other side of St. Peter's pearly gates.

Fat tears rolled down Mary Katherine's cheeks.

Nothing would ever be the same.

FOURTEEN

Shanna Perry looked more put together than most of the mothers Nikki had interviewed over the years, especially those who'd just been told their daughters were missing. She'd come straight from the airport, letting everyone know she'd been in meetings all day and hadn't had time to freshen her face, despite the perfectly applied makeup. Her plump lips glistened with gloss, and she had the sucked-in-cheek look that accompanied buccal fat removal. The person's new face looked great until age and gravity took its toll, which made older women look like their face was melting off. Shanna wasn't there yet, but Nikki could tell by her smooth forehead and unmoving eyebrows that Botox users had.

Shanna fluffed her shoulder-length auburn hair. Alexia had inherited her mother's ocean blue eyes and defined jawline and symmetric nose, but not Shanna's fair skin. She had the sort of delicate complexion that required a strict sunscreen regimen, and Alexia's social media over the summer was full of photos from the beach and pool as she soaked up the sun.

Nikki offered Shanna something to drink, but she declined.

"I have to admit, I had a couple of drinks on the flight home. Benefits of first class. Where is my daughter?"

Her tone seemed more agitated than concerned, but Nikki had learned a long time ago that no parent handled a situation like this the same, and her sitting in judgment only stymied her ability to ask the right questions.

"We don't know." Nikki walked Shanna through what they'd discovered about the last twenty-four hours. "She's been missing now for twelve hours. Her car is gone too. We've had multiple people who know Alexia insist that she wouldn't leave anywhere without her phone, which was at the scene, along with her wallet and other personal items. Right now, we're treating her as a possible victim of the same person who murdered her friends." Nikki glanced at Liam. They'd already discussed him taking the lead about the documentary since he knew more about the overall process.

Shanna swayed in the seat, her trembling hands bumping against the table. "Alexia must be hiding somewhere. She's a very fast runner. She probably ran for help and got lost. What about her car? Are you looking for it?"

"Yes." Nikki felt a pang of sadness at the desperation in Shanna's voice. Missing kids never got any easier, no matter their age. "Sheriff Miller is handling the ground search for her, and he's got drones in the air looking for her car."

"One thing, before we ask any questions," Liam began. "My girlfriend is Caitlin Newport, the documentary maker. I normally wouldn't share that information, but since the show is clearly tied to whatever happened, I want to be upfront."

Shanna's eyes burned with anger. "Then why isn't she here?" She didn't wait for an answer. "Alexia told me about the documentary Saturday morning, when I was out of town and it was far too late for me to do anything. She said they want to do another episode with information taken from my diary." Shanna glared at Liam. "You can tell her that's not going to happen."

"To be clear"—Nikki managed to speak before Liam, who fumed beside her—"Caitlin was against all of that. There are emails to prove that. Unfortunately, your daughter went over her head to the producers and dangled a carrot they just couldn't resist. Since Alexia is eighteen, she has every right to participate."

Shanna scowled. "That woman's producer called me months before Alexia's birthday. Apparently, he'd received a 'tip' that we might have information that could change the course of the investigation. I said that was absurd and hung up on him."

Nikki shot Liam a knowing look. The day she'd done most of her on-camera interview with Caitlin, she'd mentioned the same tip. "Who else could have called production?"

"Oh, Alexia called them." Shanna slowly exhaled. "She's really gotten into true crime, and it's my fault. I told her I knew the Kline family a few years ago, and she never forgot it. She did a research paper on the case last year and has been obsessed ever since."

"Alexia discovered the diary you kept in 2001. She took photos and showed them to producers," Liam said. "That's why they took her information seriously."

"She did what?" Shanna stammered.

"Do you remember the diary's contents?" Nikki asked.

Shanna's cheeks turned pink. "Some of it."

"Look, Shanna, we're not judging your past choices, and we know you have an alibi for the Kline murders, so there's no need to dance around this," Nikki said. "Alexia told Caitlin that you had an affair with Mr. Kline while you were an intern."

Shanna's jaw tightened. "I'm not proud of it, but yeah, it's true. I was an intern at the cancer research institute, in the accounting department. It was a brief affair and that was it. My life went on, and we all know what happened to the Klines. I don't understand what this has to do with the attacks on my daughter and her friends."

"Have you ever met Matt Kline?"

"Maybe when he was a kid, if he came to the firm." Shanna looked between them. "Why?"

"It appears that Alexia had a relationship with Matt," Nikki said. "He shared a few things, including that he'd seen the man that night, from the side. That's part of the reason they're wanting to do a follow-up episode with her."

"She did *what*?"

"It seems she did her research on Matt Kline and knew where to meet him," Liam said. "He's not exactly the most trusting guy, but she got his guard down enough when he was drinking to get the information."

"I can't believe her," Shanna said. "She's been an attention-getter from the day she was born, the apple of her father's eye. He encouraged it, of course. Always let her have her way. I put my foot down and I'm the bad guy. She barely has any bound-aries. Do you think Matt's hurt her? Have you searched his home?"

"We have, and she's not there," Nikki admitted. "We're checking alibis and talking to everyone who saw Alexia over the weekend. Is there any place Alexia might go? Maybe she managed to get out of the house but is now terrified." It appeared her daughter wouldn't have been able to count on Shanna for emotional support.

"Not really," Shanna said. "Alexia doesn't fear much. If anything, she would have gone after whoever did this." Her voice trembled as her show of bravado began to crack. "Do you think the same person who killed the Klines could have done this?"

"We can't rule it out," Nikki answered. "If he's alive and saw the documentary or heard about it, it is possible he could have come back. Right now, I think it's more likely this was someone the girls knew and trusted. But we don't know how far Alexia dug into the Kline murders or what she found out."

"If she's anything like Caitlin, she won't stop until she gets to the bottom of things," Liam added. "It is possible she turned up some information that spooked someone. But, as Agent Hunt said, right now that's probably the less likely scenario."

"She talked about being an investigative journalist too," Shanna said. "That way, she could travel instead of being stuck in a grimy city. Oh, Alexia, what have you done?"

Nikki handed her a tissue from the box on the table. "I know this is really difficult, but you haven't heard from Alexia since yesterday afternoon, correct?"

"That's right. She told me everything was fine and she'd be home today around noon." Shanna seemed to rein in her emotions. "What are you doing to find my daughter, Agents?"

Liam unlocked his tablet and turned it so that Shanna could see the photos Courtney had taken of the personal effects in Alexia's room at the Airbnb. "Her phone was discovered in the bathroom, shattered. Her bag and wallet were left behind as well. These are in evidence, but we wanted you to look at the photos and tell us if anything is missing."

"The credit card," Shanna said immediately. "Her Chase card is gone." She dug into her purse, her hands shaking. They waited as she struggled to keep from dropping the device. "She hasn't used it in three days. You can track it if she does, right?"

"Yes," Nikki said.

Shanna promised to stay in touch and let them know if she heard from her daughter. She also didn't mince words about her ex-husband. "I'm not surprised he's not answering. He doesn't care."

"We need to get a look at Alexia's personal things," Nikki said. "She may have kept a record about what she's done."

"If she did, it would have been on her phone. She hates the feel of paper."

Nikki knew she needed to chase Miller. He'd said the Cellebrite software would speed up the process of unlocking the phone, but perhaps something was slowing them down.

She also called Volvo, but their customer service department was closed on Sundays, and Shanna didn't have a number for Google Assistant. She planned to contact Volvo first thing in the morning and request the last several days of data from the vehicle. Alexia's new car was equipped with Google Maps and several other high-tech options. Once they had access, finding Alexia's car shouldn't be too difficult. Finding her with it, however, was another story.

"The deputy who picked me up at the airport said that the sheriff has drones in the air looking for her and that the K9s are coming," Shanna said.

"That's correct," Nikki answered. "We split up the investigative duties, with my team chasing down leads so Miller and his deputies could focus on the search. They're much more familiar with the terrain."

"She's alive." Shanna's jaw set hard. "Alexia's too scrappy. She's a fighter."

"I promise we're doing everything possible to find her. I know you said that she wouldn't have written anything down on paper, but could you go through her room when the deputy takes you home? Or allow him to? He can just do a quick search to make sure there's nothing that would give us an idea of why this could have happened. Her bag for school, any place she could have put a notebook."

"That's fine," Shanna said. "Her room is as impeccable as her car, so it shouldn't be too hard to find stuff, although her laptop is a Mac. Aren't they really hard to get into?"

"They can be, and if you try too many times, you're locked out and that drags things out," Nikki answered. "Fortunately, we should be able to access her iCloud, hopefully today or early tomorrow."

Shanna rocked back and forth in the chair. "I don't know what's more awful—that someone she knew could have done this or if the same person who killed the Klines... No, I can't think that. It's just too outlandish, right?"

"Mrs. Perry." Nikki kept her tone gentle, the same way she spoke to Lacey when her little girl was overtired and seconds away from a breakdown. "Alexia inserted herself into something much bigger than her, and things may have gotten out of hand. We're hoping she managed to run off. Does she wear a smartwatch?"

"No, she's got sensory issues. Can't stand to wear rings or watches. I always tell her that's good because I don't have to share." Her voice caught.

Nikki wished she could think of something that would make her feel better, but the reality was grim.

"How are Vivienne's and Libby's families?" Shanna asked quietly.

"Devastated," Nikki said. "Do you know the other parents well?"

Shanna shook her head. "I guess I'm a bit of a snob, but I'm really not interested in getting to know other parents beyond making sure they're not dangerous or whatever. But the girls were sweethearts."

"I'll walk you to the lobby." Nikki and Shanna left Liam with his notes, walking in strained silence down the corridor past the bullpen. As they exited the security door into the public lobby, Nikki spied a familiar head of blond hair. Unfortunately, Shanna Perry had seen Caitlin as well. Before Nikki could stop her, the woman strode across the lobby toward the reporter.

"You stupid bitch," Shanna shouted. "I told you to leave us alone. Now my daughter is sucked into this mess and her friends are dead."

Caitlin set the two plastic tubs she'd lugged into the

building down. "Mrs. Perry, I'm so sorry for what happened, but my producer is the one you should be angry with. I told him you weren't comfortable about any of it, but Alexia's an adult."

"And you have zero ethics," Shanna shot back. "Getting an innocent man out of prison made you famous, so you've got to follow up with something even more sensational to stay relevant. Now two teenagers are dead, and one is missing. Are you happy?"

"All right." Nikki stepped between the women before Caitlin could react. "Mrs. Perry, you have every right to feel the way you do, but this"—she gestured to the room at large—"isn't helping anything. You're upsetting yourself and Alexia needs you to be strong right now. Please let us do our jobs and find your daughter."

A deputy fresh out of the academy, stuck on the night shift, had been instructed to make sure Shanna Perry made it home safely and to keep an eye on the house in case Alexia made an appearance. Shanna spouted off a few nasty things to Caitlin but allowed the deputy to lead her outside.

"Christ." Caitlin sagged against the lobby wall after Shanna left. "That woman is a piece of work."

"She's upset her daughter's MIA," Nikki said. She could understand the woman's anger. There had been times in their relationship when Nikki had questioned Caitlin's ethics, too, though she'd come to the conclusion that she did have her heart in the right place—that she was out for justice.

"Maybe," Caitlin answered. "Or maybe she's more worried about what you might find on Alexia's iCloud account."

Nikki hadn't thought of that. Miller told Nikki that his team were having trouble unlocking the phone. Apparently Apple took user privacy seriously, and getting past the encryption was taking some time.

"Did you talk to her about her diary?" Caitlin asked.

Nikki nodded. She didn't want to tell Caitlin too much—it was privileged information.

"But she didn't tell you exactly what was inside, did she?" Caitlin didn't pause long enough for Nikki to respond. "Shanna didn't tell you she'd spoken with Amy hours before the murders, did she?"

Nikki grabbed one of the plastic tubs Caitlin had brought. "Grab the other and come with me." She headed through the secured doors back toward the interview room where Liam remained. "What exactly did Alexia tell you?"

"It's what she *showed* me," Caitlin corrected her. "I've seen all of the diary pictures on her phone, but this is the only one she actually sent me." She balanced the box on her hip and reached into her purse. "Here." She thrust a nearly blank sheet of paper at Nikki. "I printed it."

Nikki's pulse accelerated. The two lines, written in impeccable cursive, appeared to be the beginning of an entry dated the day of the Klines' murders. The entry was marked by a crudely drawn set of devil horns.

Just got off the phone with lil miss perfect Amy. Guess she found out her mom had secrets too.

FIFTEEN

"This is all of it." Caitlin set the last box on the table. "Chisago County handled a lot of the original investigation, which I still can't believe."

Since Bone Lake was just a few miles from the county line, deputies from the neighboring northern county had reached the scene first in 2001. Normally, they should have taken a back seat to the Washington County sheriff, but as Nikki had learned when she'd agreed to analyze the Kline murders for the documentary, the Chisago County sheriff had refused, claiming they all needed to join forces to catch the Klines' murderer. Hardin, the same deputy and later sheriff, whose bias had caused the man who'd murdered Nikki's parents to go free for two decades while Rory's brother, Mark, rotted in prison, had just started serving his first term as Washington County sheriff when the murders happened. He argued that Chisago County wanted the "glory" of a case that would be as "infamous" as the Walsh murders in 1993.

Caitlin had warned Nikki about the information before she'd watched the film, but watching Hardin's interviews from the early 2000s had made her skin crawl. She'd forgiven him, for her own sake, but the interviews had nearly made her change her mind. Hardin had passed away from diabetes last year, so they wouldn't be able to talk to him about the case.

"Hardin and Rich Langley, the Chisago County sheriff, hated each other." Miller had joined them. "I'd just started working as a deputy back then, so I didn't have much involvement with the Kline case, but I remember the shitshow. That's why the BCA stepped in, because Hardin wouldn't budge, and neither would Rich." Miller sipped a likely cold cup of coffee. "Rich was a damn good cop, had a nose for the truth. He didn't think Hardin could handle it. The BCA took over because Peggy Hanover, Matt Kline's aunt and appointed guardian, begged them. But that was more than a month after the murders, I think."

"It was." Caitlin pointed to the two plastic bins. "Obviously these aren't official case files since it's still technically open. I've got copies of every interview each department conducted, along with transcribed notes from all the recent interviews that I did. All of that is in the blue one, and the red contains the limited access I had to the actual files. A lot of that is my notes, as I was allowed to read some of it in the presence of an officer, but I couldn't make copies."

Nikki opened the red bin. Caitlin's need for organization bordered on obsessive, so the files and research were in chronological order. "I'm surprised you got that in an open case."

A familiar spark lit in Caitlin's eyes. "Rich Langley is close with Zach's grandfather. He retired a few years ago, but you know how cops are. He kept copies of a lot of stuff. He wants the case solved, but that's why I consulted with Kent." She nodded towards Miller. "I wanted to make sure nothing we did on the documentary was detrimental to the investigation." She slumped in her chair. "So much for that. I can't believe this happened. Do you think it's the original killer? Did I piss him off?"

"We don't know yet." Liam rubbed his girlfriend's shoulder. "If it is, it's still not your fault. We all agreed this documentary was needed."

"Over a bonfire and beers."

At the beginning of last summer, Nikki and Rory had hosted a bonfire for their closest friends and family, most of which consisted of Nikki's team, Caitlin, and Rory's family, the Todds. Mark had even brought his girlfriend, who normally avoided family functions because she still resented Nikki, even though she'd met Mark after he'd been released. After everyone else had gone home and Lacey had finally passed out, Liam and Caitlin had explained the idea for the documentary as they made s'mores. She wanted Nikki and Rory's honest opinion about the documentary, since it would be opening old wounds without any guarantee the case would move forward.

"I had one goal when I did the doc about Mark," she'd said. "It was about getting him out of prison. I thought it was worth the upheaval, hard as it was." She reached around Liam and took Nikki's hand. "And I know it was hard, but it was worth it. Right?"

"Of course." In that moment, it was hard to believe she'd been so at odds with Caitlin when Nikki had returned to Stillwater in the middle of Mark's appeal. "I hope Matt Kline will be okay with it, but this does need to be made. It's an unsolved massacre. Any new movement on it will help."

Miller offered her a tissue, and Caitlin wiped the tears brimming in her eyes. "There's something I haven't told either one of you. About the Klines and the case. And I should have, I guess. But it wasn't pertinent to solving it or anything."

Surprise flickered through Liam's eyes, but he recovered. "Tell us now, then."

"You already know Newport is my professional name. And I had my first name legally changed when I was twenty-one."

Nikki tried to keep her expression neutral, but inside she

was as nervous as Liam looked. "What are you getting at?"

"My real name is Mary Katherine Kettner. Matty was my best friend and Amy..." The tears started running down her face. "Amy's the only reason I'm here today."

Nikki's eyebrows raised in shock.

"Mary Katherine?" Liam stared at her in surprise, his cheeks going red. "Wouldn't have pegged you as a Catholic."

"I'm not anymore." Caitlin wiped her tears with a tissue. "Not after what I saw that night."

"What exactly did you see?" Liam asked.

"I woke up because someone was pounding on the front door. It was Matty, shell-shocked. I don't know exactly what he said to my mother, but my father told her it was bad at the Klines' and to call the police. Matty was bleeding all over the floor from a nail in his foot. He had no idea it was even there. I'll never forget the look in his eyes when my mother asked where his parents were, and he said they were dead."

"You mentioned Amy as the reason you're here," Nikki prodded. "Did you see her that night?"

"No," Caitlin answered. "She was like an older sister. Matt and I met on a walk around the area when I was young, and we were buddies until that night. I'd been over swimming that day. Matty and I were in a dunking war when we heard Amy and her mother fighting." Her eyes darkened. "I'd never seen anyone fight with Mrs. Kline. Everyone loved her, including me. She and Amy butted heads sometimes, but this was different."

"Do you know what it was about?"

Caitlin shook her head. "Matty told me they were probably fighting about 'him,' because Amy was supposedly thinking about getting back together with Ben, and her parents were dead set against it."

"That's what he told the police," Liam said. "Not about the fighting specifically," he said to Nikki, "but the issue with Amy's ex-boyfriend."

"That's not what they were fighting about, I'm sure of it." Caitlin's eyes took on a familiar gleam. "I had to pee, and I wasn't about to go in the pool because my mother told me you could get an infection if you peed in chlorine." She rolled her eyes. "Just one of her many nonsensical words of wisdom. The hall bath is just off the kitchen, so when the yelling died down, I went inside. Amy and her mother weren't in the kitchen, but I could hear them upstairs arguing. I did my business as fast as I could because I wasn't going to get caught in the middle of their fight. I had enough of that at home. Anyway, I'd just gone toward the kitchen when I heard Amy running down the stairs."

"How did you know it was her?" Liam asked.

"Because her mother walked with a little limp and wouldn't have ever run down stairs. But Sandy wasn't that far behind, and I heard some of what she said. I didn't understand it until I was older, and years later, during therapy after losing my fiancé and giving up parental rights to Zach, I started talking about the Klines—something I hadn't done since that summer. We weren't allowed to talk about it at home, and the nuns weren't interested in hearing about it either. I spoke about Amy and how much her death had affected me, and the memories kind of emerged without my trying."

Caitlin's fiancé had been killed in Afghanistan, leaving her a single mother. Overwhelmed and desperate, she'd eventually given Zach to his paternal grandparents, who raised him as their own until Zach found out the truth about his mother a few years ago. She'd started going to therapy after attending a psychology class and realizing how much help she needed.

"What did you hear that day?" Nikki asked.

Caitlin wadded the tissue into a ball. "Sandy distinctly said, 'Well, I don't know what to tell you. It happened. It's done.' And then Amy said, 'Either you tell Daddy or I will.'"

"You're absolutely certain?" Liam sounded skeptical. They all knew memory was fallible, especially childhood ones.

"Yes," Caitlin admitted. "I'd stake my reputation on it. Plus, remember Shanna's diary entry. She said Amy found out her mom had secrets. Mrs. Kline was having an affair as well. That was the original pitch for the documentary, you know. I wanted to dig into the case and try to find out what happened because I knew the Klines. The statement my mother and I gave police is in the files I brought."

"So you did tell them about the argument?" Nikki asked.

Caitlin nodded. "I don't think they ever followed up."

"When did you last talk to Matt?" Nikki asked. "If you were childhood friends, I'm surprised he turned you down for the documentary."

"We grew apart after the murders, and I haven't used the name Mary Katherine Kettner since the day I graduated high school. He doesn't know, and I didn't want to use that as an excuse to get him to talk to me."

"But you'd already accumulated years of research about the case by the time it was pitched to the executives?" Nikki asked.

"Absolutely," Caitlin answered. "After the murders, the rumors started the way they always do after something terrible happens. Most of them were bogus or about Amy and her boyfriend. A lot of those were false too. But my mother's weren't. Mom never thought much of Sandy Kline, mostly because Sandy was beautiful and so well-liked and had her own career instead of being mired down by a religious patriarchy. She became increasingly frustrated that the gossip mill revolved around Amy and her father, while her mother's name was barely mentioned."

"You said her words weren't false like the others," Nikki reminded her. "What did she say?"

"Because she swore to my father that she saw Sandy with another man less than two weeks before the murders. I heard her tell my father that very night."

SIXTEEN

Mary Katherine was brushing her teeth in the jack-and-jill bathroom. She had to get to bed early tonight so she could be rested for their big day at the waterpark tomorrow.

"Tonya, I won't have you repeating gossip." The thin walls meant she could hear everything in her parents' bedroom, even when Mary Katherine desperately tried to shut them out.

"It's not gossip if it's true," Tonya Kettner snapped back at her husband. "I saw them not far from the lake, walking on one of the paths. They stood too close and spoke too passionately to simply be friends."

"It could have been anyone." The bedsprings groaned as Vic sat down. "Doesn't mean they're sleeping together. Sandy Kline is one of the kindest, most respected people in the community. Her family basically established half of it."

"So?" Her mother's voice rang with contempt. "That doesn't mean she isn't capable of mistakes. After all, she's human."

"Did you see any intimate contact?"

"I didn't see them kissing or anything like that, but he did grab her hands and plead with her about something. She shook her head and pulled away. She didn't see me until she'd reached

*the start of the trail, and I pretended like I had just walked up,
but you should have seen the look in that woman's eyes, Vic. Like
she'd been caught with her hand in the cookie jar."*

* * *

"Do you know if your mother ever told the police what she
saw?" Nikki asked.

"Yes," Caitlin answered. "I heard her repeat the story to the
detective when she took me in to tell what I'd overheard. My
father wasn't happy."

"Why?" Nikki knew Caitlin had issues with her parents,
but she'd never heard many of the details.

"My father dismissed it when she first told him," Caitlin
said. "And my mother knew better than to push it. But after the
murders, she wasn't going to stay quiet. Said it was her Chris-
tianly duty to talk to the police. My father said it was blasphe-
mous to speak ill of the dead." She locked eyes with Nikki.
"And before you try to find a way to gently bring it up, my
father had been home all night, and even if he did have a thing
for Sandy, she wouldn't have given him the time of day."

"I thought the families were friends," Nikki responded.

"Matty and I were friends," Caitlin corrected her. "My
mother insisted that because we lived 'as Jesus intended,
without so many material things,' the Klines looked down their
nose at our family. She thought a lot of things that were probably wrong."

Caitlin's relationship with her mother had clearly been
strained. Nikki wanted to ask if they'd made peace before her
mother's death a few years ago, but it wasn't the time, or her
business.

"The producers loved the idea of turning around the narra-
tive and exploring other motives and suspects, but without Matt
participating, we couldn't sell them the idea. I finally decided

that as long as the facts were presented accurately, even if some were left out, it was worth moving forward to get the case back in the public's minds." Caitlin nudged the blue box. "The full interviews I did with all of Amy's friends, her ex-boyfriend, and the police are on a flash drive. Transcripts are there as well." She looked like she was fighting tears again. "I've had a lot of angry phone calls from her friends since the documentary dropped. I don't blame them for that. They believed their opinions were ignored in 2001 and that we did the same thing with the documentary."

"How so?" Liam asked. "You interviewed all of them several times."

"In the official report, the medical examiner, Roger Norton, said Amy had been raped," Caitlin answered. "But all of Amy's friends said they felt like the investigators were looking for a motive for Ben. They had heard Amy was a virgin and assumed she'd denied Ben. Amy's friends said there was no way Ben would have forced himself on her. He was respectful, loving, understanding. They think the ME was biased, that he created that report to fit. And Netflix didn't do much to change that opinion. They cut a lot of the friends' interviews where they explained all of this in the final documentary." Caitlin looked at Nikki. "I debated bringing this up to you when you consulted on the file, but my producer assured me Roger Norton's reports had been vetted." Caitlin slammed her hand down on the table. "This is what I get for taking their money and giving them control. I knew I should have made the documentary on my own, just like I did Mark's, and shopped it. But I got greedy."

"That's not being greedy. I absolutely believe you did this for the right reasons and taking the deal with Netflix made sense. No one would turn down the exposure for their case—or the money. This is not your fault."

Caitlin squeezed her hand. "Thank you."

Something about the medical examiner's name sent a wave of nerves through Nikki. "Why does that name sound familiar?"

"Because Roger Norton lost his license and was investigated after it came to light he'd botched cases," Caitlin answered. "The police—specifically Hardin after Washington County finally got full control of the investigation—based their investigation on the theory that Amy was the target, likely murdered by her ex-boyfriend, with her family as collateral damage. How could they find the killer if they're starting from the wrong hypothesis?"

"Christ Almighty." Liam thrust a copy of the original autopsy report at her. "What a joke."

Nikki's stomach turned as she read. No seminal fluid had been found with Amy, nor any hair or other biological evidence, yet Norton maintained she had minor injuries consistent with sexual assault. Caitlin didn't have the medical examiner's photos of the genital area, but Norton's report mentioned bruising and some bleeding, which could indicate sexual assault. No further testing had been done.

Forensic science and crime scene investigation had advanced light-years ahead of 2001, including incidences of rape, but by the early 2000s, more and more hospitals and law enforcement agencies had access to incredible sexual assault resources and investigators, and thanks to shows like *Law & Order SVU*, some of the culture surrounding rape victims had changed, their voices becoming more important. At the time, coroners were often elected officials who weren't required to have a medical background. Lack of experience and an overwhelming workload meant corners were often cut. But Norton had been a certified medical examiner working in the Twin Cities metro, with access to cutting-edge medical techniques and technology, and yet his language in the reports reminded Nikki of some of the reports she'd read from the eighties and nineties. If Norton had believed the killer raped Amy, the evidence should have been periodically tested over the years, but it would appear that former Sheriff Hardin had shelved the case.

"You didn't find any record of Hardin having anything retested, did you?"

Caitlin shook her head. "No, and a lot of the conclusions Norton made at the time were unfounded and reeked of bias. For God's sake, we knew before 2001 that hymens break all the time and aren't a conclusive indicator of sexual activity, but he claimed that it was evidence of the contrary. Hardin and the BCA agreed."

"I assume you don't have full copies of the Klines' autopsies?" Nikki asked.

"Just the final page of the reports, with manner of death," Caitlin said. "Minnesota is fiercely protective about privacy, even after someone is long dead. Unless Matt signed off, I wasn't allowed to get them. And I wasn't going to ask."

The full autopsy reports should have photos and detailed information about every wound the Klines suffered, along with toxicology and other test results. "We'll have Blanchard look at them, just to make sure Norton's findings were accurate."

"Do you think the 2001 killer is behind this?" Caitlin's tone didn't have her usual fervor. Nikki knew she was blaming herself.

"So far, we haven't found any evidence to suggest that, but given Alexia's digging around in the case, it's a possibility."

After Caitlin left, Nikki and Liam settled into the conference room to try to make some sense out of the streams of information and go over the security videos the property manager had emailed, starting with Sunday's footage. It didn't take long to confirm that day's events, but they also had hours of videos to go through from Friday, when Alexia and her friends had arrived at the house.

"We should be able to cross-reference drivers' license records with anyone who enters through the front door. Olivia said that everyone came through that door."

Kendall and Jim, the junior agents on Nikki's team, had spent the day contacting the kids on Olivia's list. Every single one had alibis, either in the form of parents or CCTV confirming they'd arrived home and hadn't left other than to go to work or another planned event. "Did you get in touch with Kendall?"

"She and Jim are going over the interviews from the Kline murders," Liam answered. "We also need to talk to Shanna about the affair. And her knowledge of Mrs. Kline's 'secrets'. She's not telling us everything."

Nikki had been thinking the same thing. "The sheriff's deputy is in front of her home for the night, and she's trying to get information from Volvo about tracking Alexia's car. I thought I'd talk to her in the morning and see if she's heard anything. I want to see Alexia's room for myself." She snapped her fingers as an errant thought hit her. "While we're going through Friday, let's cross-reference Olivia's list and make sure we have everyone's names."

Nikki handled the security videos while Liam used the DMV records to confirm faces and names. The process was painstaking even with technology. Liam cued up all of the DMV photographs of the kids on Olivia's list, and with each new arrival, Nikki had to pause the video so Liam could do the research and catalog the results.

The first to arrive on Saturday were Luke and Brett, around 11 a.m., each carrying a duffel bag that looked like it held a lot more than clothes. A familiar red bottle cap peeked out of Luke's bag's side pocket. "Guess we know who brought the vodka."

Alexia looked thrilled to see them, and not long after, a steady stream of kids started arriving. Nikki understood the property manager's reasoning for not having the security videos automatically download to her phone when the motion was triggered. Lilydale was an Airbnb, and even with a limited number of guests, the door was probably always opening and closing during a visit. The notifications would drive anyone crazy. She thought back to the haunted look in Sera Everett's eyes when she'd talked about not trusting her instincts with Alexia. "Sera suspected a party and thought about changing the security setup for individual notifications, but she ultimately decided against it, since she would be two hours away at a funeral and family gathering. She didn't get home until midnight on Saturday, and she didn't think to download the security videos. If she had, things might have been different. Sera says she would have broken up the party and kicked them out."

Nikki understood the guilt, because she'd feel the same way, but she'd assured Sera she shouldn't blame herself. Alexia was an eighteen-year-old who'd paid the deposit and knew the rules of the house. And if the killings weren't related to the documentary, they likely would have occurred somewhere else.

So far, everyone who'd come through the door had all been on Olivia's list. Each one knocked on the door and waited for someone to let them in through the front vestibule. Alexia answered the door most of the time, greeting each with a friendly hello or hug.

"Look at Alexia's face." Nikki pointed to her frozen screen. A tall, gangly boy with a farmer's tan and tank top chewed his bottom lip. Alexia's big smile had quickly changed to surprise and then anger. As Nikki restarted the video, Alexia shook her head and moved to close the door, but then Olivia appeared over Alexia's shoulder. The two girls spoke for less than a minute, but Alexia finally rolled her eyes, seemingly in agreement.

Liam scanned the photos from the DMV website. "Eric Gannon, eighteen. Looks like he came for Olivia."

"That's right." Nikki's interview with Olivia and her mother seemed like days ago. "Alexia wasn't friends with Eric, but he and Olivia are close. She said he came to hang out with her for a little while before leaving for work."

Liam pointed to the paused video. "Alexia recognized him. She didn't have any issue letting him inside."

"You're right. I need to speak to him."

Eric stayed for twenty-two minutes, and Olivia walked him to his vehicle. She'd jogged back inside with a dreamy smile on her face. Nikki didn't need to be a psychologist to see the girl's crush. Alexia had likely relented because of her friend. Seven other kids showed up in the interim, but the rush slowed after 3 p.m. The front door remained closed until just after 5 p.m.

A man with Versace glasses set a large, red cooler down before knocking on the door. He adjusted the Titleist golf visor on his head and then checked his watch. Nikki had looked at the same Garmin for Rory's birthday present. The watch did pretty much everything but whip up a homecooked meal, but ultimately Rory would have had a fit if she'd spent so much money, so she'd gone with the Apple Watch.

The door opened to reveal Alexia, who clapped and smiled. The man grinned, making the creases between his eyes deeper. He hefted the cooler and followed Alexia inside.

Nikki and Liam looked at each other. "Who the hell was that?" Liam asked.

"Given the golf hat and expensive gear, I have a feeling it's Luke's dad." She thought back to the beer cans stacked on the counter. "Surely he isn't doing a beer run for these kids."

"What's his name?"

Nikki checked her notes. "Arthur Webb."

Liam quickly typed the name into the DMV's search

feature. "That's definitely Arthur Webb. He's a lawyer. I can't believe he's dumb enough to bring a bunch of kids alcohol."

"He's a defense attorney," Nikki reminded him. "There's a difference between being dumb and thinking you're above the law."

They watched as Arthur Webb emerged from the house a few minutes later, Luke right behind him, beer in hand. They spoke for a few seconds before Arthur laughed, clapped his son on the back, and left.

"Luke didn't mention his dad being there, did he?" Liam asked.

"Nope. My guess is because he didn't want to tell me his father was there to bring them booze."

"Either way, given the timestamp, we should talk to him. He's likely more observant than the teenagers. He might have noticed something odd that they didn't."

SEVENTEEN

Nikki drove through the impressive suburb the Webbs lived in. Each home sat on multiple acres, giving the impression of a rural community despite the very expensive homeowner's association in the neighborhood.

Luke's father had a reputation as an excellent but also ethical defense attorney among local prosecutors, and Nikki hoped his eagerness to send the security videos over to the sheriff's station earlier meant he wouldn't mind her stopping by unannounced at 10 p.m.

The Webbs' home had been built near the end of the subdivision, on a hill that provided a bird's-eye view over much of Stillwater. As she approached the front door, she spotted the twinkling lights of the historic lift bridge in downtown Stillwater. From the distance, the bridge and river looked small, like a little snake carved into the ground. Motion lights flashed on as she neared the expansive entrance. Flower gardens surrounded the home, carefully planned out and bordered by decorative rock. Unlike every attempt Nikki made at planting flowers, these were meticulously spaced so that something bloomed all season, giving the yard a pop of color.

She glanced at the blinking security camera mounted over the front door and noted another at the opposite end of the decorative concrete covered porch, trained on the Webbs' four-stall garage. She'd already watched the tapes Luke's father had sent to Miller, noting that Luke's sports car had pulled into the garage around the time Luke had told Nikki they'd arrived home. The garage wasn't connected to the house, which meant the cameras had a clear view of both Luke and Brett walking from the garage. Luke's hands had been in his pockets, his head down, while Brett seemingly consoled him.

Arthur Webb had sent sixteen hours' worth of security film, and they hadn't spotted any red flags. Luke and Brett arrived at the time they said they had, and Luke's car didn't move the rest of the night.

Out of the corner of her eye, Nikki spotted a gray pickup truck parked on the far side of the garage. It looked a lot like Matt Kline's, but she couldn't see the license plate. Why would Matt be here?

She knew Liam would gleefully claim Matt had come to Arthur Webb's home because he needed a good defense attorney.

Nikki lifted the brass knocker with the name 'Webb' engraved across the middle and rapped it against the wooden door. A large-sounding dog barked, followed by a pissed-off-sounding little dog. Nikki wasn't sure which option intimidated her more. Little dogs tended to bark and attack without real provocation, just to prove they could.

The door cracked open, and Nikki braced for the dogs.

"Maybelle, knock it off." Luke stood in the doorway, a strug-gling black and tan dachshund tucked under his arm. "Agent Hunt. Did you find Alexia?"

The hope in his voice sounded genuine. "Not yet, I'm afraid. I had a few follow-up questions for you." Since Luke was eighteen, Nikki didn't need to have his parents' permission to speak with him, but she wasn't going to take a chance with Arthur Webb on standby to defend his son. "Is your dad able to talk too?"

"Yeah, come in." He stepped aside and Nikki cautiously stepped inside. She halted at the sight of a large, panting Mastiff at the end of the hall. "That's just Bob," Luke said. "He'll lick you to death. This one will bite your ankles. Literally." He motioned for her to follow him down the hall. "Dad's in his office. Matt's here too."

Nikki kept her eyes trained on the big dog as she maneuvered around him. Bob huffed and started licking his paws. "I thought I spotted his truck. Is he here on business?"

Luke glanced back at her in confusion. "What kind of business would he be here for at this time of night?" He stopped in front of a partially open door and knocked. "Agent Hunt's here to talk to us."

"This time of night?" Arthur looked up in surprise from his desk. He looked a little older than his photo on the law firm's website, with gray temples and a few more laugh lines at the corner of his eyes. "Agent, I sent the sheriff our security footage."

"I appreciate that," Nikki said. "I'm on my way home and had a few more questions. I'd hoped I would be able to speak to you both at once, along with Luke's mom if she's available." She stepped into the room, finally spotting Matt curled up on the couch, snoring softly. "I certainly didn't expect him to be here."

Arthur looked wary. "I assume he's a suspect by proxy."

"You're his attorney then?"

"I am if he needs it, but I've known Matt for years. His aunt and I dated a few years after the murders." He smiled fondly at the man on the couch. "We found out we were better as friends. I tried to be a father figure for Matt when I could."

Nikki tried to hide her frustration with Luke. "You didn't

mention knowing Matt Kline when I spoke to you, much less being close."

Luke flushed and looked at the floor. "Yeah, Dad said that was dumb." He looked at his father. "You tell her about my mother."

Arthur flinched at the request but nodded. "I'm afraid my ex-wife, Kim, left us when Luke was almost five. She had a prescription drug addiction. I received full custody of Luke, and I think the last time Kim attempted contact, he was maybe ten. Honestly, she could have overdosed. We haven't seen or spoken to her in years." He smiled sadly at his son, who shrugged.

"It is what it is, right?" Bravado lined Luke's voice.

Nikki nodded, wishing she could say something to take the kid's pain away. She tried hard not to judge parents, but to walk away was something she just couldn't fathom.

"I appreciate you not trying to talk to Luke again without me." Arthur smiled, revealing white, straight teeth, but it didn't reach his eyes. "Despite his being a legal adult, I'm sure you understand my position as his parent."

Nikki wasn't intimidated by the poorly disguised warning. "I find that things go much smoother when we're all on the same page."

Luke sat down on the leather couch across from his father's desk. Maybelle leapt out of his arms and sashayed out of the room, stopping to sniff Nikki's feet.

"Agent, have a seat." Arthur slipped his reading glasses off. He reclined in his chair, stretching out his legs. Nikki appreciated his worn-looking slippers and sweatpants. Unlike the neighborhood and his reputation suggested, Arthur didn't appear to be so tightly wound. "I confess, part of the reason I sent our security tapes is because Luke told me about what happened, that Lex was missing. Then he tells me he panicked and didn't know if he should say he knew Matt, so he didn't, but he realized omitting it made him look extra petty."

Nikki glanced at Matt, who appeared sound asleep, before taking the cozy leather chair in front of the desk. "If Matt's part of the family, why didn't he recognize Alexia as your girlfriend?"

"He never met her. Matt's like family, but he doesn't come to a lot of holidays or stuff like that. It's too much for him."

Arthur nodded in agreement. "He doesn't share much about his personal life, either. If he had, I might have figured out Alexia had found him."

"She knew he was close to you guys?" Nikki clarified. That would explain how Alexia had been able to learn Matt's schedule.

"She did," Arthur confirmed. "A source of contention between Luke and Alexia was her wanting to meet Matt, as though he were some kind of celebrity."

"Do you remember when she started asking about him?" Nikki asked.

"She did a research paper on the murders last year," Luke responded. "Until then, I hadn't told her we knew Matt. I thought he might answer her questions since it was for school, but he didn't want to." He looked embarrassed. "I guess the research paper was just an excuse to get what she really wanted."

"Is she good at that?" Nikki asked. "Getting what she wants?"

Luke shrugged. "Sometimes."

Nikki wouldn't cross Luke off the suspect list yet, but she just didn't get the sense he was guilty.

"How can Luke and I help?" Arthur asked.

"I'm sure Luke's told you there were a lot of young people in and out of the Airbnb this weekend. My people have collected dozens of prints, fibers, and hair follicles. As you can imagine, sorting out fingerprints is going to be time consuming because of the sheer amount possible because of the house being rented."

"Are you asking my son to provide fingerprints?"

"We are," Nikki said. "We need to establish every person who came into the house while the victims were in it so we can rule things out."

"My son is not a suspect?"

"At this point, no."

Arthur looked at his son. "What do you think, Luke? You're an adult."

Luke shifted nervously on the couch. "What would I have to do? Like would I get fingerprinted like a criminal?"

Nikki smiled. "You'd just have to stop at the sheriff's office in the morning, and a lab technician would take your prints and swab the inside of your mouth. Takes five minutes at the most. We'll need to get Brett's samples as well."

Luke looked at his father. "I don't have anything to hide, so I should do it, right?"

"As long as you're comfortable with it, yes," Arthur said. "And if you don't, it won't be hard for Agent Hunt to get a warrant demanding testing. I assume you will be contacting every other person who came to the house over the weekend?"

Nikki nodded and retrieved the list Olivia had written out earlier. "Olivia thought this was everyone who came through the house. Can you tell me if anyone is missing?"

She watched both father and son, trying to gauge their reactions. Neither appeared to be nervous.

"I can't think of anyone else." Luke got up and walked the paper over to his father. "Except for you."

Arthur nodded as he skimmed the list. "I was about to mention that. I don't remember seeing Olivia when I stopped by." He looked up at Nikki. "Luke called and asked me to bring more alcohol. I'm not naive enough to think that being the cool dad will make much of a difference, but I figure if I'm providing the booze, then I know it's safe."

"I understand." Nikki looked at Luke, knowing he would be the one to flinch at her question. "But you drove home later in the day. After you were drinking."

His eyes widened. "No way. Brett drove my car. Check the tape."

"He didn't drink?" Nikki asked.

"Can't. Or shouldn't, I guess," Luke answered. "He's a type one diabetic, and he's got an insulin pump. Getting drunk isn't worth messing with all of that."

"Right," Nikki said.

"He's a good sport about it," Arthur told her. "And, selfish as it sounds, I'm glad he's friends with Luke. Makes me feel a lot safer when they're out running around." He grinned at his son. "Least one of them has some common sense."

Luke rolled his eyes. "Whatever, Dad. What about Alexia? Can I do anything to help find her?"

"Sheriff Miller is using every possible resource to search for her," Nikki told him.

"Matt's not a bad guy," Luke insisted. "He's just traumatized as hell."

"They have to look at every angle, son," Arthur reminded him. "Having an open mind is crucial in these cases. That's half the reason the Kline murders are unsolved."

"What do you mean?" Nikki asked.

"Well, the Chisago County sheriff made up his mind it was Amy's ex-boyfriend," Arthur said. "Chisago responded first, even though Washington County had jurisdiction."

"I've heard about the issues." Nikki tried to hide her disgust at the previous medical examiner's findings. "I'm no fan of Hardin, but he did have jurisdiction."

"Both sheriffs made the same mistake, as far as I'm concerned. The one thing they agreed on was that Amy's ex was the primary suspect. I'm sure I don't have to tell you what happens when a cop goes into an investigation with bias."

"The BCA took over," Nikki said.

"Six weeks after the murders, maybe more." Arthur sighed. "By then, both sheriffs had lost precious time."

"You don't think it was Ben?"

"I'm a defense attorney. I never agree with the cops." Arthur smiled. "Ben was a possibility, but surely not the only one. If they'd had enough evidence, they would have arrested him."

Nikki had read up on Arthur Webb before she left the sheriff's station. He was in his forties which meant he would have been in his early twenties when the murders happened. "Were you living around here then?"

"I left for law school in Wisconsin a week or two before the murders," he said. "After my undergrad, I decided to work to save money for grad school, so I took a year in between and worked with a nonprofit. I couldn't believe it when my mom called and told me the news. Still can't."

"Did you know the Klines?"

"Not then, no," Arthur said. "I'd actually attended a lecture Sandy Kline gave on business ethics, which is the only reason I knew the name. I met Peggy well after everything happened."

"Matt's aunt?"

Arthur nodded. "Like I said, we stayed friends. I tried to give her legal advice when I could, although I told her back then most of what she was doing would only end in heartbreak. If the police couldn't find out who murdered her sister and her family, then what made her think she could? She didn't like it when I said that, but it was the truth." His knowing eyes met Nikki's. "The attorney in me has to ask, Agent. Surely these poor girls' murders weren't connected to the Klines?"

"We don't know," Nikki admitted. "My team and I are

going to work up a profile in the morning for both cases and see if we can figure it out."

"That's right, you're a trained profiler." Arthur smiled. "I think that's gotten lost in the media coverage of your career these last few years. You've had some doozies."

"I have." She yawned and stood. "I think that's my brain telling me to go home and sleep. Mr. Webb—"

"Arthur, please."

"Arthur, then. Were you expecting Matt tonight?"

"No," Arthur answered. "He called in a panic about the media finding out where he lives. I told him to stay in our guest-house for a few days." He looked at the couch and chuckled. "I guess tonight it's my office."

"How's he doing?" Nikki asked.

Arthur looked at her with a gleam in his dark eyes. "Shouldn't you be asking if I think he's capable? He told me he doesn't have a real alibi, but he did get gas."

"We're working on confirming that, but yes, he's a suspect." She checked the couch to make sure Matt's eyes were still closed. "I don't like saying that, because I understand what he's going through as far as the media notoriety and lack of privacy, but he had the motive." And so far, the only real motive they'd managed to discover.

"He did." Arthur smiled at her. "And for the record, I've handled his legal matters since Peggy passed, but he didn't ask for my services tonight."

"But you're going to protect him," Nikki surmised. She switched gears. "Luke, you saw Matt last night, right? You said he seemed a bit more calm when he left. Is that the truth?"

Luke nodded in earnest. "Matt flames out quick when he's mad. Once he tells you off, he's done."

"He's learned to compartmentalize emotions, as you can imagine," Arthur added. "I spoke with Matt last night after he stopped at Bone Lake. He was grieving more than anything because he realized who Alexia was and what he'd unknowingly done to Luke."

"What time was this?"

Arthur reached for his cell phone and swiped to unlock it. "Around 10 p.m. He was worried about Luke more than anything."

"So your honest impression is that he'd calmed down?" Nikki clarified.

Arthur nodded. "I'd say that under oath, Agent. Nothing about Matt's tone last night suggested anything but sadness and regret."

EIGHTEEN

Nikki fought back a yawn as Rory filled her large travel cup with fresh, strong coffee. She'd managed to get a few hours of sleep in the early dawn hours, dozing off on the couch with her notes from the day. Thankfully, Rory had been ready with coffee when her alarm blared at 6 a.m.

"The news is already talking about Matt Kline being a suspect." Rory leaned against the counter, dressed for work in paint-splattered jeans and a Minnesota Twins T-shirt that had seen better days. Rory owned his own construction company, and his services were in high demand all year long. Nikki liked to tease him that he'd only gone into construction for the casual attire.

She jammed her notebook into her bag. "What are they saying?" If it had already leaked that Matt had stopped by the house on Saturday night, heads were going to roll. Leaks could derail an investigation and destroy a chance at a conviction later.

"Right now, it's a lot of rehashing the old stuff," Rory answered. "I've seen at least two retired therapists with no knowledge of his case discuss how his trauma could have caused him to snap." He rolled his eyes. "God, I hate the media sometimes."

"That's right, you'd remember the case." Nikki had been in the same grade as Rory's older brother, Mark. Since Rory was a few years younger, he'd graduated high school not long before the murders. "Did you know Amy?"

"Only in passing," Rory said. "I thought about attending the funeral, but it was massive. Pretty much everyone in the area attended, and I didn't need people whispering behind my back about Mark and your parents."

"What about the rumor mill at the time?" Nikki asked. "Do you remember hearing anything about Mrs. Kline having an affair?"

"I didn't pay much attention," Rory said. "Mark had been in prison for eight years or so by then, and I worked every second I could. Kept me from dwelling too much."

Nikki believed he didn't hold a grudge for everything that had happened with Mark, but she still felt a pang of guilt.

Rory crossed the kitchen and wrapped his arms around her. "I don't blame you," he reminded her.

"I know." She craned her neck to look up at him. "What about your parents? Do you think they might remember more?"

"Maybe," Rory said. "Although I'm not sure what they'd know that wouldn't be in the records."

"The rumor mill at the time," Nikki said. "We're going to look at the original case."

He stared down at her in alarm. "You think the same person came back and murdered those girls?"

"I can't say more, but Alexia had a lot of interest in the Kline murders."

"Damn," Rory said. "I'll ask Mom and Dad if they remember anything. By the way, did you get a chance to talk to Lacey yesterday?"

Nikki shook her head. "Every time I thought of it, I was

pulled in another direction. I texted her a few times though. Did you?"

"For a few minutes last night. She's having fun and getting spoiled."

"Thanks for checking on her." Nikki sighed into his broad chest. "I need to jump in the shower. Our new boss starts today."

Henry Garcia might have Mexican heritage, but that was the only thing he had in common with Nikki's former boss. While Hernandez was warm and engaging, Garcia lacked much of a personality. Dressed in a crisp black suit with a bland tie, Garcia's small frame seemed to sink into the oversized chair Hernandez had left behind. Nikki hoped that didn't turn out to be a metaphor for things to come.

His salt-and-pepper hair was closely cropped, and a liberal helping of hair gel allowed them to see his shiny scalp. She had already done her due diligence on her new superior. His reputation as a by-the-book agent made her uneasy. Hernandez's prior experience with the St. Paul police had helped foster good relations between Nikki's unit and the police, but it also meant that he understood the Twin Cities area. He knew how to interact with the locals of all groups, and he'd been an asset in navigating the tense political landscape after George Floyd's murder a few years ago.

Garcia had grown up in Arizona, and he'd worked in field offices throughout the western states until he'd earned his shot to be in charge of an entire bureau. He'd been at Quantico at the same time as Nikki, although in a different unit. Since then, he'd worked in field offices throughout the southwest.

Nikki didn't have an issue with his promotion. She just didn't like being a guinea pig for someone she didn't know well enough to trust. Every new bureau head always brought changes, and given some of the rumblings over the past year about their "maverick" behavior, she had a feeling Garcia meant to rein her people in.

He sat up as tall as he could in the chair. His dark eyes flickered between Nikki and Liam. "Agents Hunt and Wilson, it's nice to finally meet you."

"You as well, sir."

Garcia patted the stack of folders on his desk. "You've had some incredible cases in the last few years." His smile didn't quite reach his eyes. "Impressive solve record. Methods not always so impressive."

Nikki felt Liam tense beside her. She shot him a warning look. They couldn't get off on the wrong foot, and she already had exhaustion working against her. She'd slept a few hours but had gone back to the station to check in with Miller and the deputies, increasingly worried about Alexia. They weren't dealing with the Great North Woods. The area only had so many places for a person to take refuge.

"As I'm sure you know, this is my first shot at heading my own bureau. While our solve record is very important in terms of funding, we also need to understand that playing fast and loose with the rules sometimes isn't good for the Bureau's public image."

Nikki almost snapped back that most of the things the Bureau did weren't good for its image, but she refrained. She forced a smile. "I guess that's why we have a public relations department."

Garcia didn't smile back. "They aren't there to clean up your messes."

"With all due respect, sir"—Liam sounded friendly, even relaxed, but Nikki caught the undercurrent of anger in his voice —"I believe we cleaned up our own messes. Although I think we may have a difference of opinion on what constitutes a mess."

Garcia selected the top file and opened it. "Covering for your girlfriend's son in a kidnapping investigation constitutes a mess in my book."

Liam stiffened. "You're talking about the case last July? More than a year ago?"

"The one where you upset a very prominent citizen by protecting your girlfriend's son, who was a suspect in the kidnapping."

"He was never a suspect," Nikki said. "A person of interest, but we never believed Zach had anything more than information. Agent Wilson may not have handled the situation perfectly, but he acknowledged that and stepped back from the case."

"Until he killed the man who'd taken the victims." Garcia directed his gaze at Liam. "Thereby eliminating any chance we had at learning more about his previous actions, whether he had more victims, his mentality. As a trained profiler, I would have expected more. We might have gleaned a wealth of information had he lived to go to prison."

"I understand your concern, sir. At the time, I made the decision that my partner's life—and her expertise—mattered more than whatever else he might have shared."

"I realize that," Garcia responded. "But had you not failed your partner by keeping her out of the loop regarding the boy, she may not have been in the position in the first place. You would have been there to back her up from the moment she stepped onto the killer's property."

"You're absolutely correct," Liam said. "It was a very hard lesson to learn."

Nikki didn't look at her partner, but she could feel the tension rolling off him. He'd been lectured and penalized for his decisions for more than a year.

Garcia's attention turned to Nikki. "And, Agent Hunt, for

all of your incredible accolades, you too have made poor choices during investigation. The Frost Killer—"

"Killed my best friend, my ex-husband, and kidnapped my daughter." Nikki didn't look away from Garcia's intense gaze. "Your concerns are valid, but I promise you, no one has questioned those decisions more than me. Being emotionally compromised led to Tyler's murder. I live with that every day."

Garcia's eyes softened. "I'm sure you do, and I'm sorry for your loss." He looked between Nikki and Liam. "Part of the reason I was chosen to head this Bureau is because I know how to play politics. I know how to handle departments with an image problem. And while this office doesn't have an image problem per se, we all know the issues in the metro area with race relations and crime. As I'm sure you've experienced in your careers, the average person tends to lump law enforcement into a single entity. If a cop does something heinous, then we're all bad. My goal is to change that."

"By micromanaging?" Liam asked.

"Possibly," Garcia said. "It all depends on the situation. But I can assure you that I will not be as hands-off as Hernandez. It's not my style, and not what I was hired to do. Are we all on the same page?"

"I think so." Nikki didn't like his tone or implications, but they all had a job to do. "Can I assume you'd like to start with a briefing on active cases?"

Garcia smiled, changing his entire sour demeanor. "You most certainly may. I came in over the weekend and spent time going over the open cases to familiarize myself. It seems the last few months have been relatively tame in comparison to the prior year."

They spent the next ten minutes discussing the cases Nikki's team had closed over the year and the two that were active but awaiting trial.

"Good, solid work on all of these," Garcia said. "Now, bring me up to speed on the Lilydale murders and Alexia's disappearance."

Nikki and Liam exchanged glances. They had to sell Garcia on why they needed to work the case, and she had an idea that might work for all of them. She ran through what little they knew at this point, what little evidence they had that it was the same killer, the fresh leads in Mr. and Mrs. Kline's affairs, and what few active leads they had for Vivienne and Libby's murders. "Sheriff Miller is handling the search for Alexia. The medical examiner hopes to get the autopsies finished today. We've been helping track down people who came to the home over the weekend. So far, they've all got alibis, with the exception of Matt Kline. We're working to verify his."

"What's his alibi?" Garcia asked.

"It's not great," Liam said. "He was pissed off so he drove around for hours. He stopped at a Shell station to fill up before he went home, so we're requesting the CCTV footage. He doesn't remember where exactly he drove."

"We still need to speak to Eric Gannon, reinterview Shanna Perry, and go through Alexia's things," Nikki interjected. "If this isn't someone she knew, I think Alexia may have sparked the original killer to act."

"Or Matt Kline snapped after he realized she'd used and betrayed him, and the others were collateral damage," Liam argued. "We didn't see any sign of Alexia at his place, but he's wealthy so we're searching for other property."

Garcia looked at Nikki. "You don't agree?"

She hesitated for a moment. "I don't disagree that's one possibility. I just don't feel like Matt's lying. It's a gut reaction. Which is why we have to do our jobs and verify his alibi," Nikki added before Garcia could make some comment about gut instinct not being good enough for a conviction.

Garcia steepled his hands together. "I watched the documentary. Ms. Newport is excellent at what she does. Agent Wilson, how involved is she with this investigation?"

Liam's face reddened. "Other than being devastated, she isn't." He explained that Caitlin had given them all of her research on the 2001 case, along with any pertinent files and contact information. "She has copies of the original detective's notes. He lives in Florida, but he provided her with copies for the documentary. She brought that all into the sheriff's station yesterday."

"I give you my word that Ms. Newport will stay out of the investigation," Nikki added. "She's not stupid, nor does she want anything else to happen."

"And she was against Alexia being involved with the documentary?" Garcia questioned.

"She believed using the information from Shanna's diaries was unethical, and she wanted to make sure that Alexia's claims could be verified. Producers don't listen very well."

"I don't doubt that," he answered. "Agent Hunt, you and your team know what you're doing. I'm not going to waltz in here and act like you don't, so if you're in agreement about where to go with the case, then keep digging. This case is extremely high profile, obviously, and let's be frank, Agent Hunt's involvement puts the media in a tizzy." He winked at her. "Not an insult, by the way. Just fact. If you're investigating, it's a big case. Every reporter wants the scoop, and everyone's going to hold a magnifying glass to each decision we make. That means no shortcuts, Agents. I realize it's hard when there's a possibility a living victim is still out there, but think of the brutality Vivienne and Libby endured. We can't do anything that could put prosecuting the bastard in jeopardy."

"Matt Kline is close with a defense attorney called Arthur Webb, Luke Webb's father," Nikki admitted. "He dated Matt's aunt years ago and stayed in his life." She told them about finding Matt at the Webbs' home. "He told us he was going to stay with a friend to hide from the media. That's who he meant."

"All the more reason to make sure we don't skip any steps." Garcia reclined in his chair. "And if we can solve a cold case along the way, that's even better for the Bureau."

And for him, Nikki wanted to add. She held her tongue. Garcia had been less arrogant than she'd expected, and he seemed to trust them as investigators. Nikki couldn't see him sticking his neck out for them like Hernandez did, but it also wasn't fair to expect.

"Not as bad as we thought," Liam said after they'd left his office.

"No, but you'd better believe that if this case goes south on us, he'll distance himself before he looks bad."

"Then we don't let it go south."

Garcia had a point about getting away from true profiling, which irritated Nikki even more. Part of the reason she'd left Quantico for Minnesota had been the opportunity to put her profiles into action. While she'd traveled on a few cases and had the chance to go out into the field, much of her time as a profiler with the Behavioral Analysis Unit had been behind a desk, studying victimology and trying to gather enough background on open cases. The FBI's profiling unit was nothing like television, and much of her time at Quantico involved study and research as she'd honed her craft, moving up through the ranks. By the time Hernandez started putting his special crimes unit together, Nikki was ready for a change.

Before returning to Stillwater, she'd assisted on other high-profile cases across the country, but she and Hernandez both agreed that their smaller group needed to take their profiling skills to the field, on the fly, and Nikki had agreed. Their unit served all of Minnesota and surrounding states, and Hernandez wanted the unit to be fluid, taking on major cases within a region, allowing the agents to do a lot more than research and analyze.

Initially, she and Liam started each case by sitting down and coming up with a working profile, but they both learned how to work the profile in active situations, and because the unit had essentially been the two of them in the field, Nikki spent less and less time working up actual profiles. And while her job was to assist on violent criminal cases, she had a duty to the new recruits and the victims of unsolved cases to get back to basics.

Nikki chose the conference room with the most windows to work on the profile because she'd done her time in the dingy underbelly of Quantico. Even when the unit finally moved out of the basement, the bullpen had been confined and almost as poorly lit. Floor-to-ceiling windows on the back wall meant natural light all day.

Liam had arrived before her. "Miller had someone run the file from Washington County to the office. The BCA's digitized everything, so I've printed out their case files."

"What about Chisago County?" The Chisago sheriff had tried to claim jurisdiction, eventually losing to Washington County.

"Spoke with one of their clerks," Liam answered. "She went to records and couldn't find anything related to the Kline murders. No record of Chisago doing anything."

"But they did. We need to speak with the former sheriff, but let's get started with what we have." Kendall and Jim had arrived with yellow legal pads and excitement in their eyes. Nikki had taken both of them on cases over the last year and had been impressed with their skills and quick thinking. Both had gone through the profiling at the FBI Academy and were eager to learn. "The main thing we're looking for today is whether or not the Klines' killer is also responsible for these murders."

"I've read the BCA's file." Liam handed each of them a

stapled printout. "They have some physical evidence they're sending over for Courtney to take a look at. They were able to establish a rough timeline leading up to the murders."

Nikki scanned the pages as Liam continued.

"The Klines were pillars of the community, and Sandy Kline's ancestor built Lilydale and helped settle the Scandia area. She worked as a corporate lawyer before retiring to help run a nonprofit. She was part of the original group that created the Great Northern Innocence Project. Mr. Kline was a cancer researcher who'd just been promoted to vice president of the institute. He'd also just received a large grant, which two of his colleagues had also competed for. The BCA checked them out, and both had alibis for the night."

"What about others Ted Kline worked with?" Kendall asked. "Are any of them still alive, and can we dig out anything more about the affairs?"

Nikki smiled at her enthusiasm. "All good questions. He was very well respected at work, and there's no indication of any other turmoil at his job. Sandy Kline is another story." She glanced at the notes she'd made last night at home. "She had a reputation of doing whatever it took for her to win a case."

"Said who?" Kendall asked. "All of her colleagues? Her boss, or a male attorney who was intimidated by a woman who wouldn't back down? Someone who she had an affair with, who was wounded when she ended their relationship?"

"Colin Swan was her biggest rival," Liam said. "His alibi was flimsy—he and his girlfriend went to dinner and a movie, but he paid cash and didn't have stubs. She backed him up. I checked public records to see if they wound up getting married, and they didn't. So I'd like one of you to track her down and double-check the alibi. Ask if there was anything else going on."

"What about Colin?" Jim asked. "Is he still in the area?"

Liam nodded. "He's actually the only one on the list of people Mrs. Kline had issues with who hasn't moved out of the area." He glanced at Nikki. "I think you and I should try to talk to him today."

"Can you handle it?" she asked. "I'd like to go by the fire department and talk to some of Matt's coworkers, get a feel for how he's been acting. I know you spoke to the fire chief yesterday, but what about the head paramedic?" Like so many firefighters in large cities, Matt Kline also worked as a paramedic through the department. "They're going to know more about the day-to-day stuff."

"She wasn't there," Liam said. "You hit the firehouse and I'll look for Colin."

"What else do we know about the original investigation?" Jim asked.

"Not a lot," Nikki said. "At the time, the sheriff fixated on Amy's ex-boyfriend, based on the medical examiner's report stating Amy had been raped. He based this on some bruises on her thigh, but we have doubts about his findings. Dr. Blanchard is going over them today."

Liam turned on the smartboard, and crime-scene photos from 2001 populated it. "Mr. Kline had been stabbed twice in the chest before his throat was cut. His body was near the bottom of the stairs, which is consistent with Matt's memory of hearing his father get up, go downstairs, and confront another male."

"Quick." Jim thrust his right hand in a stabbing motion twice. "Incapacitates him, and then the cut to the throat did him in."

"Slitting a throat isn't as easy as writers would have you believe," Kendall reminded them. "Even with a sharp knife, it takes strength and commitment. No hesitation marks?"

"No," Nikki said. She pointed to the photo of Sandy, her body stiff with rigor, curled into the fetal position. Her throat had been slit as well, but the hesitation marks were evident. "There are some on Mrs. Kline's body."

"Was there any sign of sexual assault or indication he spent more time with her?" Jim asked.

"According to the file, no. Her underwear was tested for semen, along with Amy's, whose underwear was found near the dock along with her shirt. The original investigators believed she tried to escape, he caught her, raped her, and put her into the water. She was found nude."

The photo of a pale, waterlogged teenaged girl next to the dock bothered Nikki. The water impacted decomposition, speeding up the process, and Amy was already out of rigor when she'd been spotted the next morning. Police had brought her body to shore and laid it out on the grassy bank to photograph.

"I thought she had bruises on her legs," Kendall said.

"Showed up the next day, which isn't unusual," Liam said.

"Do we have photos of the evidence?" Nikki asked. "Clothing, personal items, everything found with the body?"

Liam nodded and typed something into his laptop. More photos populated the smartboard. "All of these were taken by the Chisago people, along with most of the evidence. Fortunately, they did give all of that to the BCA when they took over the case."

Ted Kline's pajama top had been soaked with his blood, just like his wife's nightgown. According to the report, Sandy had been wearing pink, cotton panties, and no biological material had been taken from them. Amy's black, silky panties had also been photographed front and back.

Nikki stepped back from the smartboard to look at the photos. She studied Sandy Kline, nude on the autopsy photos. Average height, she'd maintained a curvy figure in middle age, but Amy was still young, and at least thirty pounds lighter than her mother. "What size do you think Sandy Kline was?" She directed her question at Kendall.

"Her dress size?"

"Her underwear size."

Kendall considered the question as she looked at the photos. Her eyes lit up. "Not small enough to wear those black panties."

A look of horror crossed Liam's face. "You're telling me the evidence was mixed up and no one caught it? Not even the BCA?"

"I think they mislabeled Amy's underwear as her mother's." Nikki said. "We need to look at that evidence. And Courtney needs to test everything."

NINETEEN

Shanna Perry lived in southwest Stillwater, in the exclusive area known as Liberty on the Lake. The homes were beautiful, but the idea of living in a homeowner's association soured the prospect for Nikki, even if they could afford it. The associations certainly had their benefits, but she'd rather have control over her space, instead of being confined to suburbia.

She spotted the deputy's cruiser in front of Shanna's two-story gray home and pulled in behind him. He appeared surprised to see her. "Did they find Alexia?"

Nikki shook her head. "Not yet. Have you seen Shanna this morning?"

"No," the deputy answered. "My shift started at 3 a.m., and the house has been quiet. Deputy on before me said he'd gone into the house with her, doing a full sweep. No one has been in or out since then."

Nikki followed the curved sidewalk, admiring the blooms surrounding the home. She rang the doorbell, relieved not to hear any barking dogs.

Shanna answered looking much less glamorous than yester-day, wearing leggings and an oversized sweater. Smudged mascara lined her red eyes. She stared at Nikki in fear. "Please tell me this isn't bad news."

"It's not," Nikki answered quickly. "I just wanted to check in with you and clarify a few things."

Shanna looked wary but motioned Nikki inside. Nikki slipped off her tennis shoes, careful not to leave footprints on the gleaming maple floors. The open floor plan provided sweeping views of the lake.

"I'm about to drive to Volvo headquarters and strangle someone." She pulled her hair into a ponytail as Nikki followed her down the hall into a large, spotless kitchen. "The vehicle is in my name, but Google Assistant is still fighting me since Alexia set it up. They want proof of identity and a warrant and I'm just ready to scream." She slumped onto a bar stool. "They don't care that my daughter is missing!"

"Call Sheriff Miller after I leave," Nikki instructed her. "He'll be able to get a warrant quickly. He's also got drones in the air looking for Alexia and the car." She looked around. "Are you here alone?"

Shanna nodded. "My family's out east. My piece of shit ex-husband can't leave California right now because his new, young wife is scheduled to have a C-section tomorrow." Shanna didn't bother to hide her bitterness.

"You shouldn't be here alone," Nikki said. "Ask Miller to have the victims' advocate stop by. She can help you navigate things."

Shanna locked eyes with Nikki. "Do you think my daughter is dead?"

Nikki wanted to lie and be positive, but that wouldn't help Shanna. "I'm not giving up hope. But you haven't been completely honest with me, Shanna. I've seen evidence that suggests you knew Mrs. Kline was having an affair. Is this true?"

Shanna bristled. "I didn't know anything for certain, but I heard things, yes."

"And did Amy know?"

"She had suspicions. And I was glad. She thought her mother was perfect, but she wasn't, and when I realized she was seeing the truth, I was glad. Look this was all a long time ago – how is any of this helping you find my daughter?"

"Did you know who this was with?" Nikki knew that if Mrs. Kline was having an affair, this person was a suspect.

"No." Shanna said. She glared at Nikki impatiently. "Can we focus on my daughter?"

Nikki knew she needed to prioritise Alexia. She wanted to get the truth out of Shanna, but perhaps she didn't know any more. She looked at the woman carefully and decided to believe her. "That's actually one of the reasons I stopped by. Would you mind if I looked in her room?"

"The deputy did that last night. He didn't find anything."

"I know," Nikki answered. "This is more about getting an idea of who Alexia is in order to hopefully figure out who did this and why."

"Her room's upstairs, the last one on the left." Shanna rummaged around her walk-in pantry. "I'll make some fresh coffee while you look. God knows I need it."

"It won't take long." Nikki headed to the stairs near the front entrance. A handful of family photos lined the stairwell, all happy memories of Alexia and Shanna. Would they be able to add new photos?

Nikki ignored the lump in her throat. Alexia could still be alive.

Her bedroom door was open, the curtains pulled over the east-facing windows. The double bed wasn't made, a few well-loved stuffed animals left to wait for Alexia's return.

Nikki checked the nightstand and underneath the bed, looking for anything that might give her a sense of Alexia's last few days. She found old shoes and wrappers under the bed, along with a sock. The nightstand contained lotion, cell phone chargers, a portable battery, tissues—nothing out of the ordinary. The desk beneath the window was tidy, with a few new notebooks and school supplies waiting to be used.

Nikki spied a plastic storage bin sitting in the corner near the desk with dozens of paperback books. She crouched to inspect the titles. They were all about true crime, many written by Ann Rule, whose career as a writer had been launched by her personal connection to Ted Bundy. More familiar names appeared; Alexia had both of Bob Keppel's books, the King County detective who'd led the Bundy investigation and spent far too many hours with the man; a first-edition copy of *Mindhunter*, signed by John Douglas.

As Nikki scanned the notes Alexia had written in various books, some of them observations and others questions she'd like answered, more sadness washed through Nikki. Alexia had a natural ability as a profiler, a keen eye and an understanding of behavior that most kids her age didn't have.

As she put the books back into the bin, she saw one on the floor beneath the desk she hadn't noticed earlier. *Terror on Bone Lake: The Kline Family Murders* had been written by a local reporter who'd since passed. Nikki had no idea how well the book did, but Alexia had likely used it for her research paper that she'd done on the murders last year. She flipped through; the highlights and comments appeared to be typical research notes.

A bright green sticky note caught her eye. She immediately recognized Matt Kline's address. It was impossible to know when she'd written the note, but it confirmed something more important: Alexia's digging into the case could have triggered the attacks.

Liam's voice rang through her head. He would see this as more evidence against Matt, but even if he did want to punish Alexia, he had no reason to slaughter the other girls.

But who did?

. . .

Nikki had been back in Stillwater for a few years now, but she still wasn't used to the fire department's new digs.

Stillwater had begun as a lumber town in the 1870s, so a fire station became crucial as the town grew. The firehouse built in 1887—now the post office—had served as the main station when Nikki was a child. During Lumberjack Days, a festival the town held each summer, Nikki's parents had always used the fire station as the meeting point if they'd been separated. A blond-haired, blue-eyed young fireman had been Nikki's first love. She'd been around Lacey's age when she'd seen him handing out flyers for a demonstration. Nikki had told her mother that was the man she was going to marry someday. She smiled at the memory of her mother giggling and telling Nikki to keep her options open, the world was full of good men to choose from.

The fire department had moved out of downtown on a large complex across from the Minnesota National Guard's Red Bull Unit. Nikki found a spot near Stillwater Fire Department's administration building. The campus was impressive: a burn town, smoke currently creeping out of the top, with several fire-fighters in training prepared to make entry. A pint-sized female wearing a captain's uniform barked orders at the men, who rushed to follow commands.

EMS Chief Janie Reece greeted Nikki at the administration desk. "Agent Hunt, Chief Reece."

Nikki shook her extended hand, impressed at the grip. Reece wasn't much taller than Nikki, but she looked like a triathlete. Nikki felt frumpy in her lightweight pants and FBI polo shirt. "Thanks for meeting with me."

Instead of taking her to her office, Chief Reece led Nikki to a private break room for officers and staff. Two men in crisp blue shirts emblazoned with the SFD logo and black utility pants stood to greet her.

Nikki recognized Fire Chief Stuart. The second man introduced himself as Assistant Chief Becker.

Assistant Chief Becker wasted no time. "Agent, I already discussed this matter with your superior yesterday."

"My superior?" Nikki echoed. "I wasn't aware Agent Garcia had contacted you." She knew exactly what the gray-haired, sullen-faced man was trying to do. "You spoke with someone from my team, Agent Wilson. Given the severity of the events, I'd think you'd be happy to speak with us to help clear suspects."

Chief Stuart shot Becker a look. "I'm sorry if we seem defensive, Agent. We all really like Matt."

"I understand, but since he's also a paramedic, how much time have you two actually spent around him?"

"All three of us take part in the hiring process," Chief Reece said. "Chief Stuart has final say on the firefighters, and I've got EMS. Our department isn't that large in comparison to the bigger cities, so it's hard not to know everyone fairly well."

Nikki could buy that. "Before we get to the last few days, tell me why you hired Matt given his prior addiction. I understand he's beaten it, but I think you'd agree it's a bit unusual to have a fighter also working as a paramedic with that kind of history."

"I'll take this one," Chief Reece said. "Before moving to EMS, I worked as an ER trauma nurse, and I've also done shifts in the ICU and psych ward. Point is, I've dealt with trauma victims for twenty-plus years. I have a unique perspective that other EMS chiefs may not. When Matt applied for the job, he was very blunt about his past drug addiction and the causes. He wanted to follow in his father's footsteps, and those were huge shoes to fill. Dr. Kline graduated from Johns Hopkins, you know. Anyway, as you can imagine, Matt just couldn't handle the pressure. Not because he wasn't capable of the workload, but because all of that trauma still simmers under the surface. But he was passionate about wanting to help people, and he had a unique perspective on emergencies, so I decided to do a trial run, pending drug tests. Chief Stuart and Assistant Chief Becker supported the decision."

"And Matt did well?"

Reece smiled. "Extremely. He's a quiet guy, kind of intense. Very private. But in an emergency situation, he's another person. His bedside manner with both victims and families is some of the best I've encountered. That's why we hired him full-time."

"Matt wanted to continue the routine drug tests past the ninety-day probationary period. All of our personnel are subject to random testing, but Matt really wanted his coworkers to understand that he was sober. He continued them for the first eighteen months working here, and that was something like six years ago now."

"What about disciplinary issues?" Nikki asked. "We know he got into it with a coworker last week. Assistant Chief Becker told Agent Wilson it was a misunderstanding, but that Matt was given five days' leave as punishment. He was vague on the details of what happened, however."

The assistant fire chief bristled. "Because I like Matt, and I'm not going to have him backed into a corner so the police can get an easy close." He looked at his colleagues. "We know Matt isn't capable of doing something like this, right?"

The other two nodded.

"For the record"—Nikki directed her irritation at Becker— "I'm not the police. I'm the FBI, and I don't look for easy routes to solve cases. I look for the truth." Police and fire had a long-standing friendly rivalry that usually resulted in various athletic battles throughout the year, but most of them got along well. Nikki had done her research, and Becker had become a firefighter after failing out of the police academy more than twenty years ago. She guessed he carried the grudge around like a weight on his back. "And with all due respect," Nikki continued, "Merrill was a firefighter with the department for several years, well-liked and trusted by everyone, until he kidnapped those two sisters more than a year ago at Lumberjack Days. He turned out to be a serial kidnapper and murderer."

"He was a volunteer," Becker snapped. "We didn't know him all that well."

"My point is, most of the time, the people close to the bad guy say the same thing." She held up her hand before Becker could start in again. "That being said, Matt Kline is a common-sense suspect. That doesn't mean that I think he did it, but we have to do our jobs. Vivienne Beckett and Libby Brown deserve that much. So does Alexia Perry."

A palpable shift went through the room at the mention of her name.

"Have you ever seen her around here?" Nikki took out the photograph they'd taken from Alexia's driver's license photo, along with a photo of her standing next to her new Volvo and handed them to EMS Chief Reece. "Or this car?"

Becker looked away, while Chiefs Stuart and Becker exchanged tense glances. Nikki waited.

"This girl is the reason Matt was suspended."

TWENTY

Nikki cursed the city for moving the fire station out of downtown. With road construction going on in the majority of the city, it was nearly impossible to go anywhere without a delay. For the first time in her life, Nikki looked forward to winter, when the roads would no longer be lined with orange cones.

She'd called ahead to the sheriff's station, letting them know she'd been delayed. Her interview with Eric was supposed to start ten minutes ago, and she hated making people wait. She whipped into the county government center parking lot and parked in the first available spot. Nikki checked to make sure she had her phone and notebook in her bag, before locking the jeep and speed walking toward the sheriff's office.

By the time she'd rushed inside, sweat beaded across her forehead. She spied Olivia sitting with Eric on one of the benches that lined the wall. "I'm so sorry for making you wait."

Olivia looked like she hadn't slept since Nikki last saw her. She'd spoken to Olivia briefly last night, confirming that she didn't know Alexia's iPhone password. Hopefully the techs would gain access to it today anyway.

"How are you doing?" Nikki asked the young woman.

"I think I'm in still in shock." Olivia's voice quivered. "Please tell me you know who did this to my friends. And that you've found Alexia?"

"I'm sorry, we don't have any new information," Nikki answered. "But we've got the whole day ahead of us."

Eric wrapped a protective arm around Olivia. "She's exhausted." He stuck out his other hand to shake Nikki's. "I'm Eric. I don't mean to be rude, Agent Hunt, but I have to be at work in forty minutes, and my boss is a jerk about being late."

"Of course." Nikki glanced over at the administration desk. "Sydney, would you mind keeping Olivia company while Eric and I chat?"

"Of course," Sydney said.

"I can't come with him?" Olivia asked.

"It's better if we do a formal interview, so that it's done," Nikki said. "We shouldn't be long."

She led Eric down to the big interview room.

"Have a seat."

Nikki sat down across from him, unlocked her phone, and opened the voice memo. "You're okay if I record?"

"Sure," Eric said. "Not sure how much help I'll be, though."

"That's okay," Nikki said. "Have you known Olivia a long time?"

Eric shrugged. "Not really. I mean, I knew of her because we go to school together, but she's a popular kid. We didn't really hang out until last summer. We both had jobs as camp counselors."

"I see," Nikki said. "Did you grow up in Stillwater as well?"

"Yep. But I don't know most of the people Olivia hangs out with. At least not very well."

Nikki took the opening he'd given her. "We know you came to the Airbnb on Saturday and Alexia wasn't pleased. Can you tell me about that?"

He pushed his dark hair off his forehead and sighed. "I'm not in the cool crowd. Never have been." He shrugged. "I had to work anyway, but Olivia asked me to stop by, so I did."

"How long did you stay?" Nikki already knew the answer, but she needed to make sure Eric was telling the truth.

"Not long, maybe fifteen, twenty minutes. Alexia was giving me the stink eye the whole time." He tried to laugh but looked sheepish instead. "She's not always nice, but she doesn't deserve to be murdered. Neither did the other girls."

Nikki found it strange that he assumed she was dead. "How well did you know them?"

"Not well, like I said. But Libby was in one of my classes last year. She seemed okay." He looked down at his fidgeting hands. "I still can't believe it. How could they have made someone so mad? They haven't lived long enough to do anything all that awful, you know?"

"I understand."

"Aren't you going to ask me about my grandpa? I figured that's part of the reason you wanted to talk to me. Or did you talk to him already?"

"I'm sorry, I don't know your grandfather," Nikki said.

He looked surprised. "Oh, I just assumed you would have been in contact by now, with everything that's happened. Rich Langley's my grandpa. The Chisago sheriff who worked the Kline case."

Well, that was an interesting piece of information, Nikki thought. How much did Eric know about the original case? "My team in Minneapolis has tried to reach him, but the home number we have is out of service."

Eric rolled his eyes, retrieving his phone from his pocket. "He ignores the landline because he's certain it's all telemarketers. Won't give it up because he might need it in an emergency, though. Here's his cell. Don't call after eight our time, 'cause he'll be in bed and crabby."

Nikki jotted the number down. "I assume you grew up hearing about the case then?"

Eric shrugged. "Not a lot, at least not from Grandpa. It was more from everybody else. Most people blamed him for the case not being solved since he was first on the scene. He'd retired by the time I was born, but these things have a habit of following you for years."

"Did Alexia know he was your grandfather?" Nikki asked.

Eric nodded. "Yeah, she wanted his number when she did the research paper on the murders. I shouldn't have given it to her, but she doesn't take no for an answer." He shrugged. "Sorry, but it's true."

"I know you turned eighteen a week ago, but I assume you live with your parents?"

"My mom. Grandpa helped raise me until he moved to Satan's armpit."

"Did you notice anything at Lilydale when you stopped to see Olivia?"

He considered her question. "Other than the usual people drinking and partying, no. I didn't think it was very cool that Alexia rented Lilydale to watch the documentary, and I told her that. She didn't care."

"Were you there when Arthur Webb brought more alcohol?"

Eric's eyebrows raised. "Yeah, but I didn't drink any. I had to work."

"I assume you don't know Luke well, either?"

He shook his head. "Olivia says he's a nice guy. Just besotted with Alexia. That's the word she used. Personally, I thought it was bullshit that his dad brought alcohol and then Luke possibly drove home. Olivia says Art's cool and just wants them to be safe. That's cool and all, but like, you see the double standard, right?"

"I do," Nikki said. "It's an unfortunate part of life. Just to back up a second, you became friends with Olivia last summer working at the same place as camp counselors. What kind of camp?"

"Summer camp. I probably wouldn't have gotten the guts to talk to her since she's in the popular crowd, but she's not like the others. She came right up and said we'd had algebra together and she was excited to see a friendly face." Eric flushed. "I couldn't believe it."

Nikki was starting to wonder why a girl as sweet as Olivia had become friends with someone like Alexia at all, but they'd grown up together. Nikki certainly had her share of bad relationships in high school, and she could remember hanging on to more than one toxic friendship.

She asked him a few more questions about the other people who'd come to Lilydale at some point over the weekend, but Eric couldn't think of anyone Olivia hadn't already mentioned.

After walking them out, Nikki called the number Eric had given her for his grandfather. It went to voicemail, but at least there was an invite to leave a message. Nikki explained who she was and the reason for calling, making sure to mention she'd been given his personal number by his grandson. Her next call was to Sheriff Miller.

"How's the search going?"

"Getting the K9s ready to go," he said. "Drones didn't pick up anything yesterday, so we've got them back in the air, searching a wider perimeter. Our priority is the Volvo, but we're also looking for vultures circling."

The big vultures were sorry-looking creatures, but they also acted as a guidepost toward biological remains. Anyone who'd grown up in the country knew that vultures circling meant they'd found something dead. If they found Alexia before the searchers did, her remains would probably be scavenged. Nikki pushed the thought out of her head. Alexia could still be alive.

"Did you get my message earlier about Amy Kline and her mother's underwear being mislabeled?"

"Yeah." His disgust oozed through the speaker. "I got hired mid-2002, out of the police academy. Back then, we only had two full-time criminologists to collect evidence, so I'm not surprised mistakes were made, but this is a big one, even if no biological evidence was taken from either pair. What the hell else did they miss?"

"That's why I'm calling," Nikki said. "I'd like to get into the evidence room and see what's actually in the Klines' personal effects."

"I'll let Sydney know," Miller said. "She can unlock the room for you. Liam tell you about the Shell station footage?"

Nikki's stomach flipped the way it did when the roller-coaster first began its ascent up the steep track. "I haven't seen him. What about it?"

"I'll let him tell you," Miller said. "I've got to get back to the search, and I still need to call Sydney for you."

"Keep us posted."

Nikki decided to find Liam before having Sydney take her to the evidence room. She found him in the large space they'd commandeered as an office. "Miller said the gas station footage came in."

Liam looked up from his laptop. "Yeah. Blanchard just emailed the autopsy results too. Cause of death for both girls was blunt force trauma, but get this: they were both stabbed between the third and fourth ribs, puncturing their lungs. Vivienne on the right, Libby on the left."

Nikki sat down next to him. "That sounds like an experienced hunter or maybe someone who's worked in a slaughterhouse." She couldn't imagine the fear the girls had suffered in those few miserable moments, and she was certain the killer saw them as obstacles to his true prey. He surely had worse in mind for Alexia, and their time to find her alive was running low. "He must have snuck up behind Vivienne first, and then attacked Libby from the front. He incapacitates them before he beats them senseless. The beatings were so personal, so violent. Who would do this to two teenaged girls?"

"Well, Matt Kline's not looking too good." Liam switched windows on his laptop. "This video was taken at 3:47 a.m., at the Shell station where Matt said he'd stopped."

Nikki reminded herself to breathe as she watched Matt Kline's gray Chevy pickup pull into the gas bay. He got out of the driver's side, adjusting the ballcap he wore, and started pumping gas. She gasped as he walked around the back of the pickup and knelt to inspect something. "What the hell's on his shirt?" The footage wasn't great, but the dark splotches all over Matt's shirt and jeans looked wet and sticky, and she could see similar patterns on his boots. "Maybe it's not blood."

"Maybe not, but this is the only CCTV video we have. Can't find him on anything else." Liam tapped the screen. "And if this isn't blood, then what is it? He said all he did was drive around."

"I don't know." Nikki didn't want to think Matt Kline capable of kidnapping Alexia, much less beating Vivienne and Libby to death. "But Matt told us he hadn't seen Alexia in a couple of weeks, because she ghosted him. But that's not true." She told him what Matt's superiors had told her.

"So that's lie number two," Liam said. "Because she didn't ghost him. Our guys finally got her phone unlocked. Kid's smart, because all of her notes about the case are in iCloud, in an encrypted file."

"She didn't want her mother to know what she's doing." Shanna didn't seem like the type to care enough to snoop in her daughter's phone, but Nikki knew better than to make snap judgments based on a single interview. "She didn't ghost Matt?"

"Maybe at first, but she tried calling him four times over the past week. He didn't answer. She called the firehouse Friday morning, I assume to find out if he was working."

"And she showed up and they argued." Nikki didn't like where this was leading.

"He's staying with Arthur Webb?"

"As far as I know."

"That's no good," Liam said. "I don't want to interview him on his defense attorney's turf, and bringing him here will cause a massive shitstorm. I don't want to do that without Miller giving the okay."

"Let's have him come to my house," Nikki said. "Rory's working late on a project, and it's a lot more private than anywhere else."

"You think he'll do that?" Liam asked. "Even if he's innocent in all this, he doesn't seem like the sort to accept a dinner invitation."

Nikki ignored the sarcasm in his voice. "That's why I'm going to look at the Kline evidence before we speak to him."

TWENTY-ONE

CHRISTMAS 2001

Matt sat down in front of his aunt's living room television and opened the new Nintendo GameCube his aunt had gotten him for Christmas. She'd been so excited for him to open it this morning, and part of him was excited to start playing new games. But the other part kept thinking about playing video games with Amy. Ever since he could remember, Amy had played Mario Brothers, and as soon as he was old enough, she started teaching Matt how to use the controllers. They'd spent hours playing and talking trash to each other. He missed his mom and dad for sure, but he missed his big sister even more.

He wiped the tears off his cheeks. Matt didn't want Aunt Peggy to see him crying after she'd worked so hard to make this first Christmas a good one. He read the directions on the Game-Cube box, but he was pretty sure he could figure out how to hook the system up. Aunt Peggy kept asking him if he was going to play, so he figured he'd better at least try.

Matt shifted to his knees so he could reach the power button on the television and then went back to the directions. The ESPN announcers said something about Allen Iverson after the commercial break, but Matt didn't really pay attention until he heard the familiar Nike jingle about being like Mike.

Matt stared at the commercial he'd probably heard a thousand times, his heart beating against his chest. Should he tell his aunt about the shoes?

"Sixers vs. the Lakers." Arthur, his aunt's boyfriend, sat down on the couch behind Matt. He didn't know Artie that well, but his aunt really liked him, and he'd been cool to Matt instead of treating him with pity like most adults did now.

Matt shifted to look at Artie. "You're a lawyer, right?"

"That's right."

"Are you like the kind of lawyer my mom was?"

"I'm not sure. What did she practice?"

"Corporate." Matt didn't really understand what the word meant, but he knew that before his mom had retired to work for the nonprofit she helped start, she'd practiced that sort of law.

"Ooh, that's way too much politics for me. I'm a defense attorney. Do you know what that is?"

Matt nodded. "You help get criminals off the hook."

Artie laughed. "Well, I suppose. My firm doesn't take on anyone they don't believe is truly innocent. And the cornerstone of our entire system is innocent until proven guilty." He sipped the beer he'd brought from the kitchen. "Why? You thinking of a career change, bud?"

Matt didn't smile back. "I think I need legal advice."

"How so?"

"I didn't tell the police everything I saw that night."

The grin vanished from Arthur's face. "Well, I didn't expect to hear that. I'm going to call your aunt in here if that's okay. I don't feel right talking to you about this without her here." Artie called out Peggy's name, and she hurried in from the kitchen, her cheeks flushed.

"The apple pie is cooling." She looked at Arthur and Matt. "Why so serious?"

"I'll let Matt tell you," Arthur said. "He wants my legal advice, and I thought you should be here. It's about the murders."

Peggy stilled and then sat down next to Artie. "What is it, sweetheart? Did you remember something?"

Matt shook his head, shame building inside of him. "I didn't tell police because I thought the killer might be able to find me if I did." He couldn't keep the fear out of his voice.

"The killer won't find you," Peggy said. "That's not going to happen, is it, Artie?"

"Nope. And the police won't tell the media if that's what you're thinking, kiddo. I know it was really nuts for a while with reporters, but they don't hold power over the police." Artie smiled encouragingly. "What did you see?"

Matt took a deep breath, and the confession burst out of him. "I saw him kneeling by Amy. From the side."

"You told the police that already, sweetheart," Peggy said. "You tried to sit with a sketch artist and you just couldn't remember well enough. Did you get a good look at his face?"

"His shoes. He had on the red and black Air Jordans. The Retros."

Peggy looked at Arthur. "Does that make sense to you?"

"Jordan's got so many shoes out now, but I do remember hearing about this release because they're the ones the NBA banned him from wearing in '86. Don't ask me why, but he did it anyway and Nike paid the fines." He winked at Matt. "You get away with stuff like that when you're the GOAT, right?"

"I guess so."

"How can you be sure?" Peggy asked. "You didn't see his face so—"

"The lights on the path to the dock," Matt answered. "I saw the shoes and felt jealous for a split second because I'd been trying to get my mom to buy me a pair." His eyes filled with tears. "I'm so selfish."

"No, you're not," Peggy said firmly. "You're a child. You're not supposed to go through horrific things like this. Right, Artie?"

Arthur nodded. "I don't know a lot about trauma, but my gut tells me that if you saw this monster with your sister, your brain focused on the shoes to keep you from seeing anything else."

"But maybe if I'd told the police then, they could have found the guy. Right?" Matt asked him.

"If only it were that easy, buddy. You know how many people bought those shoes? We could go to the Cities right now and probably see ten people wearing a pair."

"You don't think he should tell the police then?" Peggy asked.

"Oh no, I think you should, just in case. It's a good piece of information to have once they've got a viable suspect."

"Why?" Matt asked.

"Well, I highly doubt it would hold up in court, but the shoes could be a way for the detectives to eliminate people. Bottom line is, they need to know, just in case."

Matt hated how his lips trembled like a baby's. "Will I be in trouble? For not telling sooner?"

"Absolutely not. We'll call them tomorrow," Peggy said. "After all, it's Christmas and after four months, another day won't make a difference. Do you want Artie to help you set up the Nintendo?"

Matt didn't want to, but he liked Artie and he wanted his aunt to be happy. "Sure."

TWENTY-TWO

"Unfortunately, the evidence room's in the basement," Sydney said to Nikki as they stepped into the elevator. "The building's not ancient, so it's not too awful, but hopefully you're not allergic to dust. All the physical evidence of open cases is kept in cardboard boxes."

"I'm good," Nikki said. "Have you found out what you're having yet?" The building may not be ancient, but the elevator lumbered slowly.

"A girl." Sydney beamed. "My mom and I are so excited." Her smile disappeared. "She thinks I should quit the sheriff's office unless I can stay behind a desk and work regular hours."

Nikki heard the guilt in the young woman's voice. "What do you want to do?"

The elevator bumped to a stop, the doors slowly creaking open. "That's the thing—my parents say it doesn't matter what I want, I have to think of my daughter now."

Nikki managed to keep from rolling her eyes. "What does your partner say?" She'd never seen a ring on Sydney's finger. Not all cops wore their rings, especially if they had any real

monetary value, and Sydney might not even be with the baby's
father for all Nikki knew.

"He says my parents are old-fashioned." Sydney sneezed as
they walked up and down the aisles. Like every other evidence
room Nikki had been inside, there were far too many unsolved
cases, with too many families out there waiting for answers
they'd likely never receive unless Miller had a true cold case
unit.

"I don't have to work," Sydney said. "Nick makes enough
money, but with the baby coming, things could get tight. But
daycare costs so freaking much, I might just be working to pay
for that."

"No matter what you decide, there will be times when you
question the decision," Nikki said. "Your partner works regular
hours?"

Sydney nodded.

"Well, I won't lie to you, when I was pregnant with Lacey, I
went through this, and frankly, I still do. My late ex-husband
was able to be really flexible, so she always had a parent around.
Those first few months after she was born were awful. I loved
my job, but I wanted to be with my baby too. And part of me
felt like it was selfish to love working." She stopped walking and
faced Sydney. "I'm telling you right now, that's a load of bull.
Women shouldn't have to choose their jobs or kids, even in law
enforcement. It doesn't make us less of a parent because we
want to work and make a difference in the world—and make it
safer for our kids. But the key is a support system. I had Tyler,
and then when he died, Rory and his family really stepped up. I
think spending time with his mom and dad helped her process,
and Ruth is a nurturer. I knew if Lacey had a terrible day, Ruth
would make it better. They have a connection." The lump in
her throat caught her off guard. "My point is, your parents mean
well, but you have to do what is best for you. Some women
aren't made to be stay-at-home moms. That doesn't mean you

don't love your child just as much. It's okay to still have goals and dreams even after becoming a mom."

Sydney smiled, her eyes misty. "Thank you. That means so much coming from you." She crouched down in front of the dusty metal shelves. "Two boxes. Amy Kline has her own. Hopefully you can find something to test for DNA." She started to heft one of the boxes, but Nikki stopped her.

"Why don't you grab that dolly over there?" She pointed to the standing cart in the corner. "We can stack the boxes and take them up in the elevator."

A few dusty minutes later, Nikki wheeled the boxes into their makeshift office.

Liam glanced up from the notes he'd been reviewing. "Two boxes? Maybe we'll find something useful."

"Let's hope so. Sydney had to go back to the desk. She said Miller told her to lock the boxes in his office when we're done. He wants to have a look too." She retrieved a couple sets of latex gloves from her bag and tossed a pair to Liam. "My hands are sweaty, damnit." Nikki rubbed the moisture off on her jeans, cursing as she wriggled her fingers into the gloves before removing the lid off the box containing evidence taken from Mr. and Mrs. Kline. She skimmed the log lying on top of everything else. "Mr. Kline's pajamas, slippers. Mrs. Kline's nightgown and black silky underwear, which the sheriff's office correctly labeled as Amy Kline's." Nikki set the bag aside. She wanted Courtney to retest both sets of panties. "Here are the swabs taken from Mrs. Kline—we'll have her test those again, too." Given the former medical examiner's errors and former Sheriff Hardin's habit of cutting corners, they needed to retest anything that might contain biological material.

Liam opened Amy's box. "Nightshirt she had on, a pair of pink panties, muddy socks. Photos of her body, the dock. She was in the water, so not a lot of evidence taken from her body. No semen sample, nothing from under her fingernails. I guess that makes sense given the year and the water, but they could have taken them to test just in case."

"Too much money and work for Hardin without enough payoff." Nikki's heart hammered in her chest as she looked at the bagged evidence. She held it up for Liam to see. "I guess that's why these scrapings taken from Sandy Kline's nails were never tested." She held up the evidence log. "They're not even listed."

"Hardin was that incompetent?"

"Look what he did to Mark, all over his own bias and circumstantial evidence. He was certain the boyfriend did it." She wished Hardin were still alive so she could tell him what a lazy, incompetent fool he'd been. "He wouldn't see the point of wasting resources to have this tested."

"Fingernail scrapings this old are iffy at best," Liam reminded her. "If they're not collected within a few hours of the crime, the sample deteriorates. I don't know how long it would last in evidence if it were bagged right."

"Courtney will know." Nikki swore. She'd read the Kline file more than once, and there hadn't been a single mention of the hair. "I think the strands of hair wrapped around Sandy Kline's right fingers might be the first thing she should test."

TWENTY-THREE

Nikki parked the jeep in front of the Webbs' large house. She didn't see Luke's car, so Arthur must have found a way to get his son out of the house. Luke had certainly been humiliated enough, and even if he forgave Matt since Alexia had lied about her identity, the dynamic between them couldn't be great with her still missing.

Arthur opened the door before they could knock, ushering them inside. Nikki was about to ask what the hurry was when Maybelle the dachshund skidded around the corner, barking like mad. Arthur rolled his eyes. "Sorry. That's what I was trying to avoid." He gathered the dog in his arms. "I'd kennel her, but that makes the barking worse. Matt's in my office."

Matt sat on the corner sofa, a baseball cap pulled low over his head. "Matt, you've met my partner, Agent Wilson. Arthur, Agent Wilson."

Arthur nodded and asked them to have a seat in the cozy chairs across from Matt. Arthur sat down at his desk. "You don't mind if I record this, do you?"

"Not at all," Nikki said. "I take it you're acting as his attorney, then?"

"If he needs one." Arthur looked solemn. "The tone of your voice when you called earlier definitely has us curious."

Liam eyed Matt. "Is he actually going to talk, or are you answering for him?"

Matt sat up straighter, glaring at Liam. "Ask a decent question and I might."

Arthur sighed. "Matt, they're doing their jobs. Agents, why don't you tell us why you needed to speak with Matt again?"

"Couple of reasons." Nikki tried to keep the accusation out of her tone. "I spoke with your superiors. I know Alexia came by on Friday."

Arthur stared at Matt. "The firehouse? You didn't say anything about that."

"Guess I forgot." He shrugged.

"What did you discuss?" Nikki asked.

"Nothing, because I didn't want to talk. She kept saying she just wanted to explain, that I'd understand if I'd hear her out. I told her I didn't care and walked back inside. I'm sure there's video of it."

"I've seen it." Nikki had watched the security video at the firehouse before she'd left. Matt's version matched what she'd seen on the tape. "Did you know about her involvement in the documentary by then?"

"No," he said. "But I knew she was Luke's girlfriend. He's the one who told me about her staying at the Airbnb for the weekend. He assumed I knew who she was, but I didn't. When he showed me a photo of her, I almost lost it." Matt dragged his hands over his face. "I think he must have suspected, because he looked really sad and said yeah, 'She'll do anything to get what she wants.' Luke said that she'd been nagging him for months to let her talk to me, and then right around the time I met her, she stopped. I'm sure you can put two and two together."

"Luke and Alexia are complicated and that's putting it mildly," Arthur said. "This isn't the first time she's cheated, I'm afraid. Doing it to get to Matt is a whole other level of manipulation, though."

"You had to be mad as hell," Liam said.

"I told you that already," Matt answered. "That's why I went to the house in the first place."

"Right, and then you drove around for a few hours. Stopped to fill up at Shell." He unlocked his tablet and handed it to Arthur. "Just hit play."

Matt looked disinterested as Arthur watched the footage from the gas station. "Son, you're going to have to answer their questions. I know you didn't do anything, but look at this."

Matt snatched the tablet from him and played the video. His dark eyebrows knitted together, the muscle in his jaw twitching. The anger turned to snickering. "That's mud, Agents."

Nikki had wondered as much, but the video quality wasn't great and the shirt appeared wet. "How'd you get that much mud on you?"

"It rained half the day Saturday. I was out driving back roads. Got stuck in the mud, made a mess getting myself out."

"Then why's your truck clean?" Liam asked.

"Because I drove it through the car wash next door before I filled up." Matt looked at Nikki. "It's on the west side of the building, so this camera doesn't pick it up."

"We'll need to test the clothes you were wearing," Liam said.

Matt shook his head. "Threw the shirt away. Washed the jeans."

"Why would you just throw the shirt away?" Liam demanded. "That's awfully convenient."

Matt leaned forward, his gaze on Liam. "Because it was a $10 white T-shirt from Target."

"What about your shoes?" Arthur asked. "I assume you had mud on them?"

"Yeah, cleaned them off with the hose before I went in the house when I got back."

"We'll need them," Liam said. "To test for blood. We can't just take your word for it."

"Wouldn't expect you to," Matt retorted. "They're in my truck."

Liam didn't react to the sarcasm in Matt's voice. "For an innocent guy, you've got a hell of a lot of attitude."

Anger burned in Matt's eyes. "You know why? Because I've been interviewed twice already, you guys aren't looking for any other suspect. You're doing the same thing Hardin did to Ben."

"Your sister's boyfriend?" Nikki clarified. She wished they could tell Matt about the biological evidence they'd just sent to Courtney for testing, but even if she could, she also didn't want to give him false hope.

"Ben wouldn't hurt anyone, and I told Hardin Ben wasn't the guy I saw with my sister. He never owned a pair of Jordans."

"Wait, back up," Nikki said. "There isn't anything in any of the files about a pair of Jordans."

Matt's face turned red. "I told you, Artie. I told you and Aunt Peggy they didn't take me seriously. You're telling me they didn't even keep a record of it?"

"Obviously not, because we don't know what you're talking about," Liam said. "Why don't' you explain?"

Matt closed his eyes. "I told the cops that the man I saw with Amy had on the red and black Retro Air Jordan 1s. They first came out in the eighties, and the NBA banned him from wearing them. I remembered seeing them that night because I'd been begging my parents for a pair."

"You told investigators this?" Nikki asked. "When?"

"Not right away," he admitted. "Those first few days, all I could see was blood."

Nikki struggled against the swell of emotion in his voice. "I know."

Matt looked at her, the pain behind the mask of anger visible in his eyes. "Is that what you went through when you found your parents murdered?"

More than thirty years later, it was still hard for Nikki to grasp that people she'd never even met knew as much about her parents' case as she did. "Yes. And my parents' bodies. My mother—" She took a deep breath. "My point is, I get not saying something right away. I was sixteen and the shock was just unimaginable. At your age, it had to be worse."

"He told Peggy and me that Christmas Day," Arthur said. "Peggy debated even telling the police because the shoes were so popular, but I encouraged both of them to do so. You know how those kinds of things can help break a case if they're used right."

"You're certain you told Hardin?"

Matt nodded. "Plain as day. I told Aunt Peggy and Art that day nothing would come of it. Now you're telling me Hardin didn't even put a note in the file." His entire body tensed, and Nikki half-expected him to start throwing the first thing he could reach. "And I'm not supposed to be pissed that I'm the only one being hounded about what happened this time?"

"How do you think Alexia found you?" Nikki asked. "If Luke wouldn't share your information with her?" She wanted to see if talking more about Alexia would elicit an emotional response from Matt. How truthful had he been about their relationship? Did he want to see her suffer? "Everything about you is unlisted, although I suppose she might have paid for the information."

"Luke admitted he might have said something to her." Arthur shook his head. "Matt's always been a family friend, but he's older than my son, so they didn't know each other that well, and I certainly didn't want him to bug Matt about his past. When Alexia started showing interest in the case, Luke told her." He rolled his eyes. "I think he felt it looked good, made him seem important to Alexia. He wanted to impress her. She tried to talk to me about it, and I shut her down. But once she knew, I guess that was it."

"And Luke had no idea she was meeting with him?"

"I don't think so," Arthur said. "Luke wears his emotions on his sleeves. That's how I knew he'd gotten into it with Alexia because he came home upset and carrying on about it with Brett. His pride was understandably hurt. Point is, if he knew before, he wouldn't have been able to keep his mouth shut. My son tends to be impulsive, like I used to be: shoot first, ask questions later."

Nikki was satisfied with their information. She looked at Matt. "Now that you've had some time to think about it, can you remember anything Alexia might have said that could help us find her or find who did this?"

Matt's face reddened. "We didn't talk that much, and when we did, it seemed like she got me to do most of it. I played right into her hands. I mean, she had a whole story about a friend of hers in California who had been strangled by a guy who wouldn't take no for an answer, that she blamed herself because she hadn't helped the friend when she asked for it."

Nikki looked at Arthur, who shook his head. "I've never heard any story like that. If it's true, she never told Luke."

Alexia had picked up some of her mother's manipulation skills. Who else had she lied to and upset?

"Can you try to remember what you told her?" Nikki asked. "We might be able to retrace her steps and figure out if she crossed the wrong person's path."

Arthur looked confused. "You really think her investigation has something to do with these attacks?"

"I think it's more likely than the killer just showing up at Lilydale at random on the anniversary," she said. "Bottom line is, Alexia made a major enemy of someone. Matt, can you tell us what you shared with Alexia? All of the details matter."

"She asked if I remembered that night or if I'd blocked it out. I told her how I woke up because Dad was yelling. Then I heard a man's voice." Matt looked at the table as he spoke, on autopilot. Nikki wondered how many times he'd had to tell the story during the investigation. When her parents had been murdered, she'd lost count of the number of times she had repeated what she saw that night. She'd learned to control the memories over the years, but it had taken a lot of therapy. "I went to Amy's room. I didn't knock because I didn't want anyone downstairs to know I heard them." A tear rolled down his cheek and dripped onto the table. "She was so engrossed in writing in her journal she didn't even realize I'd come into the room at first. I told her what I heard, and she thought I was being silly until she heard the arguing. She told me to go down the dumbwaiter and go for help. I was terrified, but she made me. If I'd been faster..."

"Son," Arthur said, "we've been over this so many times. You were a child. None of this is your fault."

"Peggy was your mother's sister, right?" Liam asked.

Matt nodded.

"She and her sister were relatively close. Did she have any theory on what happened? Did she know about anyone in her sister's life who might have had reason to hurt her and her family?"

"If she did, she never told me," Matt answered. "We didn't really talk about that stuff. She wanted me to forget it. She might have said something to Art, though."

"I'm trying to remember," he said. "She didn't like Ben, the ex-boyfriend. I know she didn't believe his alibi. But, other than that, she struggled to find a motive as much as the police. As far as she knew, there were no financial issues, no big secrets."

"Obviously that's not true," Matt snapped. "They obviously pissed somebody off, but the idea that my mom was having an affair is preposterous. My dad, yeah, but not Mom. Caitlin Newport made most of that up."

"Caitlin's an investigative reporter," Liam said. "She did have a solid source about the affair but didn't think they had enough information to put it in the documentary. Her producer disagreed. She was stuck between a rock and a hard place." He glanced at Nikki, confusion in his eyes. Nikki knew Matt didn't know Caitlin was really his old friend Mary.

"I don't care," Matt said. "I'm sure you've interviewed her. What other angles did she investigate?"

Matt had refused to speak to Caitlin regarding the documentary, and she hadn't wanted to use their past connection to influence him. She could tell by the look on Liam's face he'd realized the same thing.

"She's being cooperative." Liam barely managed to hide the edge in his voice. "We need those shoes out of your truck to test for blood. And we need Matt to start from the night he met Alexia and go over it all again. Don't edit it—things that seem innocuous to you may not be to us." He unlocked his phone and opened the video recorder. Nikki had worked with him long enough to know he intended to catch Matt changing his story.

For the next forty minutes, Matt described the night he'd met Alexia, what he remembered about the bar and her demeanor, to the handful of trysts and conversations they'd had over their short time together.

By the end, Nikki was more confident than ever that Matt Kline wasn't involved. Liam followed Matt out to his truck to retrieve the boots he'd worn the night of the murders for testing. Nikki hung back with Arthur.

"How's he doing?"

"Okay, I think. But he's great at hiding his emotions and not asking for help."

"I think that's part of the male DNA," Nikki said.

Arthur grinned. "Truer words were never spoken, Agent. If

you need Matt, he's staying with us until it all dies down. But I'd like to be present any time you question him."

"Understood, although, for what it's worth, I don't expect to find blood on Matt's boots. Fortunately, our criminologists at the lab are fantastic. I'll have them rush the testing."

"We appreciate that, Agent, but don't let Matt's bluster sway you from doing your jobs the normal way," Arthur said. "I'm confident he didn't do it, but he can't see your point of view rationally."

"I get it," Nikki replied. "I always try to balance how much I talk about my parents in interviews like this, because it's easy to make it all about me, but in this case, Matt and I have so much in common. I understand what it's like to think you've made peace with it and then some little thing reminds you of them and sucks you right back into the miserable abyss. I'm glad he's able to stay with you through all of this." She started to walk to the jeep, but her own emotions were riled up. Nikki turned back to Arthur. "Let Matt know that whatever happens with this case, my team is going to continue trying to find out who killed his family."

"Thank you, Agent," Arthur said. "He will be thrilled to hear that, I know."

"I'm not sure we really gleaned anything new from that interview." Liam took the big evidence bag she handed him and slipped the boots inside. "Except for these."

"Sure we did." Nikki craned her neck to look up at him. "We've seen all the evidence logs. There's no mention of Amy Kline's journal. I don't remember seeing it in evidence photos taken of the house." She glanced toward the front door, where Matt and Arthur stood talking.

"Jesus, you're right," Liam said. "Maybe it was just missed?"

"Possibly," Nikki said. "But one of the first things I learned as an investigator in the days before everyone had a cell phone is that a teenaged girl's personal belongings can be a goldmine of evidence. If they were focused on Amy and her boyfriend, how could they miss something like that?"

The journal was likely long gone, but Nikki still had hope. She wondered if Blanchard would find something helpful when she reviewed the Klines' autopsies, but none of that brought them any closer to finding Alexia.

TWENTY-FOUR

Nikki hurried down the hall to Garcia's office. She'd dozed off at her desk going over her notes for the tenth time. She'd missed Lacey's call again this morning, but instead of being upset, her daughter had just left a message, giggling that Nikki was it.

She knocked on Garcia's open door before taking the seat next to Liam. "Sorry."

Garcia waved her off. "How's the Bone Lake case going? Have you ruled anyone out yet?"

"Colin, Sandy Kline's rival at the firm," Liam said. "His alibi for the night was ironclad, and he died in a car accident four years ago."

"Kendall and Jim have now spoken to everyone who came to the house that day and confirmed their alibis," Nikki added. "So far, our only person of interest is Matt Kline, and that's a stretch, in my opinion. Agent Wilson disagrees."

Garcia looked at Liam. "Explain."

"First off, he didn't tell us everything." Liam went over what Nikki had learned at the firehouse before showing Garcia the security footage from the Shell station. "He said it's mud.

Tossed the shirt and washed the pants. Had the shoes in the truck, so we're testing them. But he said he'd cleaned them."

Garcia studied the still images Liam showed him of Matt in the shirt. "It's really too bad this footage is lousy quality. It's impossible to tell."

"Actually, I don't think it is," Nikki said. "Not if we think about how Vivienne and Libby died. They were so badly beaten in the face we couldn't identify them right away. If Matt killed those girls, in this shirt and jeans, we'd see blood spatter all over it. Instead it's wet."

"What about these?" Garcia pointed to the oblong marks on Matt's left shoulder and sleeve.

"Those look like globs of something rather than spatter."

"Fair enough," Garcia said. "While we're waiting on the results on the shoes, you've got some circumstantial evidence against Matt."

"Sir, I think we have more than some," Liam said. "At least enough to get a search warrant for his vehicle and house."

"We looked through his house," Nikki reminded him.

"Yeah, for Alexia," he shot back. "If he'd told us about the supposed mud, we could have probably found the clothes and tested them. But he didn't. That bugs me."

Nikki rolled her eyes. "He was half asleep. And innocent people don't think of things like that."

"I don't care," Liam said. "He is the only person we've uncovered that has any real motive."

"What about Alexia's phone?" Garcia asked. "Surely they're into it by now."

Nikki explained that Alexia had kept her notes about the Klines in an encrypted file in her cloud account. "It's going to be a while before we're into it."

"She didn't have notebooks or anything in her room?"

"Shanna and a deputy went through Alexia's room and

found nothing regarding the Klines or her involvement in the documentary. I believe her, but I also wanted to go through the room myself." She told him about the sticky note in the book about the Kline murders. "Matt's current address was written on it."

"Miller called me this morning. After they got the warrant, Volvo informed Shanna Perry that the navigation features have been turned off, so they don't have access to them," Liam said. "They need the actual car and can download the data, but that doesn't help us right now."

"Anything new in the Kline murders?" Garcia asked.

Nikki told him about the new information on Shanna, the mislabeled panties and the discovery of hair and fingernail scrapings taken from Mrs. Kline. "Never tested. Not even logged."

"That could be a problem in court," Garcia said. "Chain of custody, that sort of thing. Have you spoken to any of the original investigators?"

"I've left a message for Detective Langley. I plan to ask him about the hair, as well as Amy Kline's journal. Matt said she was writing in it when he came into her room that night, and she left it there. Now, if the original investigators thought her boyfriend did it, you'd think they would have collected that diary. Langley was first on the scene, because police already knew they were going into a homicide since Matt had gone for help. I want to ask him if he remembers seeing it."

"Any investigator worth their salt would have collected it," Garcia said. "Even with the jurisdictional bickering that went on, it's hard to believe someone wouldn't have seen that journal and bagged it."

"There's someone else we haven't talked about, and that's Shanna Perry." She handed him a copy of the printed diary page that Alexia had sent to Caitlin. "Amy knew something about her mom that caused a big fight. She wrote in her diary that night, and it disappears after the attack. I think she might have known who her mother was having an affair with, and that's who killed them. He took the diary because Amy wrote his name down."

Liam nodded. "I agree with all of that. Shanna isn't telling us everything about what happened in 2001, but I don't think she'd do something to her own daughter, or to her friends."

"Agreed," Nikki said. "Her grief is genuine. She's also been cooperative about her financials and dealing with Volvo. And I don't think she knows who Mrs. Kline's affair was with."

"I think we need to look at Matt Kline more closely," Liam insisted. "Right now, he makes the most sense."

Nikki turned to her partner. "You might be right. I really hope not. That's why we need to make sure we follow everything up, everything is tested."

Garcia looked between the two of them. "What about Luke Webb? Sounds like this kid really got screwed in all of this."

"His alibi checks out," Nikki said. "His father provided us with security footage that shows him getting home when he said he did and not leaving. He and his friend were both visibly stunned when I told them about Alexia."

"So you see why it's down to Matt or the original killer," Liam said.

"You really think Matt Kline did this, Agent Wilson?"

"I think it's certainly possible and we have enough for a warrant."

"Let's see what the tests from the shoes reveal," Garcia said. "If he's innocent, it's going to look like we didn't do our jobs. Public sympathy will be enormous, as it should be." He shook his head. "No, we need solid evidence for a warrant. I can't back that, I'm sorry. We need to speak with Langley, we need the test results and, frankly, we need more motive. I'd be more inclined that Matt did this if only Alexia was missing. Why in the world would he beat those girls to death?"

"I don't have an answer, sir," Liam said.

"Let's see if you can find it," Garcia replied. "If it's not mud on the shoes, then we'll talk warrant."

TWENTY-FIVE

Nikki hadn't been inside a rent-to-own store since she first lived in Virginia years ago. Hinson's Rental and Leasing resembled any other furniture rental store, with appliances, living room and dining room, and kitchen sections. Price tags dangled from every item, and Nikki almost gasped out loud at the thirty percent interest rate. She knew stores like Hinson's were vital to lower-income families, but the interest rate was higher than the worst credit cards she'd seen.

A tall, twenty-something young woman with a ponytail greeted Nikki with a smile. "Have you been to Hinson's before?"

Nikki shook her head and showed her badge. "I'm here to speak with Mr. Hinson. He's expecting me." Normally, Nikki didn't like to call ahead and alert a possible suspect or person with information in a case in order to ensure a more honest reaction, but they needed to find Alexia and with three stores throughout Washington and neighboring counties, Hinson was a hard guy to pin down.

"I'll take you to his office."

Nikki followed the young woman down a short hall, past gender-neutral bathrooms and a storage closet.

She pointed to the open door at the end of the hall. "He's expecting you."

Nikki thanked her and approached Ben Hinson's office. He sat at his desk reading some sort of document, his brow furrowed in concentration. He wore the same blue polo as his employee, and his sparse office made him seem relatively approachable. Nikki cleared her throat and gently knocked on the door. "Ben Hinson? Special Agent Hunt with the FBI."

Ben's head shot up. "Yes, I've been expecting you. Is Alexia all right?"

Nikki didn't bother to hide her surprise. Referring to Alexia by her first name interested her a lot more. "I take it you've seen the news."

Ben stood, nodding. "Excuse my manners. Please, sit."

His fair skin had likely been protected from the sun, as he looked younger than mid-forties. They were about the same age, but Ben's ginger hair had more gray than red in it. Nikki had been lucky in that department, with a few scattered grays in her dark waves. Father Time would eventually catch up to her.

"To answer your question, no, we haven't found Alexia yet." Nikki sat down and took her notebook and pencil out of her canvas bag.

Ben dragged his hands down his face. "Jesus, poor Shanna. I should reach out, but we haven't spoken in years, and I'm sure I'm the last person she wants to speak to right now."

Nikki struggled to hide her surprise. Shanna Perry had made no mention of knowing Ben Hinson or any connection her daughter might have had with him. "You knew Shanna when you were younger?"

"She's the one who introduced me to Amy." He studied her for a moment. "You didn't know that, did you?"

"Is my poker face that bad?"

Ben smiled. "No, Agent. I suppose you won't have made the connection. She was my alibi for the night Amy died, but she used her mother's maiden name when she spoke to police."

Nikki was shocked she hadn't caught this. But she hadn't had enough time to comb through the files, and it didn't surprise her that the original team didn't get Shanna's real name. She could add it to the long list of things they'd done wrong.

Ben leaned back in his chair. "Shanna and I were foster siblings for a few years." Nikki nodded. Nikki had known Ben's history in the foster system, but she hadn't heard anything about Shanna's. Ben continued. "I'm afraid my speaking with Alexia might have put her in danger."

"When did you speak with Alexia?" Nikki didn't bother to hide her reaction this time.

"Few months ago," he said. "She came in with photos of Shanna's diary and said she had some questions about her mom's involvement with the Kline family. I should have told her no, but she piqued my interest. I hadn't spoken with Shanna in more than twenty years, and I wanted to know how she was doing. She meant a lot to me. She was the one who introduced me to Amy." His green eyes were filling with emotion. "Amy was the best thing to ever happen to me. I'd do anything to find out who killed her."

"You told the police the two of you broke up because she wouldn't have sex with you," Nikki said. "Her friends confirmed that."

Ben smiled and opened his desk drawer. He took out a black and white photo of himself and a handsome, dark-haired man wearing tuxes and showing their gold bands to the camera. "This is my husband. We've been married six years now."

"Congratulations," Nikki replied. The picture was getting clearer. "Did Amy know you were gay?"

"No one did, not even Shanna, until Amy and I broke up," he said. "Back in the early 2000s, coming out of the closet was harder than it is today, especially when you didn't have a support system. Amy was the first girl I'd dated in a while, and I think she figured it out fairly quickly. Not long before we split, she decided she was ready to lose her virginity. I should have been thrilled, but I panicked. Eventually I broke down and told her how confused I was, and she didn't get upset. She told me she'd suspected and that she'd support me." He met Nikki's gaze. "We never fought about anything. The only thing her parents didn't like was my being four years older, but once they met me, they weren't threatened. I wasn't ready for anyone to find out the truth, and she wanted to move on since she was about to start her junior year of high school. At the time, I still wasn't sure of how I really felt, and I was terrified someone would figure it out if they asked me why we broke up. Amy came up with my breaking up with her because she wouldn't have sex idea. Stupidly, we both thought it made me seem more masculine." He rolled his eyes. "We waited until my summer job with her mom's nonprofit ended."

"You worked for Sandy Kline?" Nikki asked.

Ben nodded. "Basically grunt work, helping offices get set up, stuff like that. Her mom was great to me. The only photo I have of Amy was taken my last day, with a bunch of the other interns."

"She helped her mom that summer?" Nikki asked, thinking about the alleged strain between the two.

"Here and there, but they were kind of like oil and water, you know?"

Nikki nodded. "Did Alexia know about the photo?"

"Sure," Ben said. "Shanna was in it, too, because she'd stopped by to say hi. She sucked up to Mrs. Kline a lot, you know."

"I thought Shanna interned in accounting at the cancer institute," Nikki said. "How did she manage to get close to Sandy?"

"That's Shanna," Ben answered. "She made it a point to meet her when Mrs. Kline came to his office. I don't know if the affair had started then, but I have no doubt that Shanna was sizing up her competition. Anyway, I have a copy of it in my Dropbox. And on my hard drive. Like I said, it's the only photo of Amy that I have." He picked up his phone, searching for the photo. "I can send you a copy if you want," Ben said as he handed Nikki his phone.

Frustration rolled through her as she spotted a young Shanna between Amy and Sandy Kline, a big grin on her face. "What was Alexia's reaction to the photo?"

"She was upset at first," he answered. "She kept asking if the photo had actually been taken that same summer. I think a part of her thought her mom might have had something to do with what happened, but there's no way. Shanna was a lot of things back then, but most of them revolved around bettering her own life. She might screw someone over, but she wouldn't have physically hurt anyone."

"Do you think Alexia believed you?"

"She said she did, but the kid's a hard read." A smile crept over Ben's face. "I could tell she's got a lot of her mom in her. Shanna and I weren't actually together the night Amy died." He worried the inside of his cheek. "I'd asked Shanna to lie for me because I'd gone to a gay bar in Minneapolis, and I didn't want anyone finding out. I wasn't ready." He looked at the wall, trying to control his emotion. "It sounds so pathetic now. Who cares if I wasn't ready? Amy and her family were murdered!"

"I can't imagine being in the position you were, so there's no judgment from me," Nikki replied. "Did Alexia say anything about the documentary?"

"No," he said. "And I haven't watched it yet. A friend told me the filmmaker seemed to be on my side, though. Why were Alexia and her friends staying in that house, of all places?"

"She contacted the documentary makers. That's all I can really say."

"Do you think her interest in Amy and her family is what caused the attack?" Ben paled. "If I hadn't spoken to her and confirmed her mother's diary, she might have dropped the whole thing."

"We don't know yet," Nikki said. She believed Ben; he was sincere and sad, and nothing about his demeanor made her think he was lying. "We're following up several angles. Is there anything else you haven't told the police about Amy? If you trusted her enough to come out to her, then surely she confided some things in you."

"She did," he said. "Her parents were having issues. Her father's affair with Shanna was over by the time Amy and I started dating, but the damage was done."

"Did Amy know Shanna was the woman her father cheated with?"

"No," Ben said firmly. "I didn't even know until after the murders. Shanna finally told me a few days after it happened. She was just as devastated as me. The Klines were nice people. They deserve justice."

Nikki thought about the two lines in the photo Alexia had shared with Caitlin. "Do you know when Shanna last spoke to Amy?"

"Not until Alexia showed me the shots she'd taken from Shanna's diary. Until then, I thought Shanna had spoken with her several days before the murder." Ben looked weary.

"This may seem out of left field, but do you know if Amy kept a journal?"

"I don't know," he admitted. "I know her little brother gave her one for Christmas. Britney Spears was on the cover. Amy and I were both Beastie Boys fans, and she'd kept her Britney obsession secret from me." Ben smiled, his eyes misting over. "When I found out, I said I love Britney too." He tried to stop the tears from escaping his eyes. "Find Alexia, and then find out who killed Amy and her parents. Please. They deserve to rest."

Nikki left Ben with her card and cell number in case he remembered anything else. She tossed her bag into the jeep just as her phone started ringing. Nikki frantically dug for the device. "Agent Hunt."

"We found Alexia." Miller's flat tone told Nikki all she needed to know. "I'll text you directions."

TWENTY-SIX

Pain thundered through Alexia's head. How long had she been stuck in this derelict place? Not that she could see through the duct tape over her eyes. But she didn't need to see to know that wherever he'd taken her reeked of decayed wood.

She still couldn't figure out how he'd gotten into the house. Had she left a window open? Her battered mind tried to sift through the memories of the last few days. They'd all been having so much fun at Lilydale, and the documentary was supposed to be the big reveal. She'd planned on telling all her friends about her plans for her new true crime podcast, knowing they'd take her more seriously since she'd been on television. Clearly, she had a connection to the Klines, and it was a lot more than her mother's long-ago affair with Ted Kline.

Alexia's mother had barely told her anything about the affair. She'd found most of the illicit information in her mother's old journals, locked away with her college books and other keepsakes. Shanna had been a fresh-faced intern in accounting at the cancer institute when she'd met Ted Kline, but she'd immediately been hooked by his dark hair and green eyes, along with his wallet. His recent promotion to vice president of research had meant money and prestige, at least in Shanna Perry's eyes.

It quickly became clear from the diary that Shanna had kept track of every single encounter with Mr. Kline as she'd lured him into her web. Somehow, she'd managed to persuade the brilliant researcher that cheating on his wife was a good idea. From the entries, it appeared the affair had gone on for months. Shanna had even gone to a company event hosted by the Klines, befriending a naive Amy, who saw the recent college graduate as some sort of cool girl. Through the teenager, Alexia's conniving mother had learned about the family dynamics, which enabled her to continue to manipulate Mr. Kline. He eventually grew tired of Shanna's demands and paid off her college loans in exchange for silence.

Alexia's stomach had turned when she'd read what her mother had set out to do. Months before the murders, she'd been the one to drive the stake between the Klines, and she'd used poor Amy. That's why she'd set her up with Ben Hinson, the twenty-year-old community college student with an attitude and a motorcycle. Her mother had been intertwined in the Klines' lives right up until the day of the murder. Shanna's excited scrawl from the day of the murders was imprinted in Alexia's brain.

> *I'm laughing so hard right now! I just spent two hours on the phone with poor little Amy. I still don't understand how she hasn't figured out that I'm the one her dad had an affair with. I'm the reason her mother has gone from a domineering perfectionist to all-out bitch. Kline told me how miserable his wife could be, and how she'd seek revenge if she found out the truth. As far as I know, Mrs. K caught him after we broke up because of hotel charges on his American Express, but that's secondhand info from Amy.*
>
> *Point is, Amy told me she'd caught her mother in the act*

today! Guess she surprised her at the office. I tried to get her to
tell me who it was, but she didn't know. She went on forever
about how her mother was ruining their family and a bunch of
other crap that I barely listened to. No wonder Ben dumped
her when she refused to put out. All she does is whine about
her perfect life.

I hope the real world smacks her in the face one day so
she'll see how easy she's had it. But in the meantime, I'm going
to sit back and watch their world burn.

Alexia still felt dirty thinking about her mother's callous
words. That had also been her last entry in the diary. Her
mother couldn't have had anything to do with the murders,
she'd told herself. What would the motive be? She'd already
blackmailed Kline. Shanna was coldhearted, but she'd also been
three hours away that night. Could she have done this?

She'd tried to talk to her mother about it without letting her
know she'd read her diary, but Shanna remained tight-lipped.
The most she'd talked about the Klines was the day Caitlin
Newport had asked about Alexia's participation in the documentary.

She'd laughed when Alexia had suggested Ben could have
masterminded something, albeit with help.

"He couldn't bait a damn fishing hook. Let alone slaughter
those people." Her face had taken on a more serious expression.
"Look, I'm not making excuses. I was a terrible person with a lot
of issues. But I've worked hard to get through them, and there's
nothing I could provide the investigation. You understand me?"

Alexia had said she did. She knew the documentary makers
would never agree to her participating without Shanna, unless
Alexia could bring more to the table.

So she'd set her sights on Matt Kline.

Tears built in her eyes. All she'd wanted was to uncover the
truth. Why had he done this to her and her friends?

She stilled, the sound of metal scraping against metal sending her heart into overdrive. A door opened and then closed. Alexia scooted into the corner and tried to make herself as small as possible.

His boots clunked on the splintery floor. She caught the scent of soap and braced for his attack. He hadn't raped her yet, but why keep her alive if that wasn't the plan?

He kicked her foot. "Get up."

She managed to speak despite her dried-out mouth. "Why?"

"Gotta stretch your legs. Don't want to cramp." A rough hand closed around her wrist, yanking her to her feet.

"I need shoes."

"Nah." He leaned in close, hot breath in her ear. "You won't get far."

TWENTY-SEVEN

MAY 2009

The screams of Luke and his little friend sent chills down Matt's spine. Why did four-year-olds screech like banshees?

He stretched his legs out on the new deck Arthur and Kim had built around the above-ground pool and watched Aunt Peggy play with Luke and the other kid.

Aunt Peggy laughed as the little girl splashed her. Matt still thought it was weird that his aunt hung out with Artie and his wife sometimes, but Peggy was lonely and probably still in love with Arthur. She'd never said as much, but Matt knew his aunt well enough she couldn't hide it.

"How's it feel to be a high school graduate?" Kim sat down next to him. Arthur's wife was soft-spoken and gentle, much like his aunt. He guessed Artie had a type. Everybody did.

"Weird," Matt answered. "But I'm glad it's over." Eight years after the murders, the case remained unsolved and Matt still felt kids' eyes on him at school when he walked the halls. Teachers still looked at him with pity. "College is going to be better, right?" He hoped to follow in his dad's footsteps all the way to Johns Hopkins. Matt knew he had a big task ahead of him, but he was smart and determined and didn't have a family, so he had plenty of time to study.

"Sure is," Kim said. "Long as you don't go wild, you know?"

"That's over, Kim." A couple of years ago, when Matt had finally got his driver's license, the freedom had gone to his head. He'd be out all hours of the night, just driving and thinking about everything. It was better than tossing and turning when he couldn't sleep because Amy's scream wouldn't stopped playing in his dreams. "I'm a man now. And I promised Aunt Peggy."

Kim patted his knee. "I know. I think you're going to be great. And it's going to be so good for you to be in another place, where no one knows your name or story. You'll be safe."

A chill went through him at the seriousness of her tone. "I'm not safe now?"

"Of course you are," she backtracked, flushing. "I meant emotionally safe. Fresh new start for you."

Matt shrugged. "Until someone finds out who I am."

"You don't have to tell anyone, Matt." Kim shifted to face him. "Listen to me, your parents left you enough money you can write your own ticket. You can change your name and move to California or New York or wherever you want to go, and start over."

"I wish," he said. "I couldn't go that far from Aunt Peggy. She doesn't have anyone else."

"She has us, and her job," Kim reminded him. "Your aunt doesn't want you to make decisions based on her, anyway."

Matt had never heard her talk this much at once before, at least not directly to him. As kind as Kim was, she always seemed intimidated by everyone else. Being liked was very important to her, so she didn't cause many waves. "You really think so?"

"I know so," she said. "If you want, I can help you."

"That's okay," he replied. "If I need help, I have Art."

"Of course." She bit her lip. "It's just that Artie's more emotionally connected to you. I love you, too, of course, but it's different with you guys, you know what I mean?"

"I guess."

"Artie will try to talk you out of starting a new life," Kim said. "He's not able to see what's best for you like I can."

Her serious tone was starting to freak him out. "What's best for me?"

"Escape. Sooner rather than later."

TWENTY-EIGHT

Nikki parked at the trailhead entrance to Tanglewood Nature Preserve, a pretty chunk of land south of Stillwater. Tanglewood was an important conservation area as part of a large continuous corridor of natural areas, full of big oak and maple trees, creating a canopy of shade. Most leaves remained green, but in a few weeks, the fall colors would be glorious.

A few feet ahead, near a mass of fallen evergreens, Blanchard and Miller stood over the body while Liam knelt beside it. Bruises dotted her long legs. It was Alexia.

Nikki pressed her lips together to keep from screaming in anger. After seeing Alexia's room and realizing how much she'd studied killers and their behavior, Nikki had foolishly allowed herself to think they still had a chance to find Alexia alive. So much life snuffed out the last few days, and they were no closer to solving the case.

Alexia wore the same clothes as Saturday night, her long blond hair tangled, as though someone had been pulling on it. Three of her red fingernails were missing. One fingernail, Nikki knew, had wound up in Vivienne's hair, but the others could be anywhere. And, she hoped, might help them find her killer. Her left eye was swollen shut. She had been missing for less than thirty-six hours, and her shiner had been in full bloom by the time she'd been killed, which meant at least some time had passed between the kidnapping and murder. Her half-opened right eye looked milky white, her jaw slack. Alexia's arms lay above her head, her legs at a weirdly perpendicular angle, bruises dotted along them.

Miller caught Nikki's eye. "She was still warm when they found her."

Nikki shivered. "Who found her?"

"A couple out for a walk. Husband's a retired nurse. He knew she was dead but said she still felt room temperature. We've got cops combing the entire area. We're far enough from the lake the killer had to have driven here."

Nikki stood at Alexia's dirty feet. She didn't see any fatal wounds on Alexia's torso or neck or any sign of dried blood on the ground around her body. "Head trauma?"

Blanchard knelt down next to the dead girl and gently rolled Alexia onto her side. "Gunshot wound to the upper thorax. She likely bled out internally."

"She was shot in the back?" Nikki pointed to the dirty feet. "Maybe she'd gotten free and made a run for it?"

"Yes, look at these indents on her wrists and ankles." Blanchard let the body down and pointed to Alexia's wrist, where restraints had left deep, red marks. "I'll measure the wound to be sure, but this looks like zip tie marks."

"No one's getting out of those without help if they're on right. Did he let her go and then shoot her?"

Nikki scanned the wooded area, trying to imagine what might have happened in Alexia's final moments. It had been too dry for anyone to leave footprints, but her body had been left close enough to the main trail that Alexia's killer had to have brought her out there at night. Like all of Minnesota's prized nature preserves, the trails in Tanglewood were clearly marked, but the area wasn't so huge that getting off the main paths meant you wouldn't find your way back. Still, where had he carried her body from? Alexia was about one hundred and thirty pounds alive, and much heavier as dead weight. Her body also bore telltale signs of a massive struggle. She'd put up a fight, which meant her killer had a size advantage over her.

Nikki tried to imagine what might have happened that night. Since the side porch door had been left unlocked, it was likely the killer had gained entrance that way. She'd tested the wooden floors out herself, and while they squeaked, much of the Victorian's original hardwood floors were protected by high-quality runners and throw rugs. Three teenaged girls in one place meant noise and distraction, but Nikki was certain the killer must have had the gun in order to subdue all three girls. Blanchard hadn't found any defensive wounds on either Vivienne or Libby. How had one person managed to subdue all of the girls? When she told Chandler to hide, Libby knew someone was in the house. She asked the question that had been nagging at her. "Why didn't the killer look for Chandler?"

"What?" Miller and Blanchard asked in unison.

"We agree the killer entered from the unlocked side porch. Someone unlocked it during the party."

"Or Matt Kline used his key." Liam shot her a look, sweat beading across his forehead. "I see where you're going with this, and it's leading you right to Matt."

"Enlighten me." This time she didn't hide her irritation. Blanchard and Miller exchanged nervous looks. Nikki and Liam disagreed all the time, but this time seemed different. He thought she couldn't see past the emotional connection with Matt, and that royally pissed Nikki off after all they'd been through the last couple of years.

"Matt Kline wouldn't have known Chandler was even there. That's why he didn't look for him."

"Fine." Nikki didn't believe Matt Kline had been involved,

but she'd humor her partner. "Alexia was the main target. Whoever did this obliterated anyone in his path to get to her."

"Again, Matt Kline."

Nikki swiveled to face him. "You're trying to shoehorn Matt."

"I'm following the evidence," he snapped.

"Circumstantial. Matt allowed us to check his shoes and he let you look in his truck, didn't he?"

"Courtney's testing the shoes. And it was dark. All *circumstantial* signs point to Matt."

Anger surged through Nikki. Why was Liam deliberately pressing her buttons? Liam couldn't possibly understand the trauma that Matt Kline carried with him every hour of every day. Liam knew what it was like to have his entire family ripped away from him. If Alexia had been the only victim, then Matt had the motive, she supposed, if he snapped, but why would he shatter two other families' lives like his had been? He could have gotten back at Alexia a number of ways, including legal. Unless he suddenly turned into a monster that night, the motive just wasn't there in Nikki's opinion.

Miller looked between the two of them. "You've both got good points. We can't eliminate him; we certainly can't arrest him. Not at this point."

"Alexia has plenty of superficial wounds," Blanchard said. "She fought back."

"She was a strong kid too. Whoever did this is strong enough to handle the fight she must have put up. He hated her." Liam looked at Nikki. "Another point for Matt."

"Nothing in Vivienne's or Libby's lives raises any red flags," Miller reminded them.

"She's got plenty of surface wounds, including a cut in her shoulder," Blanchard said.

Nikki circled the small area, careful not to touch any of the foliage in case Courtney found evidence. The squawk of a blue jay brought her attention to the big oak tree near Alexia's body. Nikki stared, wondering if her tired brain had started playing tricks on her. She grabbed the latex gloves out of her pocket and slipped them on. Her heart pounded as she approached the tree.

"You see something?" Liam asked.

"Just a sec." In the middle of the tree, where the heavy branches sagged toward the ground, some of the bark had been stripped away. Nikki stood on her tiptoes to reach the area. She was almost 5'8", and even though she used to know how to climb trees, this one would have been tough for her height.

But not for Alexia.

Carefully, she extracted the jagged red fingernails out of the oak tree. She held out her hand. "She tried to climb the tree."

"And he shot her from behind?" Blanchard looked even more disgusted. "Coward."

"Maybe." Nikki tried to picture Alexia struggling through the woods at night, with the full trees blocking out the moon. She'd certainly been running for her life, her lungs rasping and terror racing through her system. Alexia ran track and had set mid-distance records. She was fast, and she'd run for her life. With her hands no longer in zip ties, just as Blanchard said. "She couldn't have attempted to climb the tree if her hands were tied."

Liam's pale face matched the shock on Blanchard and Miller's. "Are you suggesting that the killer let her go? So he could hunt her down?"

"Look at the evidence." Nikki spread her arms wide. "Wriggling out of zip ties on her hands and feet? The nails stuck in the tree, the stripped bark?" She looked down at Alexia. Her feet were less than a foot away from the tree. "I think he let her go and made her think she had a chance, and then shot her."

"That's vindictive as hell," Blanchard said. "What would motivate someone to do such a thing?"

"Revenge." Liam looked at Nikki. "Let's go talk to Shanna Perry. We need to find out the truth about 2001."

Nikki drove while Liam combed through their case notes. "I think she's keeping something from us," she said. "But for some reason I don't believe she's a killer." Shanna had admitted to being manipulative and willing to do what she needed to in order to advance her career.

She exited the interstate near Shanna's home.

"We have to consider that Shanna and Sandy's mystery lover were involved in the Kline killings," Liam said.

"Shanna was out of state when they happened," Nikki reminded him.

"But perhaps she was working with Mrs. Kline's lover? Perhaps the killer is blackmailing her now, and is the one who murdered Alexia..."

TWENTY-NINE

"I'll let you take the lead," Liam said as they walked to Shanna's front door. "You seem to have developed some connection with her."

"I don't know about that." Nikki's knock was quickly answered by Marina, the victims' advocate.

"Agent Hunt, Shanna was just talking about calling you," Marina said. "Come in." Nikki and Liam stepped inside. "Sheriff Miller left just a little while ago. He cried with Shanna." Marina dabbed her eyes with a tissue. "He's a good one."

"How's she doing?" Nikki asked.

"In shock," Marina answered. "She just got off the phone with Alexia's father."

Nikki could only imagine the conversation. She almost asked if the new wife had given birth, but mentioning the sad irony of the new baby right now felt disrespectful.

They followed her through the expansive house to the sunroom that led out to the large back patio. The smell of cigarette smoke coming from the room made Nikki's throat tickle.

"Ms. Perry?" Marina said gently. "Agents Hunt and Wilson are here."

Her back to them, Shanna took a long draw of her cigarette, her hand trembling. "Who did this to my daughter, Agent Hunt?"

"That's what we're hoping you can help us with." Liam sat down next to Marina.

Shanna turned, her pretty face gray and her eyes bloodshot. "You want me to do your job for you?"

Nikki took the chair across from Shanna. "Nothing I can say will make your loss any easier, but I'm so very sorry. No parent should have to endure this."

Shanna's lower lip trembled, her eyes glistening with tears.

"This is incredibly hard," Nikki said. "But I think we need to talk, Shanna."

She waited for Shanna to respond, but she stayed silent, brooding.

"I spoke to Ben Hinson. We know you were closer to the Klines than you've let on. Alexia spoke to Ben a few weeks ago, and given what we've learned about her, I have a hard time believing Alexia wouldn't have come to you wanting answers. She certainly wasn't afraid of confrontation, was she?"

Shanna shook her head.

"There's a good chance Alexia learned something about the Kline murders that got her killed." Nikki leaned forward. "I don't think you're a bad person, Shanna. But you've made mistakes. We all make them. But we need to know everything."

Shanna snapped to attention. "Stop pussyfooting around and say what you mean."

"Okay." Liam, as usual, had no problem playing bad cop. He'd gotten increasingly good at it since his brain injury a couple of years ago, and Nikki wondered if the trauma had affected his personality more than they'd realized. "Do you know who Sandy Kline was having an affair with?"

"No," Shanna replied quickly.

"I think you do," Liam said. "I think you know who she was having the affair with, and I think you told him the second Amy told you. He decided he had to take action and went to the Klines' house that night."

Shanna looked like she wanted to leap out of the chair and strangle him. "That's absurd, and none of that has anything to do with my daughter or the other girls."

"It does if Alexia confronted you and you panicked," Liam said. "You may not have suspected him of killing the Klines, but I think you know who he is and you warned him."

"If I had any names to give you, I would," Shanna said. "I don't know who Sandy was sleeping with. Yes, I spoke to Amy that night. She didn't tell me who it was, just that she'd found out." She glared at Liam. "I think you don't have any other leads so you're trying to fit a square peg into a round hole. Is this why you couldn't find my daughter in time? This is your big FBI profiling at work? Why aren't you talking to Matt Kline? He hated Alexia for digging into his family history. He was at the house that night, for Christ's sake!"

"We're looking at Matt Kline very closely," Liam replied.

"Then why are you asking me about things that happened two decades ago?"

Nikki jumped in. "We're following the evidence, and we have to ask difficult questions to eliminate people."

Shanna turned away from Liam and addressed Nikki. "Do you have any real theories?"

"We do, actually," Nikki said. "I'm not allowed to share the information, but we're confident at this point Alexia was the target, and Vivienne and Libby were likely collateral damage."

"And you think Alexia was targeted because of her nosing into the Kline murders?" Shanna rolled her eyes. "It's far more plausible that Matt Kline snapped, killed the other two girls and took Alexia. He has the motive."

"As Agent Wilson said, we are investigating that angle, I assure you," Nikki said. "But your daughter was very resourceful and not one to back down. Did she say anything else you haven't told us?"

Shanna grabbed another tissue from the box on the table. "Saturday morning, she said we were going to have a come to Jesus talk." Shanna sniffled. "That I could help solve the Klines' murder and that I was going to do so." Her choking cry shifted to a maniacal laugh. "I was so impressed at her brazenness that I laughed and said we'd talk about it. That made her mad, and she said she knew the truth. She just needed the physical proof and was going to get it. I told her to leave it alone, that I hadn't told her everything, that we'd talk about it. Then I hung up. That's the last thing I said to my baby."

Liam had been focused on taking notes, but Nikki felt him tense when Shanna talked about the phone call and knew he'd caught it as well. "Shanna, this is really important. She said she was going to get physical proof of what?"

"The killer," Shanna whispered. "I thought she sounded like a little kid playing a game, you know? If the police couldn't solve those murders, how could she?"

"Ben's got a photo from that summer, with the interns from the nonprofit on his last day. Unfortunately, he didn't really know the other interns that well so he could only identify a couple of the girls. Would you take a look at it?"

"I was only there once," Shanna said.

"That's okay." Nikki showed her the photo. "Besides Ben, Amy, and Mrs. Kline, do you recognize anyone?"

Shanna studied the picture for a few moments. "No. I just... didn't care enough to learn their names." She handed Nikki the dogeared, three-subject notebook that had been sitting in her lap. "There's my journal, the one Alexia snooped through. It's all there. Foster kid does what it takes to create a better life for herself. Alexia didn't understand. But who else would she have spoken to about it besides Ben? And he's no killer."

"Shanna, you're certain Alexia didn't mention having issues with anyone? Did she ever talk about being followed or scared?"

Shanna snorted and then took another long inhale from her cigarette. "Alexia's like me. She wasn't scared of anything." Her lips trembled, the ash about to drop onto the carpet. "Now she's gone. What am I supposed to do?"

THIRTY

Nikki fought back a yawn as she headed toward the big conference room. She'd tried to sleep a few hours, but she couldn't stop thinking about Matt Kline. She couldn't let him be railroaded like Rory's brother.

"Hey," Rory had said when she'd admitted it to him this morning. "You aren't that same scared sixteen-year-old, and Miller isn't Hardin. The very fact that you're worried about it means you aren't going to let it happen. Work the case."

"I miss Lacey." She swallowed the lump in her throat. Lacey always made things better.

"Then let's call her now," Rory suggested. "She can go back to sleep."

Nikki didn't think her daughter would answer the cell phone she'd given her for emergencies, but just as she'd been about to end the call, Lacey's sleepy, excited voice answered. "Mommy!"

That had been enough to get Nikki through the day.

She joined the others in the conference room. "Dr. Blanchard, thanks for meeting us early."

"No problem," the medical examiner said. "As soon as I saw

that Norton was the medical examiner on the Kline case, I knew we were in trouble." Blanchard handed Nikki a heavy envelope. "Copies of all three Kline autopsies. With all the reporters, I didn't want to send this digitally." She sat down across from Nikki. They had all convened at the sheriff's station to go over what Blanchard had found. "I try very hard to give my colleagues the benefit of the doubt, because our job is hard. But it's clear the previous coroner knew he was already on the way out, with complaints mounting up, and he phoned the Kline autopsies in. Amazing considering the magnitude of the tragedy. Fortunately, someone took a lot of photos. Norton's assistant had voiced concerns about him and during the trial that led to Norton losing his license, the assistant talked about taking extra photos of a lot of murders because he had a bad feeling about Norton. We'll get to the photos in a minute."

Nikki laid the copies of each report on the table in front of her. Blanchard had marked errors on transparent sticky notes with a red marker. The previous coroner had sketched the scene, albeit poorly, but the layout of the Victorian appeared to be accurate.

"Norton said Amy had been raped based on bruising, the location of her panties, and her hymen not being intact." She looked at the group. "Of course, we know that's not a real indicator. Plenty of other things can cause that to happen. She did have some premortem bruising on her thighs that suggested a possible assault, but no semen was found in her underwear or during the exam," Blanchard said. "No other significant forensic evidence was found on her body because she was floating in the lake, and that's the only reason I trust the coroner's notes about that. There's no tearing, even miniscule, that you expect to see with violent attacks. Amy wasn't raped." She handed Nikki a black and white photo of Amy Kline lying on the autopsy table. "What's the first thing that sticks out to you?"

Nikki tried to ignore the pale, serene face of the beautiful girl whose life had been taken so early. The superficial wounds on her arms and legs had been cleaned, along with the rest of her body, revealing the deep gashes to her heart and stomach. Nikki grabbed her pencil, wielding it like a knife. She pretended to stab Liam, sitting to her left. "She struggled with him, he pinned her down and went for her vital organs. They found blood on the shore, supporting the theory she tried to crawl to the boat and wound up in the water."

"She drowned, there's no doubt about that," Blanchard said. "The poor child suffered, but you're still not seeing what bothers me most. A good coroner—doesn't have to be a medical examiner, but anyone with medical training—should have a solid understanding of bruising and the patterns it leaves. Look at her thighs." She slid a compact magnifying glass across the table. "You might need this to see the whole pattern."

Nikki held the instrument in front of the autopsy photo, focusing on the bruises on Amy's thighs. "She was grabbed from behind. The palm prints are on the back of the legs."

Blanchard nodded. "These photos were taken the day of the murders. Had they taken ones the day after, I don't think we would need the magnifying glass. But the coroner didn't bother to do so, which is negligence in my opinion. Her body wasn't released to the funeral home for four days, so he had the time to do his due diligence. He just chose not to."

Liam took the magnifying glass from Nikki. "Is it just me, or are those superficial chest wounds in a weird spot?"

"What do you mean?" Nikki asked.

"Here, I'll show you." He motioned for her to stand. "Come toward me, like you were going to attack."

She did as he asked. Liam thrust the magnifying glass toward Nikki. "The natural motion when you stab someone from the front is an underhand motion, like this." He pushed the tool against Nikki's stomach and then her heart. "The wounds to her heart and stomach are driven straight in, as though her attacker were directly on top of her. But these?" He pointed to the wounds around Amy's collarbone. "Look at the angle and the depth."

"You're absolutely right," Blanchard said. "She surprised him. And that makes the rest of this even worse. Look at Ted Kline's injuries."

Nikki did as she asked, noting the injuries she'd seen the first time she'd looked at the file for Caitlin. "Throat slashed, likely from behind." Nikki caught Blanchard's knowing look. "I have a feeling I'm really not going to like what you're about to say."

"Sandy Kline," Blanchard said. "The coroner noted a few bruises suggesting defense, but he doesn't say anything about the faint marks around her wrists. He also noted Mrs. Kline had sexual intercourse a few hours before she died, presumably with her husband. But I looked at the photos, and *she* had vaginal tearing. They were tiny marks, but I'm confident that's what they were. Amy had none."

Nikki looked at the photo of Sandy Kline lying face up on the stone patio surrounding the pool. "We're pretty certain they mislabeled the women's underwear."

"They did," Blanchard said. "Which is going to make it easy for a good defense attorney to get any case thrown out. Short of a DNA match or a confession, getting a conviction with this mess is going to be nearly impossible."

"But you're confident the killer assaulted Sandy Kline instead of her daughter?"

Blanchard nodded as Nikki continued going over the scenario.

"We know Amy discovered her mother was having an affair and that her mother had told her it was over. Maybe she told her lover, and he couldn't handle it. Amy might have survived if she'd stayed upstairs."

"I don't know, Amy's facial bruising suggests the killer was angry as hell at her," Liam said.

"But was he angry that she'd interrupted his time with her mother or because she'd caused the demise of the affair?" Nikki asked. "In my opinion, the only evidence that actually connects these cases is the location of the crimes. Did you see any wounds on the Kline family that suggested he incapacitated them the same way Vivienne and Libby were?"

"No," Blanchard said.

"I agree, it's two different killers," Liam said. "But I don't trust Matt Kline the same way you do." He looked at Miller. "We cleared the other partygoers, including Luke Webb and his friend Brett. If he's cleared, then who else had issues with Alexia, who also knew she would be at the house?" Liam said. "Besides Matt Kline, I mean?" He smirked at her.

Before Nikki could retort, her phone vibrated on the table. She didn't recognize the unknown number, so she excused herself to take the call. "This is Agent Hunt."

"Agent Hunt, Rich Langley here. You've been trying to reach me?"

Nikki grabbed her notebook and pencil. "Yes, thank you for calling back. I'm actually here with Sheriff Miller, my partner, Agent Wilson, and the medical examiner Dr. Blanchard. Is it okay if I put you on speaker?"

"Of course." Rich coughed. "Pardon me. Eric told me what happened at Lilydale. I know he didn't have much use for those girls, especially Alexia, but he's broken up about it. Guess you're calling about the original case."

She noticed the subtle shift in his tone. Langley had fought for Chisago County to keep the case, but Hardin had waged a successful smear campaign against him, convincing the public that the Chisago sheriff dropped the ball on the Kline murders. Between her own experience with former Sheriff Hardin and what she'd learned about the case, she had a feeling Langley did the best he could. Chisago County was smaller than Washington County, with less budget and fewer officers. At the time, only the sheriff and the chief deputy had certified forensic training. On paper, Washington County's sheriff's department appeared much more suited for the job, but she knew some of the colossal mistakes Hardin had made in his tenure.

"I'm not calling to question your decisions back then," Nikki said.

"Didn't think so," Rich answered. "I moved to Florida about a month after your parents' real murderer was finally caught. You know how badly investigations can get screwed up thanks to one cop."

"Thank you for trusting me." Nikki hoped he could hear the sincerity in her voice. She kept going back to what he'd said about Eric not liking the girls. "I know Alexia wasn't happy Eric showed up at the party."

"No, she wouldn't be," Langley said. "She's always looked down her nose at anyone who doesn't live in the same income bracket—at least until she got interested in the Klines' murder and found out I was Eric's grandpa. She tried to buddy up to him so she could speak with me about it, but Eric's not stupid. He told her no and she was mad. She even tried to pay him to share my police files with her, like she had a right to them."

"When was this?" Nikki asked, waiting for Langley to realize why she was asking about his grandson. He clearly wasn't thinking of Eric as a suspect, and Nikki hadn't either.

"Before school ended for the year, I think. Anyway, what did you want to know about the original case?"

Liam scribbled a note to her about checking Eric's alibi, and Nikki nodded.

"I'm familiar with the Kline case as far as reports and all of that go. I want to know what you saw when you first arrived on scene, down to the smell, sounds, any little detail you can remember."

"You don't want to hear my opinion on what actually happened?"

"I do, eventually. But sometimes the most vital information in a case, especially a cold one, comes from the first responders or individuals who found the body, especially if the victim is recently deceased. You arrived first?"

"Yep," Langley said. "I wasn't supposed to be on shift that night, but we were short on deputies, and as my good luck would have it, I'd stopped to fill up at the gas station not far from the Klines'. I remember thinking the kid—Matt—had probably run off and gotten hurt, maybe made up a story. As you know, that wasn't the case."

Miller introduced himself. "Assume lights in the house were on when you arrived?" he asked.

"About half of them," Rich answered. "Front door was locked, so I went to the east side, where the pool is. Found Sandy there. She was still warm, but no pulse. The sliding door was standing open, and the lights downstairs were almost all on. Mr. Kline was near the stairs, blood everywhere."

"Did you call for backup?" Nikki couldn't help but ask the question. Every officer was trained to call for backup the second a victim was discovered, to ensure the integrity of the crime scene and the officer's safety in case the perpetrator was still nearby.

"Soon as I realized she didn't have a pulse. I should have waited to go upstairs, but I was afraid Amy might be up there somewhere, trapped."

"Was there any sign the killer actually went upstairs?" Nikki asked, thinking of Amy's diary.

"That's one thing Hardin and me disagreed on from the start," Rich said. "I thought it looked like her room had been searched, because it was messy and both her aunt and Matt said Amy kept her room tidy. Matt Kline couldn't remember if his sister's room was messy that night because he was scared shitless. Hardin won that battle. His theory was that Ben Hinson showed up to see Amy, her parents said no, and things went south."

"But no physical evidence linked him to the murders?"

"Wasn't much physical evidence to begin with," Rich answered. "That's one thing that bugged me about Hardin's theory. He was certain Ben did all this over not being able to see Amy, and he went so far as to postulate that Ben probably thought Amy would run away with him with her parents out of the way, and when she didn't, he killed her."

Nikki rolled her eyes. Hardin would think something like that. He had never learned things weren't always what they seemed. "I've spoken to Ben. I don't think he had anything to do with the murders."

"But you have a theory?"

"Have you watched the documentary yet?"

"Don't plan on it, Agent. I lived it."

"I understand," Nikki said. "We've been trying to figure out the motivation behind both the Kline murders and the ones over the weekend. We know one of the victims had some information about people connected to the family, and she planned on discussing them in the series. What was your gut reaction that night? Who did you think could have killed the Klines?"

"No lovesick twenty-year-old," Rich said. "Thanks to Matt's testimony, we know this person spent some time in the kitchen, and that's likely where he entered the house. Someone let him in the back door, and both Ted Kline and Amy were upstairs. Matt too."

"Sandy Kline let someone in the back patio door in the middle of the night?" Nikki had been thinking the same thing, albeit with more information than Rich Langley had ever had.

"And what mother would let her daughter's angry ex-boyfriend in the house at that time?" Rich demanded.

"None that I know."

"Exactly. But she did let him in, so she knew him." Rich paused for a moment. "My theory was that Sandy Kline had an affair, broke it off, and the guy showed up and killed the family."

The four of them exchanged looks. "Because of what you saw at the scene?"

"And because of what Amy's friends told me the day after," Rich said. "Amy had discovered a terrible secret about her mom and was going to confront her about it. She wouldn't say what it was, but Amy said she had to do it for the sake of her family."

"That was never in the reports, was it?" Miller asked. "I haven't seen that."

"Wouldn't be," Rich answered. "I had to give all my notes to Hardin and the BCA. They probably got thrown out because he steamrolled his theory over everyone else's."

"What about shoe prints?" Nikki asked, thinking of the Air Jordans.

Langley snorted. "Another bone of contention between Hardin and me. He said the shoe print by the docks wasn't fresh, and I said it was. I took several pictures that I don't think he even looked at."

Nikki glanced at the others. "You mentioned Alexia wanting copies of your files. I assume you kept copies. Do you still have them?" If Langley was like every other good cop she'd worked with, his answer would be a resounding yes.

"Hell, yes I did. But I don't have them here. They're at my old place, where Eric and his mom live."

Miller's phone vibrated, and he stepped out of the room. Before she ended the call with Langley, Nikki asked if it would be all right if she went over and got the files. He explained they were in his locked file cabinet.

"I'm the only one who knows the passcode, but I suppose I can trust you. It's 12-26-05."

Nikki assured him she would let him know when she'd secured the files. She debated asking him not to give Eric a heads-up, but she didn't want him to change his mind about the files.

"I'm going to get that file," she said to Liam as soon as she ended the call with Langley. "It'll give me a chance to ask Eric a few more questions too. Can you do me a favor and research the Air Jordan shoe releases between 1999 and 2001? We need to figure out what the soles look like and have the shoe-print analyst look at them as soon as possible."

Liam nodded as Miller returned. Nikki started to bring him up to speed, but he cut her off. "Alexia's Volvo was just located parked at an empty house for sale three streets over from Matt Kline's place."

THIRTY-ONE

"How did they find it?" Liam asked.

"Google Assistant finally came through," Miller said. "Shanna requested the information Monday morning, but since she wasn't the registered driver of the vehicle, we've had to jump through hoops."

Nikki wanted to scream in frustration. Could they have saved Alexia if they'd known where her car was earlier? "I have a hard time believing that Matt would dump her car near his house, when he knows the vehicle is high tech and can likely be traced."

Liam rolled his eyes. "You think he's being set up? Come on, Nik. Look at the evidence."

"The circumstantial evidence," she said between gritted teeth. "He let you take the boots for testing. He's cooperated. Why in the hell do this?"

"I'm not a psychologist," Liam said. "The guy's experienced extreme trauma. Who knows how screwed up his head is?"

"Not to be an ass, but I have a background in psychology." She'd never bothered getting licensed because she'd planned to go into the FBI anyway, but Nikki's graduate degree in

abnormal psychology, along with her thesis topic about childhood trauma among law enforcement officers, had garnered the
interest of the FBI. That's why her mentor, Elwood, had
recruited her. That's why she'd had access to some of the
greatest analytical minds in the history of the FBI. Douglas and
Ressler had retired, along with Hazelwood, but she'd had access
to them thanks to her mentor. None of that qualified her to be a
therapist, but no one else in the Minnesota Bureau and most of
the Midwest Bureaus had the kind of background that Nikki
had. "I experienced trauma and didn't end up killing people,
even when I could have and gotten away with it." Nikki had
been the one to finally catch the man who had murdered her
parents when she'd returned to Stillwater a few years ago, and
not putting a bullet in his head had been one of the hardest
things she'd ever done.

"You're too close to this," Liam shot back. "This is exactly
the kind of thing Garcia is talking about, by the way."

"I'm pretty sure he meant withholding information during a
case, like you did last year." Anger coursed through her even as
her mind told her to calm down. Nothing Liam had said was
wrong. Circumstantial evidence pointed to Matt. The car being
found close to his house didn't help his case, no matter what
Nikki thought. She couldn't stop thinking about the jurisdictional and personal bullshit that had played a big part in
preventing the Kline murders from being solved. Matt had
suffered for years because the system had failed. It just wasn't
right.

"I'm going with Miller to the car's location," Liam said
tersely. "I'll have Kendall track down the information on the
Jordans. Are you coming?"

Riding in a car with Liam sounded about as appealing as
being locked in a trunk right now. "We need Langley's files. I'm
going over there to get them. I'll meet up with you guys after
that."

.   .   .

Nikki waited until Miller and Liam had left before heading out
to the jeep. She was being petty, but Liam's attitude irritated
her and she needed some time to cool off. She'd get the shoe
print, scan it with her tablet and get a copy to Kendall for
research. She'd give the original photo to Courtney and let the
shoeprint analysts have a crack at identifying the shoe.

Her phone rang with a call from Stillwater Country Club.
"This is Agent Hunt."

"Um, hi. This is Brett. Luke's friend."

"How are you doing?" She was surprised he'd gone to work
given news of Alexia's death.

"Okay, I guess."

Nikki unlocked the jeep and started the engine. "Did you
remember something else about the other night?"

"Yeah, but I'm not sure if it's even important."

"Why don't you tell me, and I can figure it out?" Nikki
asked. "A lot of times it's the innocuous details that break a
case."

"Well, I guess you probably know that Alexia didn't like
Eric all that well. Actually, at all, and it just got worse over the
last six months. We expected he'd stop by to see Olivia, and
Alexia usually puts on a good fake smile even if she doesn't
like you. But she was cursing his name the whole time. Luke
told her to get over it; she said he didn't understand. She'd
needed Eric's help with a school project for a class and he
refused."

"Was that out of character for her?" Alexia must have been
talking about Langley's files, but she wouldn't have shared that
information with her friends.

"Uh, she didn't like being told no, so not really. But it kind
of bugged me that she made such a big deal out of it and was so
shitty to him. Olivia said she was just being herself and not to

worry about it, but when they found her body, I knew I had to call you."

"Why?" Nikki said.

"Look, I don't want to get anyone in trouble. I might just be talking out of my ass, you know?"

"Let me decide that, Brett."

"Yeah, okay." He cleared his throat. "Where they found her is less than a mile from Eric's house."

Nikki took a moment to digest the information. On its own, it didn't mean that much, but given what they'd found out from Rich Langley, Eric could have accessed the Kline case files.

"Thanks for telling me." She debated calling Liam, but the information about Eric was as circumstantial as the evidence against Matt, and it would just spark more argument. But if Eric was involved, she could be walking into a trap. Liam and Miller already knew where she was headed. As long as she let them know she'd gone into the house and kept her weapon close, she'd be fine.

Nikki tried to calm down as she entered the address into the jeep's GPS. She hated feeling petty, but her gut told her that she was right. Thanks to the media converging at his house, it wouldn't have been hard to find out where Matt lived. Parking so close to his home screamed set-up to Nikki.

But was Liam right? Was she too close to the situation? If she were being honest, Nikki had to say yes. But that didn't mean she couldn't still be objective, right?

She asked Siri to call Courtney at the lab as she merged into traffic.

"I'm still working on the sample taken from Sandy Kline's fingernails." Courtney answered in her usual way. Nikki wasn't sure the last time she'd heard her friend actually say "hello."

"That's not why I'm calling," she said. "I need an objective opinion. Liam and I are on opposite sides in this investigation."

"He's wrong," Courtney said.

"You haven't heard the issue yet."

"Doesn't matter. He's a man. He's probably wrong."

Nikki laughed. "Just listen." She told her about Matt's car being found and the various theories she and Liam had thrown at each other over the last few days. "I know I can't compartmentalize this, Court. I've spent the last year making peace with the fact that getting emotionally involved in a case makes me a good cop as long as I walk the line. This is the first time in a long time I'm starting to doubt my instincts. If you think I'm completely off the rails on this, tell me."

"I can see both sides," Courtney said. "And, honestly, I think it's kind of a good thing as long as you guys can use your heads. Let him and Miller run with the idea it's Matt. Follow your leads and see where they take you. That way, when you catch this piece of shit and he goes to trial, you both know you've done your due diligence."

"You're right." Nikki glanced at the interstate sign. The exit for Bone Lake was next. Maybe if she walked through the scene again, she'd be able to get a better feel for the truth and her own objectivity. "I'm going to stop at Bone Lake and walk through the house again before going to Eric's. Can you rush something for me?"

"Matt's shoes? I'm waiting on results. I'll yell at someone and get back to you ASAP."

"Thanks, Court. I don't know what I'd do without you."

"Lose your mind," she said cheerfully. "But, in all seriousness, be careful going back to that place."

"I don't think the killer's going to return, especially in broad daylight."

"That's not what I'm talking about. That place is loaded with bad vibes. I know you don't believe in ghosts, but we all leave energy behind, and every death in that house has been violent. I had to psych myself up to go inside the other day."

One of Courtney's hobbies, when she actually had time,

was ghost hunting, although Nikki thought it was more about having an excuse to go to creepy places than anything, but she could tell by her friend's tone that she was genuinely worried.

"I'll be careful. Promise." Nikki's phone vibrated with another call, Nina Barton's name on the caller ID. "I'll check in with you later." She hit end and then accepted the new call.

"Um, hi. This is Nina Barton, Olivia's mom."

"How are you? Is Olivia holding up all right?"

"I think so, but... I'm probably overreacting and wasting your time. Never mind."

"No, no, what is it?" Nikki asked.

"Well, Olivia isn't answering her phone. I've been calling and texting for two hours without a single response. She told me that she was going to stop by Eric's after work, and I checked the find-a-phone app. It says her phone is at Eric's, but I called and he said she left an hour ago. Something isn't right."

Anxiety rippled through Nikki. "I'm actually headed there anyway. I'll check it out and call you back."

THIRTY-TWO

Nikki sped through the back roads trying to avoid construction, her mind on Eric Gannon. She'd texted Liam and Miller about Olivia, letting them know she planned to find her before joining them.

His alibi was that he'd been home sleeping the night of the murders, and his mother had told Kendall when she interviewed her that Eric's vehicle had been in the driveway all night. But the property was only two miles from Bone Lake, an easy walk for a healthy kid like Eric. He had issues with Alexia; she'd treated him poorly. But what about the other two girls? Nikki couldn't shake the feeling they were missing a giant piece of the puzzle.

Kendall and Jim had already gone back over the security videos the property manager had sent over, making sure no one else had arrived at Lilydale that weekend. The security camera mounted by the main entrance covered the entire front yard down to the lake, but the rest of the house was left exposed.

Eric definitely didn't fit in with the rest of Olivia's friends, and Alexia had treated him poorly. His attacking her Nikki could somewhat justify, but not the other girls, especially knowing it would devastate Olivia.

So why say she wasn't at his house when her phone told a different story?

Nikki didn't see Olivia's blue Camry in Eric's driveway. The seventies-styled ranch home had a two-car garage, the aging Jeep Wrangler registered to Eric's mother parked in front. Despite the home's age, it was well cared for, the evergreen bushes maintained. Two planters of red geraniums flanked the front door.

Nikki texted Liam to let him know she'd arrived with no sign of Olivia's car before making sure her Glock was still loaded. She slipped it into the holster she rarely wore and grabbed her phone before quietly shutting the jeep door. On her way to the house, she peeked in the garage windows, finding it empty, save for a push mower and various other everyday tools.

If Eric was keeping Olivia in the house, he'd already hidden her car. Nikki approached the house with caution, her mind going in circles. Langley had left files here, but he'd never seen the diary. Alexia hadn't treated Eric all that well, but she struggled with motive. Eric had talked about Libby being nice to him before he met Olivia, and he'd seemed genuinely shocked and saddened when Nikki interviewed him. Nothing made sense.

As Nikki cautiously approached the house, she heard Eric shouting obscenities inside. Hand on her weapon, Nikki banged on the door. "FBI. We're looking for Olivia."

Footsteps thundered on the other side of the door. Eric yanked the door open with a confused look on his face. "She's not here."

"I heard you talking to someone." Nikki smiled. "Not very friendly, either."

Eric snickered as he held up a headset. "Playing *COD* with some dicks online."

"*COD*?"

"Sorry, *Call of Duty*. You can come in."

Nikki scanned the front room for any sign of Olivia or a possible struggle, but it looked as normal as their family room, right down to the gaming chair Eric must have been sitting in. Rory and Mark each had one and played some online game that resulted in a lot of shouting too.

He spoke into the headset's microphone. "Sorry, guys, have an important visitor. BRB." Eric tossed the headphone on the gaming chair. "Olivia's not here. She left, like, two hours ago. I told her mom that." Fear flickered in her eyes. "Is she missing now?"

"I don't know," Nikki said. "Her mom used the find-a-phone feature, and according to the app, her phone is here." She kept her gaze locked with his, but Eric didn't appear nervous. He was just a kid playing video games.

"Seriously?" He looked around the room before walking over to the oversized sectional couch and messing with the cushions. "Shit, here it is." He held up the phone. "She must have had it on silent. I didn't hear it vibrating, but I've been kind of preoccupied since she left."

"That's okay." A wave of relief swept through Nikki before it was replaced by a new worry. A teenaged girl not noticing her phone was missing for two hours didn't sit right with Nikki. Even if Olivia was the type to keep it on vibrate, it was hard to imagine she wouldn't have at least checked her phone in the last hour or so. Why hadn't she come back for it? "Did she say where she was going next?"

He bit his lip. "I don't know how much I'm supposed to say."

Nikki crossed her arms and waited.

Eric quickly got the hint. "Okay, she stopped by Luke's after her shift to see how he was doing. There's a gas station a couple of blocks away, right out of the gated neighborhood, I guess. Anyway, she stopped to get gas first and a woman came up to her. She told her how great it was to see her and how beautiful she'd grown to be, and Olivia thought she seemed familiar but couldn't place it until the woman showed her a photo of Luke's birthday party not long before she left. It was his mom, Kim Webb."

"What?" Nikki said. "Arthur said she left, had a painkiller addiction."

Eric shrugged. "Kim told Olivia that Arthur deliberately got her hooked on meds so he could get rid of her. She finally left before he could have her put in a hospital. Olivia said she just started talking, like she'd been waiting to tell someone."

"Did Olivia believe all of this?"

"She's on the fence. Kim seemed sincere, but if she's a drug addict, then who knows," Eric answered. "Kim said she'd tried to stay away, but when she heard about the murders, she knew she had to come back for Luke and Matt."

"Why?"

"She wouldn't tell Olivia. She wanted Luke's number, but Olivia said she couldn't just give it to her without talking to him first."

"Kim was okay with that?"

"She said as long as Olivia didn't say anything to Arthur, that was fine. She gave Olivia her number." Eric worried his bottom lip. "Olivia was trying to decide what to do about it because Luke's going through enough. I told her she should just tell him that she saw his mom and she asked about him, don't tell him the rest. Just give him the number and he can decide on his own. He's an adult, you know?"

Nikki nodded. "Did she say anything else?"

"She said something about a photograph that would explain stuff, but that's all she said." Eric started biting his nails. "I told her she was probably messed up from the drugs and to be careful, but Olivia really thinks Kim's telling the truth. Oh!" He snapped his fingers. "She asked Olivia if she'd read the story of Judas, in the Bible. Olivia hadn't, not really, since they aren't religious. Kim said she'd told Matt once, and he didn't listen either."

THIRTY-THREE

Before she left for Luke Webb's home, Nikki searched through the thick pile of evidence reports and personal notes that Rich Langley had taken until she found the image of the partial shoe print. The toe box area was easily visible, with the print fading around the middle of the foot. She dug her tablet out of her bag so she could take a high-quality photo, which she then sent to Kendall so she'd have the photo as she did the background research on the Jordan brand shoe. She needed to get the original photo to the FBI lab today, so they could start analyzing the print as well.

She skimmed the rest of the information in search of anything she hadn't already seen. A statement from Martin Shields, one of Sandy Kline's longtime rivals, caught her eye. She didn't remember this statement being in any of Washington County's files, and it wasn't hard to figure out why. Langley had interviewed Martin two days after the murder while the jurisdictional battle had been playing out. At this point, it didn't matter why the statement hadn't been with Washington County's evidence on the Kline murders. Nikki was more interested in the statement itself.

She could tell by the notes in the margin that Langley would follow up, but she couldn't find any notation that he actually had. According to Martin, he'd suspected Sandy of having an affair with an intern, but he knew that, without proof, he'd be labeled a gossip, so he'd bided his time. After the murders, he'd made it a point to tell Langley that Sandy had taken a few interns with her when she left to start the nonprofit, and that guy had been one of them. Martin didn't know the interns' names, as he felt that was beneath him. Nikki thought about the photo Ben had shared with her, of him, Shanna and Amy with the interns at Sandy Kline's nonprofit on his last day working for her. He hadn't known any of the interns' names either, and Shanna had claimed similar.

The law firm remained in business, but Nikki would need a warrant to ask the company to track each intern down. The Assistant District Attorney who'd prosecuted her parents' real killer had connections everywhere. It was a long shot, but she had to get the actual photo of the shoe print to the lab, anyway. She'd drop it off and then see if she could catch the ADA or set up an appointment with them.

She called Liam to check in. "I've got the print. I already sent a copy to Kendall, but I'll get it over to our analysts. I'm headed to the Webbs' right now." She told him what Olivia had said about Luke's mom. "She's probably over there with him and forgot her phone. How's it going over there?"

"Car's clean," Liam said. "But we expected that because Shanna said Alexia was militant about keeping it looking brand new. You remember the last time Matt said he was in the car?"

"Before she ghosted him. At least a few weeks."

"Then if we find his prints, they're likely going to be more recent." Liam sounded satisfied with himself. "I think half of Miller's deputies are here just to keep the media back," he continued. "No way Matt doesn't already know about the car being found. He's not at work and not answering his cell. How close are you to the Webbs' place?"

The Webbs lived in a much nicer area of town, but the drive shouldn't take more than ten minutes, pending traffic. "Fifteen minutes, probably." Liam and Miller had to question Matt, and Nikki wanted to be there. "I'll go over to the Webbs' and see if he's there."

"Bring him to the government center so we can all talk to him," Liam said.

"That's my plan."

Matt's vehicle was nowhere in sight when Nikki pulled into the Webb property. She also didn't see Luke's car, but it could be in the garage. Hopefully he or Arthur were home. She grabbed her keys and phone and headed up the Webbs' landscaped sidewalk.

Nikki smiled at the security camera mounted to the left of the door and knocked. She expected to hear Maybelle's rapid-fire barks, but only the big dog made the effort to announce her presence.

"Agent Hunt." Arthur looked surprised and a little relieved to see her. "I just saw the news about Alexia's car. I'm trying to track Matt down. He's not here and not answering his phone."

"Can we talk?"

"Of course, come in." He shooed the big dog away and shut the door behind Nikki. She finally spied little black and tan Maybelle, her nose just millimeters away from a closed door near the kitchen.

"I wondered why she didn't go crazy when I knocked."

Arthur rolled his eyes. "I swear to God, she's a toddler. She likes to knock her toys down the stairs and then look at you until you go get them, because she's afraid to walk down them herself. That's her and Luke's game. I give up pretty quickly. So far, she hasn't got the hint."

"How's Luke doing?" Nikki asked.

"Not great," Arthur said. "He's at a friend's. First time he's left the house since the news."

She followed him into his large office. "Both the sheriff's department and the FBI have excellent resources for victims' families. We have some fantastic grief counselors. I would find someone for Luke to talk to sooner rather than later."

Arthur nodded. "I plan to, but he's stubborn. I'm hoping Matt will be able to convince him how vital talk therapy can actually be. Speaking of Matt, I know you can't tell me much about Alexia's car, but is there anything you can share?"

Nikki sat down in one of the cozy leather chairs. "Actually, I haven't seen it. Miller and Agent Wilson are there now. I wanted to follow up on a lead I received from retired Chisago County Sheriff Langley." She told him about the partial print in Langley's file. "I've got agents and our footprint experts comparing them to the Air Jordans," Nikki said. "But it looks like Hardin somehow wound up with a lot less evidence than Chisago did, and I can't figure out why."

Arthur's eyes narrowed in anger. "Unbelievable. What else did they miss? If Hardin were still alive, I'd find a way to sue him." He took a deep breath and slowly exhaled. "Thankfully Langley kept copies like a good cop. Do you have the print with you? I'm not a sneaker head, but if I recall, most Jordan brand shoes have different soles with each release."

"I don't." Nikki rolled her head from shoulder to shoulder, her gaze falling on the built-in bookshelves. "Are those first-edition Fitzgeralds?" She jumped out of the chair and hurried over to look at the books that were enclosed in glass. She'd recognize the strange first-edition *Great Gatsby* cover anywhere. The tiny lips and giant, thick lashes on the woman's face were hard to miss.

"They are," Arthur said. "*This Side of Paradise* is one I hunted down myself years ago. But my ex-wife's great-great-grandfather had business dealings with the Fitzgeralds. He signed a copy of *Gatsby* and gave it to him as a thank you gift."

"That's amazing. I actually worked a case at the Fitzgerald house in St. Paul a few years ago." Nikki was about to ask if she could see the signature when she spotted the row of photographs behind the glass case.

Arthur had the same photograph that Ben had showed her, of Sandy Kline and the interns. He'd never told them he'd interned for her, much less that he'd had interactions with Ben, Shanna and Amy. But there he was, in the back row, and the pieces began to click into place.

"Everything okay, Agent?"

"Just admiring the books." She tried to think of a reason to leave without igniting more suspicion, but what about Olivia? "By the way, did Olivia come by looking for Luke?"

"Few hours ago." Arthur nodded. "She said she'd be at home if he wanted to talk when he came back."

Her phone vibrated, and Nikki almost lost her poker face. She glanced at the caller ID. "I have to take this. Excuse me."

She hurried out of the office and down the hall toward the kitchen, hoping Arthur hadn't picked up on her nervousness.

"This is Agent Hunt."

"I got some weird results back," Courtney said. "The scrapings from under Sandy's nails match the evidence taken from under Alexia's nails—100 percent match."

Nikki couldn't take a chance on her voice carrying. The vaulted ceilings and hardwood floors made the house a virtual echo chamber. "Listen, I need you to tell Liam that. Right away, since he's at another scene." Nikki willed herself to sound normal. After the chaos that had resulted in Liam's head injury a couple of years ago, they'd come up with a code phrase in case one of them got into trouble again. Nikki hoped Courtney remembered. She lowered her voice to a whisper. "Tell him the stargazers are blooming at the Webbs'."

"Shit." Courtney hissed. "You're there now, with no backup?"

"That is correct." Maybelle hadn't budged from the basement door. "But Olivia left her phone at Eric's, and she's not there. Her mom is probably overreacting. Anyway, tell Liam I'll see him soon."

"I'll call him the second we hang up," Courtney said. "But we should stay on the phone."

Nikki checked down the hall to make sure Arthur was still in his office. He'd killed at least three innocent girls to cover up his secret, so killing Nikki wouldn't be a problem for him. "Just let Liam know." She ended the call before Courtney could argue and tiptoed toward the closed door.

The door locked from the front, Nikki realized. She listened for noise downstairs and heard nothing, but Maybelle whimpered. Nikki gently unlocked the door and inched it open, praying it didn't creak. She peered downstairs. "Olivia?" she whispered.

Her heart hammered in her chest. Someone was down there.

Nikki debated walking down or getting out of the house and calling for backup. What if Arthur did something to Olivia before they had the chance to save her?

Nikki never got the chance to decide. Two strong hands came down on her shoulders and shoved, hard.

THIRTY-FOUR

"Agent Hunt, please wake up." Olivia's frightened whisper seemed to ring in her ears. Nikki forced her eyes open, but darkness still surrounded them. A sliver of light streamed into the room a few feet to her right.

"Where are we?" she managed to ask. Her head pounded and pain seared through her shoulder.

"The storage room in the basement, I think," Olivia whispered. "It's a walk-out. I think that's where the light's coming from."

Nikki reached for her phone and cursed. Arthur had taken it. "Try to stay calm. Help is coming."

"How did you find me? I lost my phone."

Nikki matched Olivia's whisper. "You left it at Eric's. He told me you ran into Luke's mom."

Olivia sniffled. "She told me that Luke needed to get out of the house, he was in danger. Then she said something about Judas and that Matt needed to know. At first, I didn't think anything of it, but I was going over texts with Alexia, just to read them. I forgot the same thing happened to her weeks ago, with Luke's mom. We had all been told she was a druggie that ran off, so I told Alexia that she was probably in a bad place and not in her right mind. I kept thinking about how it freaked Alexia out, and she started being a little more paranoid about things."

"So you came here, hoping to talk to Luke?"

"I feel so dumb. Arthur said he wasn't here, but he could tell something was wrong, and before I knew it, he'd talked me into coming inside. I told him about Luke's mom, and he said she was dangerous. I was going to leave when he knocked me out."

Nikki struggled against the duct tape around her wrists, but the pain in her shoulder was so severe she couldn't put much effort into it.

The sound of footsteps coming down the stairs made both of them tense up. "Stay quiet, and stay behind me," Nikki whispered.

Olivia shifted toward her in the darkness.

Suddenly, the room was bathed in light. Arthur stood in the doorway, tall and menacing, his wild eyes flashing between the two of them. He pointed a pistol at Nikki. "You should have taken your call outside, Agent."

"Arthur, please think this through." Nikki squinted against the light and tried to ignore the pain in her side. "My partner knows I'm here. We have DNA evidence that links the crimes. It's over. Adding two more victims, especially an FBI agent, isn't going to help you."

Arthur snorted. "I've killed six people. You think that matters now?"

"What's your plan? This place is going to be surrounded soon."

"I'll figure it out." A bead of sweat rolled down his nose.

"Alexia figured it out, didn't she?" Nikki asked. "She said something at the party to you."

"Why couldn't Alexia just leave well enough alone?" he

demanded. "I made one mistake twenty years ago and spent my life trying to make up for it."

Olivia tensed next to her but stayed quiet.

"You're calling the violent deaths of three—now six—people a mistake?" Nikki asked. She knew she had to buy Olivia and herself time. Liam would be here, but it would take him a while. She'd spent long enough trying to convince him not to suspect Matt; what if he finally agreed with her and didn't come looking at the Webbs' house? "Why did you have to kill Vivienne and Libby? Those two girls were completely innocent."

"I knew Alexia had been snooping in my office. She's the only one who would have had the balls to take it. She played innocent, but I saw it in her eyes. She would go to the police the next morning. I had to act."

"She had evidence against you?" Nikki asked.

"Obviously. Do you know how many times I told her to let the police investigate? How many times I told her to stay away from Matt? She didn't listen, just like Amy."

"You hadn't left for college that night."

"I was supposed to be, but that Friday, when I'd come to tell Sandy bye and try to figure out when she could come to Madison to visit, Amy decided to pop in without telling her mom. She saw us kissing and took off." He ground his teeth. "Sandy said she'd make Amy understand that she had to stay quiet. She wouldn't be a problem."

"But she was," Nikki said.

"The gall of that kid," Arthur seethed. "She never wanted for a damn thing, but she didn't care that I made her mother happy. All Amy cared about was herself. Sandy strung me along for months. She kept telling me she was going to leave Ted, but she never did." Spittle formed at the corner of his mouth. "If that little bitch had kept her mouth shut, they'd all still be alive. I wasn't planning on killing her that night. Too risky to go upstairs, but then she shows up and comes at me. It was her own fault."

"Still, why did you kill the Klines? Because Sandy ended it?" Nikki wasn't sure how much time had passed since she spoke to Courtney. Surely Liam and Miller would get here soon. "She was in her forties, and you were in your prime, headed to graduate school and a lucrative career. You would have had plenty of female attention."

"I only wanted Sandy's." Arthur's voice rose. "I know how badly I ruined Matt's life. Why do you think I've been here by his side all the time, keeping him sane and safe? He would have had Amy at least if she hadn't been so hotheaded."

The click of another weapon caught them all off guard. "Never say my sister's name again."

THIRTY-FIVE

Nikki watched Matt in horror. He towered in the doorway, chest heaving as though he'd been running. His eyes were bloodshot, the gun shaking in his hand. The feral look in his eyes sent off alarm bells in Nikki's head.

"Put your gun down and push it over to Agent Hunt."

"Matt, please," Arthur started.

"Shut up!" Matt brought the pistol down hard into Arthur's shoulder. He dropped to his knees, the gun coming out of his hand. Matt's long leg came round Arthur and kicked it over to Nikki. "Up against the wall, *Artie*."

Arthur did as he was told, his bravado seemingly gone. "I'm sorry, son. I was young and impetuous. I've tried to make it up to you."

Matt crossed the room in a single stride and pressed the gun to Arthur's forehead. "You kept me close to protect yourself. That's why you dated Peggy and then dumped her."

"You were supposed to be headed to my cabin in the north woods to stay with Luke," Arthur said. "Why didn't you?"

"They found her car close to my house." Matt ignored the question. "You did that, didn't you? You tried to frame me."

"With circumstantial evidence," Arthur pleaded. "You wouldn't have been found guilty."

Disgust rolled through Nikki. She'd never met a bigger narcissist. "Matt, will you get the tape off Olivia and me?"

Matt flinched, as though he'd forgotten they were in the room. Pistol still aimed at Arthur, he crouched behind Nikki and used a pocketknife to cut the tape and then did the same to Olivia's.

"I want you to go upstairs and call your mom," Nikki told her. "Tell her you're okay. Then call the police. Go."

Olivia scurried to her feet and raced out of the room, her footsteps loud on the stairs. Maybelle barked from somewhere in the house.

Luckily, she'd fallen on her left shoulder. She was pretty sure she'd dislocated it, but her shooting arm was just fine. Nikki grabbed Arthur's gun and tried to stand. Pain shot through her ribs.

Matt knelt in front of Arthur again, gun against his temple. "You're a monster. Prison's too good for you."

"Matt," Nikki warned him. "Don't ruin the rest of your life. Besides, when he goes to jail—which he will—the other inmates will punish him much better than death. He's killed, raped, destroyed young girls' lives. There will be people in there with sisters and daughters."

The gun trembled in his hand. "But Amy, she never got the chance to live her life. My parents didn't get to see us graduate or have kids. Meanwhile, this bastard continued breathing."

"You know I understand," Nikki said. "Finding out that not only had my parents' killer not gone to prison but that someone I'd grown up with had served all of that time because of bad police work and bias was bad enough, but when I found out the person who killed them had been someone I loved and trusted..." Her voice broke. "I had him in my sights. He wanted me to shoot him. But I knew that even if I could claim self-defense, my life and my daughter's would be ruined."

"I don't have anyone."

"You have Luke," Nikki reminded him. "And Kim is out there, Matt. She warned Alexia and she talked to Olivia. You can all heal together."

Matt looked at Arthur. "Kim told me to escape after graduation. She acted weird that day. She knew, didn't she? You made her leave?"

"I did what was best for my son."

"You did what was best for you," Matt shouted, tears finally streaming down his face. "For you."

"How did you figure it out?" Nikki had to get his attention off Arthur.

Matt pulled out the object tucked in the back of his jeans. A young, innocent Britney Spears smiled shyly on the book's cover.

"Your sister's journal?"

"My boss called and said a package came for me there, marked urgent," Matt said. "Alexia left a note inside that explains everything. She wanted me to have the diary back and decided to mail it just in case."

"The police are here," Olivia called down the stairs. "I mean, the sheriff and a redhead guy. He's freaking out."

"Send them down." Nikki shifted to her knees, but she was pretty certain her left ankle was badly twisted. "Matt, give the gun to the sheriff when he comes in."

More footsteps in the house, along with familiar voices.

"Nikki!" Liam shouted, running down the stairs. He skidded to a stop in the doorway, white-faced, gun pointed at Matt. "Put the weapon down, Matt." Liam's calm voice surprised her. "I know you're innocent in all of this and you saved Agent Hunt and Olivia, but once you pull that trigger, all of that goes away."

Matt and Arthur stared at each other, misery etched across both of their faces.

"Amy wouldn't want you to do this," Nikki said softly.

Matt's chest heaved. He handed Liam the gun and sat back against the wall across from Nikki, head in his hands.

Liam called for Miller to cuff Arthur while he helped Nikki stand. Miller hauled Arthur to his feet and pulled him out of the small storage room, barking his Miranda rights.

Nikki fought back a howl of pain. Her ankle was definitely twisted all to hell.

Liam assessed her. "You should let me carry you upstairs."

"Not a chance in hell, Wilson. I have one good leg," Nikki said. "You got here pretty fast. You guys didn't get backup? You just came running?"

"I would have, but no. Alexia put a GPS tracker on the bottom of her car. She initialed it, so we knew she put it there. Miller had someone get her phone from the station, and we were able to see where the car had been. Then Courtney called."

"Stargazers bloomed. Matt, are you coming up?" Nikki grabbed Liam's arm for support, and the two of them followed Miller and a cuffed Arthur upstairs. "Actually, how did you get in here without Arthur knowing?"

"Side door to the basement." He looked at Liam. "I have to give a statement, right?"

Liam nodded. "Yeah, but someone must have called the media before we got here so they could get a shot of Arthur being walked out. If you can sneak out the way you came and come to the sheriff's station, go ahead. Just go right to the sheriff's."

Matt bolted from the room.

Nikki adjusted the sling on her left shoulder and knocked on Matt Kline's door. While she waited, she put most of her weight on her right leg and moved her left foot back and forth. The ankle injury had healed well, but she still had a bit of a limp, and her left leg seemed constantly on the verge of cramping.

"Agent Hunt, come in." Matt looked a lot better than he had the last time Nikki saw him. After he'd given his statement at the police station, Kim Webb had arrived, asking to speak with him. Matt had cried in her arms for a few moments before he was able to actually talk to her.

"How are Kim and Luke?" Since Luke was eighteen, he had decided to stay with Matt for the time being while he and his mom got to know each other.

"They're actually at a therapy appointment right now." Unlike the last time she'd been here, the place smelled fresh and bright light streamed in the windows. "It's going to be a long haul, but thankfully Luke's out of high school. And he's happy being with his mom. He never understood why she left, and I think Webb let him believe it was Luke's fault."

Nikki didn't mention the switch from calling him Arthur to

Webb. The coward was currently on suicide watch at Oak Park Heights—the same prison that housed the man who'd murdered her parents. Miller was determined to make sure he stayed alive to stand trial.

"I have some new information for you," Nikki said. "I thought you might want to know the print that Langley took that night did in fact match the Retro Air Jordans you thought you saw."

"Maybe if I'd ever seen him wearing them..."

"You were a kid when it happened," Nikki reminded him. "That kind of trauma screws with memory and perception. None of this is on you." She reached into her bag to retrieve Amy's journal. "I wanted to get this back to you as soon as possible. We've made copies, so it's yours."

Arthur hadn't said much since his arrest, but Alexia's letter had helped them piece together what happened. Learning about the journal from Matt had been the first domino to fall. Alexia remembered seeing it a while ago when she'd been snooping in Arthur's office for the key to the liquor cabinet. She had also seen the photo of the interns in Arthur's office, but Ben's information helped her put it together.

Her mistake had been longing for fame. In the letter she'd left for Matt, Alexia planned to go to the police as soon as she checked out of the Airbnb. She wanted to make sure all of her ducks were in a row so that she would be the star of the final documentary episode and get credit for helping solve the case.

"When we searched Arthur's office, we found the key to the glass box that had the Fitzgerald books. He always said his ancestors knew the Fitzgeralds, but that's not true. Your mom's did. I think she either gave the copy of *Gatsby* to him or, more likely, he swiped it at some point." Nikki took the book out of her bag. Once cleared to give it back to Matt, she'd kept it safe in an evidence bag. "Read the inscription."

"To Ms. Lily, a dear friend and even better cook." Matt

looked at Nikki. "So much under my nose the whole time and I didn't have a clue."

"Arthur's a master manipulator and a true narcissist," Nikki said. "No one else saw it, either."

Except Alexia. After Arthur's arrest, something kept nagging at Nikki. She'd gone through her notes until she'd found the copy of *Terror on Bone Lake* that Shanna had allowed her to take. Alexia had put the sticky note on the page that talked about Sandy Kline's nonprofit and interns. Nikki was glad Shanna didn't want the book back. If Alexia had just taken her information to the police, the three girls would probably still be alive. But she'd wanted to put the screws to her mother, and Shanna would have to carry that knowledge the rest of her life.

Her phone pinged a text notification, but Nikki didn't have to look at the caller ID to know who'd sent it. "I hope it's okay, but I tracked down Mary Katherine Kettner. She'd love to catch up."

Matt's eyes widened. "Seriously? MK?"

"That was her nickname?"

"I never heard anyone but her parents call her Mary Katherine," he said. "I know she hated that name."

"She certainly did," Nikki said. "So much so that she changed it. Do you want to talk to her?"

"She's here now?"

Nikki nodded. "Right outside the front door."

"Hell, yeah." Matt hurried past Nikki, nearly yanking the door off its hinges. "What the hell?" He turned to glare at Nikki. "You brought her here? I'm not giving interviews."

"Matty, it's me. It's MK."

He slowly turned back to face Caitlin. "What?"

"I'm sorry," she said. "I left Mary Katherine behind when I graduated. I never forgot about Amy, and I swore to myself that if I ever had the opportunity, I would try to find out what happened. You didn't want to talk for the documentary, and I understood. My producers don't know about our personal connection. I didn't want to use it that way." Tears streamed down Caitlin's face. "I'm so glad you have closure."

Nikki held her breath and prayed Matt wouldn't react in anger. But he threw his arms around Caitlin, and the two started crying.

"You guys need to catch up." Nikki smiled at both of them when they calmed down. She squeezed her friend's arm. "Did Liam drive you?"

Caitlin nodded. "I wanted him here just in case it didn't go well."

Nikki handed her the keys to the jeep. "And no, I don't have any files or evidence in there, so don't even think about snooping."

Caitlin laughed. Nikki hugged her goodbye, and turned to say the same to Matt. He swept her up in a big hug as well. "Thank you. You saved me. Not the other way around."

Nikki headed out into the fall weather. Liam leaned against his car, feet crossed at the ankles. "You kind of look like a budget version of *Sixteen Candles* right now. Except you've got the red hair."

"Hilarious," he said. "How'd Matt react? Caitlin was so worried."

"He's thrilled," Nikki said. "I told her to stay and take my jeep. I assume my partner will give me a ride home."

"Suppose." Liam shuffled his feet. They hadn't had time to talk about anything but the case in the last week. "I'm sorry about the way I acted."

"Me too," Nikki said. "But I think Courtney's right. Disagreeing is a good thing, keeps the investigation honest. As long as we don't kill each other in the process."

Liam grinned and opened the passenger door for her. "Did you read all of the diary? I felt so icky, but Garcia wanted to make sure we knew exactly what was in it."

"Not all of it," Nikki said. "The first and last entries were enough for now." The last entry had talked about catching her mother and Arthur, along with numerous times Arthur had come on to Amy. She'd told her mother that if she didn't break if off that day, she was telling her father. The confidence in her decision, that she'd done the right thing, only made the end result more sad.

"What's next?"

Nikki checked her watch, her stomach fluttering. "Lacey will be home in sixty-seven minutes, maybe sooner. Rory and I are spending the weekend with her, in our pajamas, catching up on all of the shows she missed while she was gone." She couldn't wait to hold Lacey and smell the sweet scent of her hair. She'd missed her little singsong voice so much. Rory had cleared his schedule for the weekend, letting his foremen know they needed to be on call for an on-site emergency. This weekend was family time.

"Do we have time to stop at McDonald's?" Liam looked guilty.

"We ate lunch like ninety minutes ago."

"So? I'm a growing man."

"More like man child." Nikki settled back into the seat. Things were finally getting back to normal.

A LETTER FROM STACY

I want to say a huge thank you for choosing to read *Her Last Tear*. If you did enjoy it, and want to keep up to date with all my latest releases, including the next Nikki Hunt thriller, just sign up at the following link. Your email address will never be shared and you can unsubscribe at any time.

www.bookouture.com/stacy-green

I have always loved old houses. They have so much history, and in my experience, their own energies created by generations of inhabitants. Even as a kid, I felt like every old house I entered whispered to me, including the house that inspired *Bone Lake's* Lilydale. The lake is a real place in Washington County, and the name was too perfect not to construct the story around it.

My author letters are normally short and sweet, but as some of you know, my father passed in January 2023. His love of detective shows like Hillstreet Blues and Cagney and Lacey are the reason I love crime fiction and all things dark and twisted. I can remember watching those with him when I was probably too young. I also inherited his love for history and sports. We loved the Dallas Cowboy's Troy Aikmen/Emmet Smith era, and we cheered for Jeff Gordon every Sunday. But our real love was basketball. Michael Jordan and the 90s Chicago Bulls were everything in our household, and some of my best memories with Dad are listening to Bulls games on the radio, because we lived in the country and didn't get WGN at the time. I chose the Air Jordans and the Nike commercial to honor Dad.

We lost Mom in 2017, shortly after my parents finally moved near us, but she'd battled health issues for years. Having dad within four minutes meant we were able to spend a lot of time with him, and the two of us got closer. Without Dad, I don't think there would be a Nikki Hunt series. I don't think I'd be writing now, because Mom was my biggest supportor, and I nearly quit in 2018 before Bookouture reached out. Dad constantly reminded me of how disappointed she would be that I wasn't writing and pushing forward in one of the few things that did keep me afloat those first couple of years.

We expected him to live into his nineties, but a fall and subsequent brain bleed changed all of that. He'd recovered enough to have conversations, so the hospital shipped him off to the nursing home where a series of events spanning three days caused him to become septic. He should still be here with us, watching my daughter graduate and swim at a Division Two college.

I was fortunate enough to be with him when he passed, but there are still days when the anger buries me. What could I have done differently? Was there one little decision that could have saved his life? The practical side of me says no, but the emotional wreck that dwells deep within insists it's true. Dad's with Mom now instead of missing her terribly, so we take solace in that.

On a happier note, music always plays a role in Nikki's books, and the Beastie Boys' Sabotage seemed like the perfect song for Amy since it's been my personal anthem this last year. This year has been full of brutal truths and tough decisions, and being an orphan is still something I'm getting used to. I couldn't have made it through it all without my husband Rob and daughter Grace. I'm lucky to have them both.

I hope you loved *Bone Lake*, and I'm very excited about the next Nikki Hunt book releasing in the spring. Thank you so much for reading, and if you loved the book, please leave a review. They're vital to keeping series successful and finding new readers discover the Nikki Hunt Series.

I love hearing from my readers – you can get in touch on Facebook, X (Twitter), Instagram or my website.

Thanks,

Stacy

www.stacygreenauthor.com

 facebook.com/StacyGreenAuthor
 x.com/StacyGreen26
 instagram.com/authorstacygreen

ACKNOWLEDGMENTS

Writing a good story is hard, but writing an accurate story is even tougher. Thank you to John Kelly for all the information on Stillwater and Washington County, as well as F. Scott Fitzgerald's Minnesota history.

Thanks to the Washington County Historical Society for letting me pick their brains and sending photos for accuracy.

Thank you to Stillwater Police Chief Mueller for his help with the investigation, as well as Jill Oliviera from the Minnesota Bureau of Criminal Apprehension.

Sotheby's helped me sift through the years of Air Jordan brand shoes to ensure accuracy on the soles.

As always, special thanks to John Douglas for reminding me to always profile the victim first.

Thank you to Kristine and John Kelly, for being my true family. Special thank you to Jan Barton. I love you more than I can say!

Maureen Downey and Tessa Russ, you're both rock stars. Thank you for handling my social media so I don't have to! Lisa Regan, thanks for the virtual shoulder to cry on and the support.

My editor Jennifer Hunt has helped to bring Nikki to life since the beginning. I'm so grateful for her unwavering support and kindness, along with the entire staff at Bookouture.

Finally, thank you to my readers! I'm truly humbled by your messages and reviews, and I hope you love *Bone Lake* as much as the other books in the series.

PUBLISHING TEAM

Turning a manuscript into a book requires the efforts of many people. The publishing team at Bookouture would like to acknowledge everyone who contributed to this publication.

Audio
Alba Proko
Melissa Tran

Commercial
Lauren Morrissette
Jil Thielen
Imogen Allport

Data and analysis
Mark Alder
Mohamed Bussuri

Design
Blacksheep

Editorial
Jennifer Hunt
Sinead O'Connor